WHO
SHOT
LONGSHOT
SAM?

PAUL ENGLEMAN

WHO SHOT LONGSHOT SAM?

A MARK RENZLER MYSTERY

THE MYSTERIOUS PRESS

New York • London
Tokyo • Sweden • Milan

Some of the places and events in this book are real. But the characters are fictional, and any inference of similarity to real persons is wishful thinking or paranoia on the part of the reader.

 The Mysterious Press, 129 West 56th Street, New York, NY 10019

Printed in the United States of America
First Printing: November 1989
10 9 8 7 6 5 4 3 2 1

Library of Congress Cataloging-in-Publication Data

Engleman, Paul.
    Who shot longshot Sam? / Paul Engleman.
        p.   cm.
    ISBN 0-89296-365-4
    I. Title.
PS3555.N426W48   1989   89-42604
813'.54--dc20   CIP

This is for Larry Carney,
who bet on the wrong day to go fishing;
and for Brian Carney, who managed to beat the odds.

Thanks to my brother Mark for the title, story idea and use of the world's best junk mail collection; Kevin Reynolds for his racing expertise; Nat Sobel for his efforts on my behalf; and Barb for making it all worthwhile.

And special thanks to Bill Malloy, my morning-line favorite for Editor of the Year.

1

It was Monday, July 29, according to the racing program. The box was on, my shirt was off, and I was drinking before noon again. Hardly what you'd call an auspicious start to a busy week, but then who said anything about being busy? Besides, it was only a beer.

While most New Yorkers were slogging through the sweltering heat to their jobs, I was slouched on my couch looking at another grueling week of vacation, which is my preferred euphemism for being out of work. Unfortunately, my air conditioner had taken a vacation the night before, leaving me at the mercy of my reserve cooling system—a fan I had picked up during Dollar Days at Woolworth's back in the days when a dollar was still worth something.

The fan did little more than blow hot gusts of West Seventy-second Street air across the living room, which conveniently doubles as my office, swirling up tufts of cat fur that someone must have overlooked while running the old Hoover last week—or was it last month? This probably explains why I wasn't wearing a shirt, even if it doesn't account for why I wasn't out looking for a job. Or why I was watching daytime TV.

Unemployment is terribly disheartening to some people, but not to me. For one thing, I'm used to it. For another, I'm an adaptable guy. You have to be in my business. I'm a private investigator. My name, just for the record, is Mark Renzler.

I learned long ago that there's nothing intrinsically wrong with being out of work. It's being out of *money* that's the

1

problem. Fortunately, I was doing okay on that score. Two years back, I had come into a sizable sum, at least by my standards. With both my ex-wives happily remarried to a pair of hardworking schmucks, the alimony albatross was off my neck. Except for the speed at which my hairline was receding, I didn't have anything to worry about. I was free, white, and pushing forty-three.

Anyone who's been in the business for any period of time can tell you it's not what it used to be. Private detectives aren't much in demand anymore. But I take the good with the bad, and so far 1974 had been a very good year.

I'd had a steady arrangement all winter with an attorney who was defending thirteen harness drivers accused of fixing Superfecta races at Yonkers and Roosevelt raceways. I usually give lawyers a wider berth than a runaway garbage truck, but I met this guy at Yonkers a few years back and he seemed okay—as runaway garbage trucks go.

Even if you don't follow racing, you probably heard about Superfix, as the newspapers called the case. The indictments were announced right before Christmas, and with Henry Kissinger home from the Middle East and Dick Nixon home trimming his tree, there wasn't much news for the media to cover. Besides that, Yonkers and Roosevelt are the top harness tracks in the country. If you could believe the prosecutor, there was a full-fledged conspiracy in which twenty-eight people had fixed thirty races.

I didn't believe the prosecutor, and not just because I'm naturally skeptical. Winning the Superfecta required picking the top four horses in a race. Fixing the Superfecta required bribing four drivers to hold back their horses in the same race. It would be easier to fix a nuclear power plant.

The alleged "mastermind" of the scheme, a former horse trainer named Forrest Gerry, was accused of buying off the drivers with thousand-dollar bribes. A thousand bucks is a lot of money to some people, me included. But not to guys like Buddy Gilmour, Del Insko, and Ben Webster. They were the best harness drivers in the country. It didn't make sense that they would risk lifetime suspensions just to make a quick grand.

After checking on the government's star witnesses—"unindicted co-conspirators" in legal jargon—I soon discovered that the entire case didn't make sense. There was a plumber from Staten Island, a gas-station manager from Queens, a trucking-company owner from Hoboken. Being lowlifes wasn't the only thing they had in common. They had all managed to *lose* money betting on fixed races. That ain't easy to do. Even more amazing was that some of the drivers had *won* the races they were accused of fixing. Figure that one out.

It turned out Forrest Gerry was not so much a master*mind* as a master con. He convinced the rubes that he could fix races, then used their money in separate bankrolls to cover every possible combination for himself. Each time one group of backers won, another group lost. But he was winning all the time and, adding insult to proverbial injury, pocketing the money they gave him to pay the nonexistent bribes.

Superfix turned out to be nothing more than a tax-evasion case. And, I might add, a waste of taxpayers' money. In return for my efforts, I cashed a tidy payoff. There weren't any fixed races, but I was fixed for the year. So I guess you could say I really was on vacation.

That doesn't explain why I was watching daytime TV. It was a habit I picked up last summer when the soap operas and game shows were being preempted for what the networks call "special programming." There was a circus called Watergate on, and it filled a certain void in my life when I could have used a few assignments.

Before the Watergate hearings, I used to flip right to the sports pages in the paper, stopping only for the occasional plane hijacking or random unprovoked shooting spree. But I came to enjoy the daily parade of Dick Nixon's sulking aides across my TV screen, not to mention the pompous posturing of their holier-than-thou inquisitors. Watching Watergate turned me into a regular news junkie.

Withdrawal didn't come easy once the hearings ended, but the events of 1974 provided plenty of therapeutic distractions. First there was the so-called fuel shortage, with angry motorists cussing about greedy Arabs from OPEC and coming to blows with each other over spaces on gas lines. And all the while the heads of America's oil companies were trying not to gloat over the killing they were making.

Then Patty Hearst, heiress to the California newspaper

fortune, was kidnapped by a group calling itself the Symbionese Liberation Army. It would have made a great name for a rock band, since nobody could figure out what it meant. Even harder to figure was the SLA's ransom demand—$200 million in food for the poor. Before Patty's daddy could dig up the clams, a Berkeley radio station came up with a tape on which Mr. Hearst's daughter announced that she had joined the SLA cause and changed her name to Tania. This came as something of a shock to her parents and her fiancé, a grim-Jim by the name of Steven Weed. No sooner had they finished insisting that she must have been coerced into making the tape than Patty did a network news cameo, toting a machine gun during a videotaped bank heist. In addition to sending her parents' blue blood to the boiling point, the episode put the freeze on Mr. Weed's wedding plans.

Just as Patty went underground and dropped out of the headlines, news of Watergate started to resurface. Every day it seemed like one of Nixon's closest friends or advisers was being indicted, convicted, or sentenced. In addition to his other problems, The President, as Nixon liked to call himself, was found to owe half a million in back taxes. An honest mistake, I'm sure. Things had really heated up the week before when the Supreme Court ordered Nixon to turn over his tapes to the special prosecutor. Then the House Judiciary Committee got into the act, announcing that it had adopted three articles of impeachment.

There was no doubting that Dick Nixon was a survivor, but it looked like his time was finally running out. I planned to be watching in living color when he made his exit, not to mention I had some money riding on when it would happen. I was in a pool with my friend Nate Moore and my bookie, Angelo Albani. My day was Monday, July 29.

By noon it was looking like I had lost my bet. There had been a news bulletin during "The Price Is Right," but that turned out to be a false alarm: the indictment of ex–Tex governor John Connally on some dirty dairy dealings. Strictly small potatoes.

I was working up the energy to see about a new air conditioner when the phone rang. I figured it was Angelo or Nate calling to needle me. Angelo likes Nixon, so he was giving him until August 8. Nate despises him, so he had bowed out by the end of June.

I figured wrong. It was my friend Al Phillips, the harness-racing writer for the *Chicago Tribune*. I met Al at Yonkers ten years ago when he worked for the *Daily News*, but he quit in 1971 after a messy divorce and moved to Chicago. Al was an oddity among handicappers—not only did he know his stuff, but he was also a literate guy. He'd even written a book on racing that was published in hardcover. This was quite an accomplishment, since most stuff on the subject is written in crayon.

"How's it going, Renzler?" he asked. "You got any hot tips you'd like to share with me?"

"Bet on Nixon to be out of office by the end of the year."

"End of the *year*? Try end of the week."

"You know I've always been a conservative bettor."

"Yeah, that's right. Mr. Two-Dollar Window. Well, how would you like to get in on something big for a change?"

"That depends on what you have in mind." Al was a guy who always had a scheme. So am I, come to think of it. That probably explains why we got along.

"Have you been out to this new harness track in Jersey—Garden State Downs?"

Garden State Downs was New Jersey's latest attempt to lure bettors out of New York. So far it had failed miserably. And with good reason; it had been built faster than a McDonald's and had all the amenities of a rest area on the Jersey Turnpike.

"Sure, I've been there—once." I'm the sort of guy who'll try anything once.

"What's it like?"

"Worse than you could possibly imagine. The horses are about two steps from the glue factory."

"And how'd you do?"

"I got skunked. Didn't cash a winner all day, and then I got a flat tire in the parking lot."

"Correct me if I'm wrong, but isn't that car of yours about two flat tires from the junkyard?"

"I got rid of the Corvair, if that's what you mean. I'm driving a Pinto now."

"A Pinto! Maybe someday you'll explain this attraction you have to death traps."

"I like to live dangerously," I said. "Maybe you'll explain why you're interested in Garden State Downs."

"I'm coming out there next week."

"Why in the world would you want to do that?"

"To win a hundred thousand dollars."

"What are you planning to do—rob the place? I've got some bad news for you, Al. The betting pool at Garden State Downs is about the size of a birdbath."

Al snorted. "They're having a race-handicapping contest out there. It's called Super Pick. You haven't heard about it?"

"I guess I did see an ad in the paper."

"Yeah, I figured you did. Okay, here's my plan. There are two separate contests—one's open to pros, the other's for amateurs. The prize money is fifty grand for each. The way I figure it is I enter the pro, you enter the amateur. We'll work together on it, a fifty-fifty split."

"Is that legal?" I asked.

"Of course not. But if we're discreet about it, who's to know? If we're lucky, we win both contests and come away with a hundred grand. Even if we're not, I figure my picks will at least be good enough to win the amateur part. The worst we can do is walk away with twenty-five grand apiece. Simple, huh? And not bad for five days' work."

No, not bad at all. And probably not so simple. I'd be lying if I said I didn't like the sound of fifty thousand bucks. But I wasn't as confident as Al Phillips. And as much as I liked Al, I knew he was a hustler. There had to be a catch.

"Tell me a little about how the contest works," I said.

"There's not much to tell. Each contestant starts out with a thousand-dollar bankroll. The amateurs compete with the amateurs, and the pros compete with the pros. The person with the most money left after five days of betting is the winner. There's one pro winner and one amateur winner. What do you think?"

"From what I know about Garden State Downs, I think we'd be better off betting on cockroaches."

"No, that's where you're wrong. I've got a friend out there who's *cleaning up*. It's an easy track once you get to know it."

"We don't know it."

"Exactly. Which is why I want you to go out there this week. You know—to get the feel of the place."

"I see." The prospect of ten days in New Jersey made the idea of a quick killing sound a little more like slow death. But I'd be willing to spend ten weeks there if it meant making fifty grand. Or, in Al's worst-case scenario, twenty-five.

"If your friend's doing so well, why haven't you talked to him about teaming up?" I asked.

"Yeah, well, that's the problem. He's entered in the pro side of the contest. Barring a miracle, I'm afraid Sam's got that part of it locked up."

"Did you say *Sam?*"

"Yeah, that's right. Longshot Sam."

"Oh, Christ."

"I guess you've heard of him, huh?"

2

I had never seen Sam Natoli, but I was familiar with his reputation. Longshot Sam was to handicapping what Minnesota Fats was to billiards. I didn't know he had started hanging out at Garden State Downs, but it made sense that he would. For one thing, he lived in Jersey. For another, there are lots of variables at a new track that a good handicapper can use to his advantage. Longshot Sam was the best.

"So basically we're talking about twenty-five thousand tops," I said to Al Phillips.

"Yeah, probably. But that's still a lot of money. Even after the entry fees."

"Entry fees?"

"You didn't think it would be free, did you?"

"To be honest, Al, I hadn't thought about it."

"It's two large for the pro and five small for the amateur."

"I take it you want to split the fees, too."

"That would only be fair, don't you think?"

I figured I should play hard to get. You don't want a guy like Al thinking you're an easy mark. He took my silence as an invitation to do some arm-twisting. "Come on, Renzler," he said. "We could make the killing of a lifetime, for Chrissakes."

"I don't know, Al. This could be the week Nixon resigns."

"Who cares about that?"

"I do. I've got two hundred bucks riding on it." I didn't see any gain in letting him know I had already lost my bet.

"You can watch it on one of the TV sets at the track."

"Not at Garden State Downs, Al," I said. "This place only has radios."

"Very funny. But let's get serious. I'm talking about a serious proposition here."

"What makes you so sure we can win this thing?"

"Because there's practically nobody in the contest."

"Nobody except Longshot Sam," I reminded him.

"Forget Sam for a minute. I'm talking about the amateur part. They were expecting a hundred entrants and so far they've only signed up half that many. Those are pretty good odds."

Maybe so, but fifty people was still a lot to compete with. Few casual bettors are willing to drop five hundred bucks at the track, so you could be sure even the amateurs were good pickers.

"The worst thing that could possibly happen is you'll learn something about handicapping," Al continued.

"I thought the worst I could do was win twenty-five Gs."

"Okay, so I exaggerated a little."

"Are any of the other pros lining up amateur partners?"

"Christ, I hadn't thought of that." Al hesitated, but he was only momentarily daunted. "You see. That's why I'm glad you're in on this. You're already keeping me on my toes."

"And what's the answer to my question?" I asked. "*Do* you think any of the other pros are bringing along ringers?"

Al paused, and I could hear him lighting a cigarette. That was a good sign. I hate when friends stop smoking. Nine out of ten become fresh-air fiends, an insufferable breed.

"No," he said at last. "Not these guys. They're too dumb."

"What about Sam?"

"No, not Sam. He's too honest."

That was more than you could say for Al or me. I like to think of myself as an ethical guy, but when it comes to the track, I'll take any edge I can get. I'm one of those people who think winning is everything. It's a philosophy I picked up playing Little League baseball.

"How many pros are in the contest?" I asked.

"Ten. It's basically the same group as last year, when the contest was held at Ak-Sar-Ben."

"That's the one in Nebraska, right?"

"Yeah, in Omaha. Ak-Sar-Ben is Nebraska spelled backward. Cute, huh? The place is a dump."

"Wait until you see Garden State Downs," I said. "So how did you do in last year's contest?"

"I came in second. Sam finished first. It wasn't too bad. I walked away with ten grand."

"You mean there's second-place prize money, too?" Super Pick was sounding better all the time.

"Of course, Renzler. It's like a racetrack. Win, place, show. Remember?"

"Yeah, I remember." You didn't want to ask Al too many dumb questions about the track. He wasn't what you'd call a patient guy. "Who else is on the pro side? Maybe I've heard of them."

"Yeah, you probably know some of them. Sol Epstein, Lou Larson."

"Oh sure." Sulky Sol Epstein and Lucky Lou Larson were New York guys. I was amused that Al knew them by just their first names, instead of their full racing monikers.

Sulky Sol published a tout sheet. He got his nickname from the carriage that a harness driver sits in. Lucky Lou was Al's successor at the *Daily News*. I figured he got his nickname because he was fortunate that some enraged bettor hadn't killed him. They were both lousy handicappers, but you'd never know it to see all the dummies who carried their picks around Yonkers and Roosevelt. If five percent of them were betting the car payment on the selections of Sulky Sol or Lucky Lou, there was a lot of repo work to be had in the New York area.

"Then there's Tommy Stevens," Al said.

"Not *Tote*board Tommy."

"Yeah, that's right. You've heard of him?"

Tommy Stevens sold betting systems through the mail. Until that moment, I didn't know he was a real person. I figured Toteboard Tommy was just a goofy name invented by some direct-mail shark.

Tommy's specialty was watching the toteboard for overlays, which occur when horses are underbet in relation to the total betting pool. At every track except Roosevelt, the toteboard only projects the win odds. For place and show, it only tells the amount bet. Since the size of a payoff is determined by the percentage of the pool wagered on each horse, it's possible to calculate if certain horses are underbet. When a horse is an overlay, it might pay $4 to win but $5 to place or show. Betting to show in this situation is a better bet, because a horse that finishes first also pays off for place and show.

Unfortunately, spotting overlays requires an aptitude for making complex calculations in a matter of seconds—even, it turns out, if you are using the Toteboard Tommy Racing Computer, which is supposed to do all the math for you.

"Sure, I know who Toteboard Tommy is," I said. I didn't confess that I had dropped seventy-five bucks on his computer, which proved about as helpful as one of those metal detectors that winos use to find coins in the park. Al would sneer at me if he found out.

"He sells that idiot computer. It's not even a computer, for Chrissakes. It's just another dumb logarithmic calculator."

I didn't much care about the computer. I didn't even care about hitting Tommy up for the refund I had coming as set forth in his "no-questions-asked" money-back guarantee. There hadn't been any questions asked when I called for my refund. That's because I got a disconnect recording from Ma Bell—or maybe it was *Mrs.* Toteboard Tommy. At the time, I was so furious that I could have driven all the way to his post-office box in Council Bluffs, Iowa, to smack him in the chops, but now I was simply curious to find out what a guy named Toteboard Tommy looked like.

"Who else is in this with you?" I asked.

"Well, there's Timmy the Geek."

"You mean Timmy the Greek?" It was harder to control my enthusiasm for that one.

"Yeah, that's right. We call him the Geek."

I'd been wanting to get a look at Timmy the Greek Malkos for ten years, ever since I got a flyer in which he offered to sell "the key to unlocking the secret of the racetrack AND the door to unlimited wealth"—all for a mere ten bucks. The key to a storage locker at Grand Central Station cost more than that.

If you've never seen the junk mail put out by the bandits who sell systems for winning at the track, you don't know what you've been spared. I know a guy who buys mail-order pornography, and even he's offended by it. Targeted strictly for losers, racing offers are filled with the most astonishing collection of fractured phrases, phony testimonials, and bald-faced lies ever to see the printed page. P.T. Barnum said there's a sucker born every minute, but based on the volume of stuff that these charlatans crank out, I'd say his estimate was off by about forty-five seconds.

In the world of racing junk mail, Timmy the Greek was king of the heap. I should know. I'm on every sucker list you can imagine.

It's not that I'm dumb enough to fork over the dough for this stuff. My purchase from Toteboard Tommy was an exception, a hasty decision reached when I was feeling flush one day. And Tommy's system does work—if your name happens to be Einstein. But I do subscribe to a couple of gambling magazines, and they'll sell your name and address to anybody—no questions asked. The guys who peddle racing systems buy names like they were cornering the market on cancer cures.

A woman I dated who works in the subscription department of *Time* magazine told me some companies make more money selling names than they do selling products. She also told me I was the smartest guy she ever went out with, so you should probably take her info with a grain of salt. I had two years of college, but even my mother used to say I was a slow learner.

One of the side benefits of having your name sold and resold to semiliterates with bad typewriters is a free change of identity. About half my mail is addressed to a fellow named "Dark Penzler."

"Does Timmy the Greek really have three houses?" I asked Al, recalling one of the claims in his mailings.

"Are you kidding? The Geek? He lives in a trailer park in Maryland."

"How much does he weigh?"

"Oh, I don't know. He's got to be up around three hundred pounds."

"I thought it would be more than that." I had never seen a full picture of Timmy Malkos, just the mug shot in his offers. But I figured his head alone must weigh fifty pounds.

"The thing you've got to remember," Al said, "is he's only five foot five. You should've been there last year. He got stuck in the turnstile, and they had to cut him out with a blowtorch."

"Well, he'll be glad to know there's no chance of that happening at Garden State Downs."

"Why not?"

"They don't have turnstiles. The entrance is a length of rope thrown over a pair of horses. *Saw*horses, that is."

Al laughed. "Yeah, I knew what you meant."

"Of course, that might have changed. When I was there, they had a PARDON OUR REMODELING sign up. I thought it was strange that they were already in the process of *re*modeling."

Al went over the other four contestants. I take some pride in keeping up with this stuff, but I was glad I only knew two of them.

Dr. Dave Higgins was a former racetrack veterinarian who peddled about twenty different systems. Regardless of which one he was selling, he invariably described it as "an Rx for beating the races." Clocker Callaway put out pamphlets on speed rating, a handicapping method based on a horse's past-performance times. Speed rating is a valid approach, but it requires a lot of calculation. That's probably why Clocker also peddled a special stopwatch with four separate rings on it to time each quarter of a mile. He also offered a higher-priced model called King Clock, which had his smiling mug right on the dial.

The two pickers I didn't know were Track Jack Jones and Serendipity Red McCall. Al said Track Jack published a tout sheet at Jackson Park in Michigan. He had come in fourth at last year's contest. Serendipity was a female picker from California.

"I assume she's nicknamed Red due to her hair color rather than suspected ties to the Communist party," I said.

"Yeah, but she's still a dingbat," Al said. "She's got a huge set of knockers. We call her the Daily Double."

Ah, you can beat the racetrack, but you can't beat racetrack humor. "And how is she at knocking down winners?" I asked.

"Terrible. She bases her picks on astrology."

"What do you mean . . . astrology?"

"I mean astrology. You know—like you see in the newspaper. She does goddamn horoscopes for the horses!"

"Is that so?" I thought I'd heard of every imaginable system, but evidently there was a whole other world out there.

"So what do you think?" Al asked.

"I think I'd like to get on her mailing list."

"I mean about the contest, for Chrissakes. Are you in or not? Come on, Renzler—shit or get off the pot."

Until then, my racing pen pals had been oddball names living in post-office boxes in unimaginable towns. Confirming their existence was reason enough to attend Super Pick. But I had a feeling the novelty would wear off fast. It was a good thing there was money to be won. Of course, there was also money to be lost. Big money. At least to me it was big money.

"Tell you what, Renzler. I'll spring for the fees. When we win, I'll take your share of the nut right off the top."

That's what I was waiting to hear. If Al felt that strongly about it, he had to be on to something good.

"That's okay, I'll cover it," I said.

"No, no, I insist. That way, I won't have you second-guessing me."

"Well, how do I register?"

Al chuckled. "I already took care of that. I registered you a month ago."

"Thanks for the advance notice, partner."

"Hey, I've been busy."

"On what?"

"On our system for winning this thing. You want to hear about it?"

Just then, I heard the announcement of a special news bulletin on TV. "I'll have to call you back, Al. I think Nixon may be about to resign." Maybe I was going to get lucky after all.

I put down the phone just in time to see a somber-faced Dan Rather appear on the screen. "Monday, Monday, sad Monday," he said. "Singer Mama Cass Elliot is dead at the age of thirty-three."

Sad for Dan maybe. I switched off the set without waiting to hear the cause of death.

3

Garden State Downs was a straight shot west of Manhattan, twenty miles as the crow flies and twenty-five as the traffic crawls. It was located near the town of Pequannock, an old Indian name that probably means "close to shopping centers and schools." Lots of towns in Jersey have Indian names, but the place has undergone a remarkable transformation since the "dollah" replaced wampum as the standard unit of currency. It has also changed considerably since I lived there, but that was twenty-five years ago.

Starting at the Lincoln Tunnel, North Jersey is basically an unending strip of eight-lane asphalt bordered by factories, diners, gas stations, and car dealerships. That's if you take the scenic route. The one break in the man-made landscape is a vast expanse of swamps near the Jersey Turnpike called the Meadowlands. They're not much to look at, but they serve some vital social functions, like providing a burial ground for mobsters who have fallen out of favor.

A couple of years ago, state fathers and real estate developers devised a plan to build a sports complex in the Meadowlands that would include, among other things, a racetrack. It was one of those greedy schemes that politicians like to hail as "partnerships" between the public and private sectors. I tend to be cynical about such ventures, but there was a certain logic to this particular proposal. It amounted to a marriage of the state's two largest industries—gambling and landfill.

By the time you reach Pequannock the asphalt has narrowed to four lanes, the diners have been supplanted by fast food

15

franchises, and the car dealerships are big enough to permit test drives right on the lot. The dirty old factories have given way to shiny new office buildings and to factory-outlet stores, where smart shoppers go. If you look carefully, you can even catch sight of some trees, a sure sign that you're closing in on the "nice" part of Jersey.

I hadn't been out there since my ill-fated trip to Garden State Downs a few months before. I try to keep my distance from Jersey, but the prospect of winning fifty grand had tempered my resolve. Plus, when it came right down to it, I had nothing better to do. Even so, the week flew by like a thoroughbred and it was Friday by the time I made my stretch move.

I knew the Pequannock area a bit, because my parents lived in the nearby town of Wayne after my father retired and before they decided Florida was a better bet. That was in the fifties, when the place was mostly farmland and there was no mystery why Jersey was called the Garden State. Nowadays the only evidence of agriculture is the roadside fruit-and-vegetable stand set up on a vacant lot next to a LANDFILL NEEDED sign.

I guess you can't quibble with progress. The last time I did, I got an earful from my brother-in-law, dear old Dick Derkovich. If my memory serves me correctly, that was also the last time I saw him—two short years ago.

"You don't live here, so what the hell right do you have to complain about it?" he had demanded.

I didn't have an answer then, and still don't, except to ask a question of my own: Why would anybody *want* to live there?

Dick and my sister, Karen, resided in my hometown, Clifton, until a year ago when they moved to Pompton Plains, which borders Garden State Downs on the other side of Pequannock. GSD, as the track is called, was built on an unincorporated tract that the mayors of both towns laid claim to the moment construction plans were disclosed. Say what you will about small-time politicians, they sure can sniff out a tax base.

The land in dispute had been a barren stretch of sand and gravel quarries until thirty years ago when someone filled a quarry with water, planted some trees, and opened a private bathing and picnic area called Sunnyside. In recent years, Sunnyside had been overrun by "undesirables," which is suburbanese for "busloads of blacks from the Bronx." The locals stopped swimming there, and the owner shut the park down.

Sunnyside was a local landmark of sorts, so the decision to close was the stuff that suburban tragedies are made of. But a concerned state legislator named Carmen Vitello located the perfect buyer for the land in his cousin, a developer named Billy Bonnardo, who, as contractor for half the shopping centers in North Jersey, was something of a local hero.

Most people expected Billy B., as he was known, to build an indoor shopping mall. He decided to put up a harness track.

Now I don't have any right to complain, but it seems to me that if you want to keep undesirables out of your town, building a racetrack sure ain't the way to do it.

Quite a few people, including my brother-in-law, agreed. But Billy B. was a popular guy, and Carmen V. was a lout with clout. While Bonnardo assured folks that the track would be more beautiful than any shopping mall they had ever seen, Vitello persuaded his legislative cronies to withhold their approval on the Meadowlands project unless the GSD plan was also adopted.

The measure might have failed if fate hadn't intervened a week before the crucial vote. While dining on surf and turf—as was his custom on Saturday nights—at a mob steak house on Route 46 in Totowa, Billy B. bit off more turf than he could chew or swallow. He suffered what is known as a café coronary, losing control of most bodily functions but not the ability to speak. Unfortunately, the thoughts in Billy's brain didn't always coincide with the ones that came out of his mouth, leaving him to yap unpredictably for the rest of his life.

This turned out to be a brief period of time. When Billy bid the world *arrivederci* a month later, nobody bothered to ask if he had fallen out of his wheelchair or been pushed by his wife or son. Friends and relatives agreed that Billy was better off *morte*.

Bonnardo's last brush with solid foods proved to be a stroke of good luck for the racetrack proposal. Within hours after the accident, his status rose from local hero to state martyr. The fix was in, but just to make sure, Billy's people fitted him with a clean diaper and wheeled him onto the floor of the state house for the vote. After the measure was approved, Billy showed his appreciation by grinning at the cheering throng of lawmakers and saying, "I'd like to fuck you all very much."

After Billy passed away, the ownership and development of GSD passed on to his son and partner, Billy Jr., on whom he had conferred the nickname Biff early in life. This seemed reason enough to suspect that the kid had a hand in the old man's demise. While Billy had a reputation for extravagance and perfection—due in no small part to the cost overruns that plagued all his projects—his son's first solo venture failed to live up to the legacy. Despite his dad's promise, Biff managed to make GSD uglier than any shopping mall you've ever seen.

I figured the track's shortcomings were due as much to the project's lack of public funding as they were a measure of Biff's talents, but that was still no excuse. The designer of the place was either a close relative or somebody who had snapshots of Biff in a compromising position with an old gray mare. He had spared every expense in the construction, starting with the parking lot, a dusty rectangle made of equal parts dirt, gravel, and broken bottles. It was big enough to fit five hundred cars comfortably, provided they were stacked on top of each other. Huge ruts were visible where church buses used to park while loading and unloading their undesirables at Sunnyside. For latecomers, there was an overflow lot across Route 23 behind the Quality Motor Inn. I wasn't a latecomer, but I parked there anyway in the hope of avoiding another flat tire.

The GSD grandstand was a two-story cinder-block structure that might have been an addition onto the original bathhouse at Sunnyside. The blocks were reinforced with rust-colored steel girders—let's hope they were steel—that jutted out at angles which did not look to be ninety degrees. Other than setting the color scheme for the building, the girders didn't appear to serve much purpose, except perhaps to provide moral support for the blocks. I figured they might need it on a windy day or during a sudden rush to the betting windows.

The best feature of GSD was the track itself, a half-mile oval built on the site of the old lake. This would have worked out fine if the lake had been filled to ground level. It wasn't. I didn't think the oversight was due to a shortage of bids on the work. But it had certainly proved costly.

Most tracks have drainage systems that enable them to keep

operating during any disaster short of an earthquake or nuclear war. GSD, by contrast, had been forced to close five times in six months. And this had been a year of light rainfall.

As I approached the ramshackle grandstand, I wondered if the building was really sinking into the ground or if it just looked that way. It could have been the tilt to the crooked black letters over the entrance that spelled out GARDEN STATE DOWNS and lied "Harness Racing 365 Days a Year." Or the folds in the white banner announcing SUPER PICK that looked like it had been fashioned out of Billy Bonnardo's last set of bed sheets.

Because the track itself was set down into the old lake, it was visible from the parking lot, which was a plateau overlooking the edge of the track apron where bettors congregated to watch the races. At most tracks, the apron is a vast expanse of tarmac that slants up gradually to the grandstand. But at GSD, it was a short, steep grade of dirt and gravel filled in on one side of the old lake, closer to a drop than a slope.

Before going inside, I paused a moment by the barbed-wire fence along the edge of the lot that prevented people from sneaking down onto the apron and added to the friendly atmosphere. Below me, I could see the early birds chewing on their White Owls and chatting it up about their chances. In just a few hours the place would be littered with losing tickets and lost hopes. But the old-timers weren't thinking about that right now. Like me, they were expecting to win some cashola.

4

While paying my admission, I noticed that Biff Bonnardo had come up with the cash to install turnstiles. He had probably determined it was cheaper in the long run than paying high school dropouts to press buttons on hand counters.

I popped for three bucks to go upstairs to the clubhouse. In addition to affording a better view, the clubhouse usually draws a smaller crowd, which means shorter lines at the betting windows. It also tends to draw a better class of people. This basically means that guys are more likely to use handkerchiefs than blow their noses right into their racing programs. Crowd size wasn't a concern at GSD, but the socioeconomic advantages rated special consideration.

As I climbed the stairs where the escalator should have been, a bright red tout sheet caught my attention. It was called "Longshot Sam's LONGSHOT SLAMS." Since I had been out there, Al Phillips' buddy had started selling a sheet. The four-dollar price was steep as these things go, but money was no object to a high roller like me.

I didn't have any trouble finding a beer and a seat. There couldn't have been more than a thousand people in the whole place. I could tell from the sheets in their hands that half of them were doing the same thing I was—comparing Longshot Sam's selections with the entries in the racing program.

Each horse in the program is assigned morning-line odds, set by a track official called the racing secretary. The morning line is an estimate and doesn't affect the actual odds, which are determined by how much money is bet. Longshot Sam's pick in

20

the first race, Simply Red, was 8–1 on the morning line. If the odds stayed at 8–1 after the betting was done, Simply Red would return $18 on a $2 wager—$16 in winnings, plus the original $2 bet.

Sam's selections were interesting because they were true longshots on the morning line. Most touts pick horses listed at 5–1 or less. Some of them pick morning-line favorites, which means you'd do just as well to save the money for their sheet, spend it on a beer and just bet the horses with the lowest odds in the program.

You can pick a lot of winners betting on the favorite but not enough to make any money. Favorites win a third of the time, but their average payoff is only five bucks. If you bet $2 on the favorite in nine races, you'd probably cash three winners. But it would cost you $18 to get $15 in payoffs. That doesn't sound like much damage until you start calculating your losses on $50 bets. Then you're in deep horseshit.

Longshot Sam picked a 6–1 morning-line shot in the second race and a pair of 7–1 shots in the third and fourth. The one that really caught my interest was his SLAM OF THE DAY, and not just because it was typeset in letters the size of hoofprints. The horse's name was Sugar Donut, and he was listed at 25–1 in the ninth race.

Sugar Donut was owned by Tony Lunaviva, a guy from Ohio who also owned a chain of donut shops around New York called Holey Toledo. Tony had made a name for himself by making a fool of himself. He was the star of his own low-budget late-night TV commercials, in which he popped his head through a giant cream donut and shouted: "Holey Toledo! I'm just *crazy* about donuts!"

A year ago, Lunaviva decided to plow his dough into horse racing. He bought fifty acres in Parsippany and built a house with all the conveniences of one of those bachelor pads that they used to run in *Playboy* magazine. On a tower next to his house he put a giant ring that he claimed was the world's largest donut. As far as I knew, nobody had come forward to challenge the assertion.

Tony's racing trademark was that each of his horses was named "donut." He started out at Yonkers and Roosevelt, but his horses ran as if they were on a Holey Toledo diet. He began racing them at Garden State Downs the day it opened.

If Sugar Donut's past-performance record was indicative of the rest of Tony Lunaviva's stable, he wasn't having any more success at GSD than he'd had at Yonkers and Roosevelt. I couldn't find anything to indicate Sugar Donut was capable of finishing the race, no less winning it. Evidently, Longshot Sam knew something I didn't.

It quickly became clear that Sam knew a lot of things I didn't. His selections won three of the first four races. That's good picking when you're going with longshots. There was only one problem. Half the people at the track were betting on Sam's picks. As a result, horses that should have been longshots were going off at low odds. But even if Sam's selections weren't paying off much, he was having a better day than I was. After four races, my perfect record at GSD was still intact—so far, I hadn't picked a winner.

My luck finally changed in the fifth race, and so did Sam's. I won the fifth with a $7.20 payoff, cashed $9.40 on the sixth, and hit another 5–2 shot in the seventh. Two of Sam's picks came in to show, and one finished out of the money.

Sam's eighth-race selection woke up at the top of the stretch just as mine fell asleep. I was ready for a nap myself until I noticed an oddity in the results. Longshot Sam's pick paid $5.60 to win, $5.80 to place, and $5.40 to show. That, folks, is what you call an overlay. It suddenly occurred to me that if most of the bettors were going with Sam's picks to win, there might be a lot of overlays. The problem, of course, was being able to spot them.

I considered ducking out before the last race to beat the crowd until I realized GSD didn't have a crowd to beat. And I was curious to see how Tony Lunaviva's horse would do. As I studied the program again, I thought the racing secretary was being conservative in setting Sugar Donut's odds at 25–1. I would have made him a 50–1 shot.

I've been calling Sugar Donut "he," by the way, because that was his original sex, back before some vet had nipped his manhood in the bud and changed his official status to gelding. Now, at thirteen years old, he was about ready for a change to the status of Elmer's Glue. But the bettors were clearly stuck on him. At five minutes until post time, Sugar Donut's odds had dropped to 6–1.

It was a strange situation, but there was an explanation for it. It was due to the herd mentality of the bettors—not unlike what happens when the stock market takes a sudden plunge and panic selling sets in. When a longshot's odds drop sharply, people think the "smart money" is on the horse, so they follow the herd. In fact, most insiders don't blow their money betting to win. They know people will notice, so they hide most of their bets in the place and show or exacta pools where it's less likely to be spotted. In the case of Sugar Donut, it looked like Longshot Sam had started the herd moving with his Slam of the Day.

I stood near the fifty-dollar window and watched the tote-board on the monitor. At two minutes to post, there was another odds flash. Sugar Donut was down to 4–1. With one minute left to bet, I got on line behind three guys who were pushing sixty and a woman who was flirting with thirty. I couldn't hear how much they bet, but I heard the first two guys ask for the same horse to win—number 3, Sugar Donut.

I realized the young woman was with the guy ahead of me when she turned and motioned for me to step in front of her. I could also see that she was a real thoroughbred—tall and slim, with perfect skin, sky-blue eyes, and a full mane of shiny auburn hair that hung to her shoulders. She wore a short, sleeveless cotton dress that matched her eyes and clung to her like Scotch tape. The dress was belted with a strand of white silk and ended midway between her waist and knees, revealing just enough of her thighs to make my knees want to buckle. I was sure she hadn't purchased the outfit at one of the local shopping malls.

I wondered what a dame that classy was doing watching the trots at a dump like Garden State Downs on a hot Friday afternoon. At least she was there with a guy who did his betting at the fifty-dollar window. He put a C-note to win on number 5, Lady Be Good, the morning-line favorite.

The betting clerks usually know better than to chat it up with the customers, but the guy at my window hadn't mastered the rules of teller etiquette. Maybe he had recently been promoted from the job of admission counter. "Gee, Sam," I heard him say. "I thought you were going with Sugar Donut."

"Not at those stinking odds," Sam replied.

I was sure there were lots of guys named Sam at GSD, but I would have bet the fifty bucks in my hand that the guy ahead of me was no ordinary Sam—he had to be Mr. Longshot. I knew Al Phillips' buddy was a great horseplayer, but I wasn't aware his handicapping skills applied to the field of women as well. As he pressed the ticket into his companion's slender hand, I realized the lady was his wife. Judging by the rock of Gibraltar on her finger, I figured she was a happily married woman.

I got my bet down just before the windows closed—Sugar Donut to show. Then I ambled over to the bar, where Sam and his wife were watching the race on the monitor.

I thought about introducing myself right away, but the polite thing was to wait until the race was over. It wasn't polite to stare at Sam's wife, so I tried to be subtle about it. I'm blind in my left eye, the result of an injury I suffered when I played minor-league baseball. I've still got my original, not a glass one, but it sits dead in the socket, there only for decoration. The condition is usually a detriment, but this time it gave me a natural advantage. I kept my bad eye on the TV and my good one on Mrs. Longshot.

Just for the record, I'd like to say that I'm not some lech who eyeballs every female between the age of consent and the onset of menopause. I'll admit to doing my share of girl watching—maybe more than my share—but I'm not some knee-jerk drooler. It's just that Sam's wife was the best-looking woman I'd seen in a long, long time. That she was at a racetrack in Jersey surrounded by beer-bellied buffoons and blue-haired bags only enhanced her appeal.

Down on the track, Sugar Donut stayed near the back of the pack for the first three-quarters of a mile, just like in his previous races. As the horses paced down the backstretch, the old boy moved out from the rail and into the middle of the track. The lead horses were lined up four across when they entered the final turn, but as they came out of it and headed for home, Sugar Donut put on a closing move that defied his prior record. He charged on the outside, streaking past the other horses and leaving them all behind as he crossed the wire.

Well, all except one. The number-5 horse, Lady Be Good, held on to win by a nose. At least it appeared that way to me. It was a photo finish, and the result wouldn't be official until the judges were done looking at the picture.

5

With the numbers 3 and 5 flashing on the toteboard, the track announcer reminded everyone to hold their tickets until the result was official. I've always figured that anybody dumb enough to toss out a ticket before the winner is posted deserves to lose. But then I get irritated with those consumer-product warnings that advise you not to take your toaster into the bathtub.

Longshot Sam didn't have any doubts about the results. He turned to his lovely wife, grinned and said, "Better not cash that ticket today, honey. People might get upset."

Sam had a point there. It wouldn't be good to be seen cashing a hundred-dollar bet on a horse that had beaten his Slam of the Day.

I introduced myself as they were turning to leave.

"Oh, sure!" As Sam shook my hand, he said, "Honey, this is Al's friend—the private detective that's coming out for the contest next week." To me, he said, "I'd like you to meet my wife, Michelle."

"It's a pleasure."

Michelle smiled. "We've heard a lot about you, Mr. Renzler."

"You can call me Mark." That was merely a suggestion. As far as I was concerned, she could call me anything she wanted short of shit-for-brains.

I've already noted Michelle's physical attributes, so I should also mention that her husband didn't look bad either—especially for a guy who spent the better part of his life at the track and went by Longshot Sam. Based on the moniker, I would have expected a runt in a plaid jacket with a White Owl grafted to his teeth. But Sam Natoli was only four inches shorter than I am, which made him five foot ten. He wasn't what you'd call svelte, but he had the build of a guy who knew enough to lay off the racetrack chow.

Al Phillips had told me Sam was sixty, but his black curly hair was only starting to go gray, and still had plenty left. More than I had, come to think of it. His swarthy complexion and thick eyebrows left no doubt about his Mediterranean heritage, and his brown eyes had a glint in them that told you somebody was definitely home upstairs. He had high cheekbones that seemed to stretch the skin up tightly from his sharp chin, leaving little opportunity for wrinkles, except at the corners of his eyes. It's hardly my place to speak on behalf of the fairer sex, but I thought Sam Natoli was a guy most women would call handsome. Evidently Michelle thought so, and that was proof enough for me.

A chorus of boos went up around us when Lady Be Good was posted as the winner. Sam chuckled. "I guess they thought they had a sure thing. How did you make out?"

"I had him to show," I said.

Sam squinted at the toteboard. "Hey, not bad. You got lucky and got yourself an overlay."

Indeed I had. Sugar Donut paid $4.20 to win, $3.60 to place, and $4.00 to show. That gave me a fifty-dollar profit on my bet. It also put me well into the win column for the day.

"Or maybe it wasn't luck," Sam added. "Al says you're a pretty good handicapper."

I shrugged. "It was just a hunch."

A small crowd formed around us as bettors came over to lodge their complaints with Longshot Sam. "What happened, Sam?" one of them demanded. "I blew twenty bucks on the bum."

I was amazed that anybody had the gall to gripe. If you had slavishly played Sam's picks all day, you would have left with more money than you came with. Anybody with a little sense would have cleaned up.

"Can't win 'em all," Sam said impatiently. He turned to me and whispered, "You want to join us for a drink? We've got to get out of here before the vultures arrive."

"It looks like they're here already."

Sam was hounded all the way through the clubhouse, a fifty-fifty split between jerks with axes to grind and well-wishers who didn't know when to quit. "We'll be able to talk in here," he said, stopping at a door labeled THE WINNERS CIRCLE—MEMBERS ONLY.

I followed them into a badly lit bar that Sam said was owner Biff Bonnardo's idea of an exclusive club. Based on the handful of guys in the place, it must have been very exclusive. There were about twenty booths that no one would mistake for leather, though that was clearly the intention. The tables were cross sections of oak trees coated with about six inches of lacquer finish. Instead of menus there were placemats shaped like horses that offered drinks and sandwiches with names like Sure Thing, Daily Double, and Odds-on Favorite.

Sam went directly to a booth in back. I had a feeling it was his private booth. We ordered a round of drinks without funny names from a waitress in a funny outfit. With a cowboy hat, Western-style blouse, short skirt, and fishnet stockings, she looked like a cross between Annie Oakley and the Happy Hooker.

"So what do you think of our little racetrack?" Sam asked.

"It's kind of low-budget."

"That's a polite way of putting it. But I'll tell you one thing: Once you know the trainers and drivers, it's a cinch."

"It must be exciting to be a private detective," Michelle said. I had a feeling she wouldn't mind keeping the conversation clear of racing.

"It has its moments." I could have told her the truth, but Michelle was somebody I didn't want to disappoint.

"Well, we're glad you'll be here for the contest," she said, fingering a silver necklace with a charm in the shape of a trotting horse, complete with driver and sulky. "I don't know if Al said anything or not, but we could use your help."

"No, he didn't. What seems to be the trouble?"

Michelle gave her husband a glance, as if to get his approval to talk. He shot one back that said "permission denied." There was an unnatural pause while she considered whether to explain, then a natural one as Annie Oakley put our drinks on the table.

"Well, here's to our mutual success next week," Sam said, raising his drink.

"We should tell him, Sam," Michelle said. "Just in case."

"No, it's nothing." Anger crept into Sam's voice. "Don't even bother to bring it up."

Michelle shot a furtive glance my way, almost begging me to give it a try. I did.

"If there's a problem, Sam, I'd be glad—"

"There's no problem. So let's end it right there—okay?"

Sam stared at me and I gave it right back. I didn't want to pry, but I wasn't about to let him off easy. Our eyes locked for a moment until he was forced to look away. That's another advantage of being blind in one eye: I can stare down a bull.

Sam changed the subject with the smoothness of a politician dodging a bribery allegation. "I know of you from a long time ago, Renzler. I remember when you played for Clifton High."

"That *was* a long time ago," I said.

"This guy used to be a big baseball star, Michelle. He broke every record in the state."

Michelle paused and toyed nervously with her necklace while deciding whether to ignore her husband or be polite to their guest. Her concern for my feelings won out.

"Really?" she said at last, gazing at me with wide-eyed wonderment that made me wonder if she was a baseball fan. If so, she got a few more points in my book. Not that she needed any.

"They were just high school records." I shrugged, but Michelle still looked impressed.

"I used to live down in Nutley," Sam said. "I used to go over to Clifton and watch you play. You would've been a great one, Renzler, no doubt about it." He paused. "Uh, maybe I shouldn't be bringing this up. I mean with the injury and all."

"That's okay. I don't think about it much anymore."

"What happened?" The concern in Michelle's voice sounded genuine. You can guess I appreciated it.

I hadn't told the story in a long while. It didn't upset me to tell it, but after twenty-five years it was hard to put much energy into the narrative. I gave them the short version.

"I was playing for the Richmond Sailors, a triple-A team. I was batting against a pitcher who had a reputation for being wild and fast. He sure lived up to it the day he beaned me. He cranked one up and I couldn't get out of the way in time. I don't think I ever saw it. The next thing I knew, I was on my back in the hospital and the whole left side of my face was bandaged. The doctors said I was lucky to be alive. I wasn't feeling very lucky then, but I guess they were right. I took it directly on my eye. A few inches over, and it would have hit me in the temple. Then it would have been lights out for good."

"My God, that's terrible!" Michelle gasped.

"At least it kept me out of the army."

Sam chuckled as he flagged the waitress for another round. I was tempted to beg off and send him a message about silencing Michelle, but I decided it was none of my business. Besides, if Michelle wanted to talk to me, she'd have a chance to do it alone next week. To be honest, that idea held a certain appeal for me.

Sam gave me some tips about Garden State Downs for the contest. It was good inside stuff about which drivers and trainers won consistently, and I took down notes.

"One thing you don't want to do here," he said, "is pay too much attention to the morning line."

"Why's that? Do you have a crooked racing secretary?"

Sam smiled. "Al was right. You do know your stuff." I took that as a compliment. "I wouldn't go so far as to call him crooked, but let's just say he's not above adjusting the odds a little in his favor when he sees an opportunity to make a nice bet come along. It happens at a lot of small tracks."

"And what does Biff Bonnardo think of that?" I asked.

Sam shrugged. "He turns the other way. He's kind of a sleaze if you ask me. And I'm sure he doesn't pay the guy enough money. Bonnardo's pretty cheap, as I'm sure you can tell from the design of this place."

I nodded and reached for the check, but Sam beat me by a fingertip. As we were getting up to leave, Michelle asked, "Did Al talk to you about staying with us next week?"

"He mentioned it. But I was planning on getting a room at Howard Johnson's."

"Not that dive at the Route 23 traffic circle," Sam said. "No way we're going to let you stay there."

"That's right," Michelle added. "We've got a beautiful house right down in Packanack Lake with lots of extra rooms."

I'd be lying if I said waking up in the vicinity of Michelle Natoli didn't sound appealing. But HoJo's also holds a certain appeal for me, one that goes back to the days of the Friday-night fish fry, before I learned there were greater pleasures in life than the twenty-eight flavors. It's a perverse appreciation, I'll grant you, not unlike my interest in racing junk mail. I guess it's basically a sense of nostalgia. HoJo's was the first restaurant my parents took me to, my first concept of what a restaurant is supposed to be. I was probably thirteen by the time I realized that the reason my old man went there was because he could take the kids *and* have a martini. Before that, I thought orange was the color of all things luxurious.

Needless to say, I didn't try to explain any of this to Longshot Sam and his wife. I merely told them I didn't want to impose.

"Don't be silly," Sam said.

I hemmed for a moment, then hawed for another, until Michelle began giving me the business with both barrels of her baby blues. *"Please,"* she whispered.

It was then that I realized there was more than hospitality on Michelle Natoli's mind. As I looked into her eyes, I saw something that sent a shiver up my spine. And no, Mike Hammer fans, it wasn't lust or longing or any of that good stuff. It was something more basic, much stronger.

It was fear.

"Thanks," I said. "I'd be glad to."

6

I cashed my ticket on Sugar Donut on my way out and added two crisp fifties to the stack of bills in my wallet. It was pushing five-thirty by the time I found a crawl space in the line of commuter traffic.

I let the Pinto warm up before indulging the luxury of switching on all-news radio. I've learned the hard way that the car doesn't respond well if you ask it to do too many things at once. You don't dare honk the horn while the wipers are going. It even belches when you hit the high beams.

I tuned in just in time to hear a report that Watergate songbird John Dean had been sentenced to one to four years in country-club jail. I figured his wife, Mo, was secretly hoping he'd get all four, but it was a cinch the snitch would be out in a few months.

I planned to head straight back to New York, but when the orange roofs of HoJo's beckoned my better judgment lost out to the temptation of fried clams and one more belt for the road. I told myself it would be smart to wait for the end of rush hour, but I knew I was lying. In Jersey, it's always rush hour.

Some people feel self-conscious eating alone, but it's never bothered me. That's because I'm not a self-conscious person—oblivious was the word my most recent girlfriend used. She dumped me for a "sensitive" guy. At least that's the reason she gave me. It probably didn't hurt that he was worth two million bucks. I figured he could afford to be sensitive.

The clams didn't taste as good as they did when I was ten years old. My tastes haven't changed much, so it must have been due to a decline in HoJo's standards. But the main problem was that I couldn't get the look of fear on Michelle Natoli's face off my mind.

I succumbed to another temptation when I noticed the telephone next to the cigarette machine. I happened to have a dime in change left, so I put it in the slot and rang up my sister. I was probably asking for more trouble, but my mother always said that trouble was my middle name. In that case, I used to ask, how did I end up with a middle name like Francis?

My plan was to hang up if my brother-in-law answered, but Karen did the honors. "Oh, how thoughtful of you!" she said. "You remembered!"

Apparently I was calling on a special occasion. I tried not to let on that my memory was as bad as ever while going over a mental list of the important dates in her household. It was a short list.

"Well, you know me," I said. "I've always been a thoughtful guy." Hardly true, but not a bad recovery, all things considered.

"Sixteen years. I can't believe it's been that long."

I took that to mean it was her anniversary, although I vaguely recalled that it had been snowing at her wedding. "Yeah, I know, that is a long time." Especially when you're married to a guy like Dick Derkovich.

"You wouldn't believe how big he's gotten," Karen said.

"That happens when you start getting up there in years. It's something we all have to face."

"And he's so handsome."

Now *that* I found hard to believe. I knew from experience that love can be blind, but it's usually a temporary loss of vision. My two episodes had each lasted three years.

"Why don't I put him on and you can congratulate him."

I had about as much to say to my brother-in-law as G. Gordon Liddy had to say to the grand jury. He had even less to say to me. Dick's a man of few words to begin with, and he doesn't like to waste them for my benefit.

In fairness, I should point out that I've given him lots of reasons to dislike me. One occurred five years ago when I made the mistake of spending Christmas in Jersey. I tend to suffer from the holiday blues and usually turn to alcohol for a cure. I got on a bourbon jag that resulted in my decking their next-door neighbor. I think he was whining about niggers moving into the neighborhood, but he might have merely said that he liked the Boston Red Sox. It wouldn't have been so bad if the guy's kids hadn't been there. But there was a bright side to it: I no longer get invited to Jersey for Christmas.

"You deserve some congratulations yourself," I said.

Karen laughed. She's always had a sweet laugh. She's always been a sweet girl. "Oh, you mean for putting up with him all these years."

"Exactly."

"Well, I've loved every minute of it," she said. That was a bald-faced lie, unless love was deaf and dumb as well. "Hold on a sec, and I'll get him for you."

"No, that's all right. I'm at a pay phone. You just wish him happy anniversary for me."

"Anniversary! It's Herbie's birthday! You dummy. We got married during the winter. How could you forget?"

Now that she mentioned it, I did recall that Dick's car had skidded off the road and gotten stuck in a ditch. I thought he deserved it for driving a Cadillac, but I did feel sorry for Karen. They ended up spending their wedding night on the fold-out sofa in my parents' basement.

"I guess I'm not such a thoughtful guy after all."

"You never were. But don't worry about it. I still love you anyway."

"That means a lot to me, Karen." I didn't bother to add that it would have meant a lot more if she didn't also love Dick Derkovich. That had to say something about her standards.

Just then, a gum-cracking voice informed me that it was time to ante up another dime. I scrounged in my pockets but came up empty. "Deposit ten cents or I'll have to cut you off," the operator repeated. There was just enough edge in her tone to suggest that she'd enjoy doing it.

I spotted some change on the counter that someone had left as a tip and thought about taking out a temporary loan, but the intended recipient of the windfall was only a few steps away. She had eyes that looked like a pair of man-eating moths, thanks to five bucks' worth of Maybelline mascara applied ever so carefully. Somehow I didn't think she'd go for the idea.

"Give me the number and I'll call you back," Karen said.

It was time to own up. "That's all right. I'll stop by."

"Where the hell are you?"

Miss Congeniality cut us off before I could answer.

I downed another gin and tonic, then headed up Route 23 in search of a shopping center. It took all of about thirty seconds to find one.

I went into a drug store the size of Yankee Stadium and selected a birthday card from a rack that was a hundred yards long. I stuck a fifty inside. I was about to scrawl a note advising Herbie not to spend it on booze and drugs when I remembered that he attended a minor seminary. I couldn't think of anything clever to say to a future priest, so I merely signed it, "Congrats—Uncle Mark."

When you don't have any kids of your own, you're expected to take a special interest in your nieces and nephews. It was a good thing Herbie was my only one, because there was an awful lot of him to take an interest in. As a kid, his only hobbies had been watching TV and eating, but he'd excelled at both of them. I'd been slipping in my avuncular duties of late, so I slipped another fifty in the card before sealing the envelope.

A hundred bucks should buy a guy a lot of slack, but I figured I needed plenty before going to see my sister. In addition to dodging the question of why I had tried to conceal my whereabouts, I'd have to explain why I couldn't stick around. I stopped in a flower shop and bought a dozen white roses for Karen, then hit a sporting-goods store and got a dozen white golf balls for Dick. That was the only thing short of a lawn mower that I knew he would like. For myself, I picked up a fifth of Beefeater gin. When Dick found out I was coming, the first thing he'd do was lock up the liquor cabinet. If I was lucky, the second thing he'd do was leave the house before I got there.

No such luck on that score, but I made out all right anyway. The family was going out to dinner for Herbie's birthday, and I was holding up the show. I was even spared the tour of their new house.

Dick and Karen were waiting in the driveway when I pulled up. Dick's a real stickler about being on time, and he was tapping his foot impatiently. I suspected that he had issued a five-minute ultimatum and I had arrived at T-minus-three seconds. Punctuality has never been one of my vices.

Karen gave me a hug and gushed over the flowers, then delivered the good news about their dinner plans in an apologetic tone. Dick kept a careful watch to make sure she didn't break down and invite me along.

"It's too bad you didn't call sooner," Karen said, after I told them I had been at Garden State Downs. "Herbie would've loved to go with you. He's been nagging Dick to take him there ever since it opened. But he's just been too busy."

"No, that's not the reason," Dick said, in a tone that sounded like a reminder.

Karen smiled. "Dick thinks all the races are fixed."

I knew better than to take issue with one of my brother-in-law's opinions. And in the case of Garden State Downs, there was a chance he might be right about something for once. Instead I shook hands and gave him my peace offering.

"Thanks," he said. "I usually pay a Titlist 3, but these will do in a pinch."

I felt like pinching him with one of the garden tools that he keeps neatly arranged on the walls of his garage, but I was trying to be on my best behavior. "So, where's Herbie?" I asked. It seemed out of character for him to be late for a meal.

"Oh, he just went back inside for a minute," Karen said. "And by the way, he likes to be called 'Herb' now."

"Is that so?"

She laughed. "I'm having trouble getting used to it myself."

Karen took the gifts into the house. I decided to hang on to the gin. Generosity has its limits, and I had a feeling I might need it for the ride home. In the absence of anything to talk about, I complimented Dick on the nice job he was doing with his lawn. His discourse on the proper mix of fertilizer and seed was cut short when an angel of mercy bounded out of the house.

It had been two years since I had last seen my nephew. At that time he was five feet tall and his waist was about five feet around. His skin was ravaged by acne and he had about ten grand worth of braces on his teeth. So it took me a moment to recognize the strapping youth now lumbering toward me.

Karen had told me that Herbie was working out, but the

transformation was so remarkable that I suspected the power of prayer must have been involved too. He had grown by a foot and though his weight was probably the same, the rolling layers of fat had been displaced by rippling racks of muscle. The acne had cleared up and given way to whiskers. The world's biggest marshmallow had turned into a fucking animal.

"Hello, Uncle Mark," he bellowed.

"Happy birthday, Herb."

My knuckles crunched as he clasped my hand. It hurt like a son of a bitch, but it was an improvement over last time, when he had tried to plant a wet one on my mouth. I had turned at the last second to take it on the cheek, and he caught me full force with his braces. A doctor friend of mine put me on a course of antibiotics as a precautionary measure.

"Looks like you've been hitting the weights," I said.

"That's right, Uncle Mark. I can bench-press two-fifty." I didn't doubt it for a moment.

Karen returned as I gave Herbie his card. "Is Uncle Mark coming to dinner with us?" he asked hopefully.

There was an uncomfortable pause as Karen looked at Dick. I did the dirty work for him. "Sorry, Herb. I've got to get back to the city and take care of some business."

Herbie used to stomp and pout when he didn't get his way, but now he took the news like a man—frowning momentarily as if he felt a migraine coming on. "Are you working on a case?" he asked.

"I sure am." Herbie thinks I've got the most exciting job in the world. I didn't want to dispel the notion by telling him it was a case of gin.

"Uncle Mark went to the racetrack today," Karen said.

The newfound maturity began to drain from Herbie's face. "Darn, I wish I could've gone too." It looked like he was about to revert to his old methods of coping with disappointment.

God knows what possessed me at that moment. It might have been the booze making me a friendlier guy than I really am. More likely, it was the idea that Herbie's old man wouldn't take him to the track.

When I was half Herbie's age, an uncle we called Shifty used to sneak me into Yonkers by putting a cigar in my mouth, a fedora on my head, and a program over my face. It wasn't my place to question Herbie's vocational plans, but I suspected his decision to enter the priesthood was partly attributable to lack of acquaintance with the near occasions of sin. As his uncle, I felt some sense of duty to handle the introductions.

"Tell you what, Herb," I said. "You be ready at noon on Monday, and I'll show you how to wheel an exacta."

"Really?" Herbie's face lit up like a floodlight. He rubbed his giant paws together. "Boy-oh-boy-oh-boy!"

Daddy Doom looked like he was about to blow a fuse. "But he doesn't have any money to bet with."

"Oh yes I do!" Herbie waved his pair of U.S. Grants as if he were signing up for the Union army. He put me in a bear hug that sent my clams swimming for cover. "God bless you, Uncle Mark!"

"Likewise, Herb."

7

Some people wake up with hangovers and can't remember what they did the night before. Booze doesn't affect me that way. I never forget what I did. But sometimes I wonder why I did it.

Saturday morning was one of those occasions.

The last thing I needed at Super Pick was to have Herbie tagging along. Over a breakfast of aspirin and coffee, I tried to think of a graceful way out, but the only thing I could come up with was that I should have taken him with me the day before. I'd been betting on horse races long enough to know that shoulda-woulda-coulda don'ta count. That's a quote from my bookie Angelo.

I was well into my beer cycle before I got up the energy to call Nate Moore and let him know I had taken the liberty of registering him for Super Pick. I'd been feeling guilty for letting Al Phillips pay the freight, and I figured it wouldn't hurt to stack the deck a little more in our favor. After all, if you're going to cheat, you might as well do a good job of it. And I knew for a fact that Nate wasn't busy. For weeks now, he had been doing exactly what I was doing—watching TV and waiting for Nixon to resign.

In addition to being a full-time friend, Nate is my part-time partner. He's a massive man with a passive manner that can change to a mean streak if the situation warrants. To paraphrase the poet Spiro Agnew—when the going gets tough, I call on Nate. Although he's worked with me for years, being a detective is only a hobby for him. There was a time when he needed the dough to support his primary occupation, painting. Not houses, mind you, but canvases. Nate is a bona fide arteest.

Three years ago Nate hit the big time in a big way, and I'm glad to claim a supporting role in his success. It began when he painted a green garbage dumpster with a dandelion growing out of it and a mosquito the size of a mallard grinning and nibbling on the dandelion. Nate titled it *The Garden State* in honor of my New Jersey roots. It was a present for my fortieth birthday.

If the truth be told, *The Garden State* is one of Nate's lesser efforts. I'm not trying to pass myself off as an art critic, but it only took him forty-five minutes. He even did it to scale so it would fit over my green sofa. The whole project started as a way for me to get out of painting the wall myself after a short-tempered client had pumped it full of bullet holes.

Before presenting it to me, Nate showed the painting at a gallery in the West Village. It went up next to an Andy Warhol and was promptly spotted by a crazy art collector with a Rhode Island accent and a Rockefeller bankroll. The guy offered twenty thousand dollars, but I turned him down flat. For sentimental reasons, I explained to Nate, who promptly went into a tirade about the difference between sentiment and stupidity. Guess which one I represented.

"Ask him for twenty-five," he said, "and I'll paint you another one just like it."

I did, he did, and we split the cash. After being my muscle for fifteen years, Nate Moore also became my benefactor. I don't know about you, but twelve and a half grand is the biggest ticket *I* ever cashed at one window.

In addition to getting a wad of dough and a lot of dates, Nate became an instant celebrity. He did the talk-show circuit and a college lecture tour, and he almost got a part in a John Waters movie. He got a bit insufferable for a while there, but basically he took all the attention in stride. He kept working with me unless it conflicted with a taping of "Dick Cavett."

Of late, Nate had been saying that his fifteen minutes were about up, but I think he was just starting to feel old. Nate rounded the Big five-oh last year. His star *had* faded a little, but he was still doing okay for himself.

We hadn't worked together lately because I didn't have any

work to do. But we were still hanging out and comparing notes on the Watergate soap opera. Nate had a special interest in Tricky Dick's demise because his father had been a labor activist whom Nixon had singled out as a subversive in the early fifties. Although he didn't share my enthusiasm for the track, Nate liked to cross the Hudson River now and then; after all, he owed his success to New Jersey. I knew it would take some persuading, but I figured he'd be willing to go.

I figured wrong.

"Are you crazy?" he asked, after I had given him the capsule summary on the contest. "The House Judiciary Committee adopted three articles of impeachment last week. This is the week King Richard finally gets knocked off his throne."

"You're putting far too much faith in Peter Rodino," I said. Rodino was the committee chairman, a congressman from Jersey with the voice of a cement mixer and a head full of gravel.

"Well, I'm not surprised that you'd be willing to miss the glorious moment for the prospect of making a few bucks. You've always been a front runner." Nate frequently questioned the depth of my political commitment. He was horrified a few years ago when he found out I wasn't registered to vote. I told him it was a sign of my superior cynicism.

"You're being far too optimistic. He's good for one more Soviet peace mission. Or at least another attack of phlebitis."

"Hey, I like seeing Dick with the Bear. I like it when his veins get clogged. You expect me to pass on that for five days at the track with your cretin pen pals?"

Nate had his own perverse pantheon of personal heroes, but his taste tended to run toward washed-up character actors and TV game-show guests. His favorite was Joe Franklin, host of a late-night talk show that Tony Lunaviva ran his donut commercials on. As far as I was concerned, the show's only purpose was to tell people they should already be in bed. But Nate was a faithful watcher, and had even appeared on it as a guest.

"I seem to recall you telling me that you wouldn't mind meeting Timmy the Greek yourself," I said.

"Sure, I said I wouldn't mind," he clarified. "But I didn't say I'd go all the way to Jersey to do it."

"You can watch the news on TV out there," I said, borrowing one of Al Phillips' selling points.

"*If* we make it out there. We could also break down in that shitbox car of yours again."

"I got a new tire—and a tune-up."

"That makes me feel much better. Just give me one good reason for going."

"You could make a pile of money."

"So says Al Phillips."

"That's right. You don't like Al very much, do you?"

"He's not as bad as some of your other low-life friends. But I sure wouldn't trust him. Besides, what do I need money for? You seem to be forgetting who you're talking to."

"And you seem to be forgetting that you're on a downward cycle. You ought to be saving for the nursing home, old man."

Nate snickered. I could hear him popping open a can of beer. At least I figured it was a beer. I'd be surprised if he had taken up soda pop.

"You'll get to see my nephew again," I said.

"Oh yeah?" Nate had taken a shine to Herbie after meeting him at a Yankees game a few years back. The kid told him about some financial problems in his parish, and Nate wound up donating a painting to help the cause. That should have put me in Karen's and Dick's eternal good graces, but I got right back in the doghouse with my antics at Christmas.

"How's the little guy doing?" he asked.

"He's not so little anymore," I said.

"He never was."

"Herbie's been working out. He's built like a brick shithouse. He's only sixteen, but he looks twenty-one. He calls himself Herb now, and he's studying for the priesthood."

"Father Herb, huh? Sounds like the leader of a California drug cult. Does he still try to kiss you on the mouth?"

"No. He's into crushing hands now. And I'm sure there's no hand he'd like to crush more than old Uncle Nate's."

"Well, you tell young Herbie that old Uncle Nate sends his regards."

"I don't believe it," I said, affecting a hurt tone. "You're going to make me grovel."

"No, I'm not. I'm just waiting for you to come up with a good reason."

I told him about Longshot Sam and his wife. Mostly, I told him about Michelle. That raised his interest, but not enough.

"If you run into any trouble, of course I'll help you," Nate said. "But I'm not going to hang out at that mud hole of a racetrack just for the fun of it."

"So you're really begging off."

"You're the one who's begging, Renzler."

"Next time you need a wall to hang a painting on, don't turn to me."

"Oh, break my heart."

"I'm out five hundred bucks for your entry fee."

"A mere drop in the bucket compared to what Al Phillips says you'll win. Can't you come up with an excuse to get off the hook?"

"When's the last time you collected a refund at the track?"

"Yeah, you've got a point there," he said. "Well, I'm sorry to let you down. What about that slimebag Angelo?"

I liked Angelo Albani, but he was only good in small doses. "Would *you* want to spend five days with Angelo?" I asked.

"I wouldn't want to spend five *minutes* with him. Remember, I'm the only one of your friends that I like."

"Well, thanks a lot . . . *friend*."

"Hey, wait a sec, I've got an idea. Why don't you get Herbie to stand in for me?"

"Herbie?"

"Yeah, why not?"

"He's only sixteen."

"But he looks twenty-one, and he's built like a brick shitter. You said so yourself."

I lit a cigarette and thought about it for a moment.

"Come on," Nate said. "It's a brilliant idea."

"I wouldn't go that far. But it's not a bad one."

8

I hadn't seen so many cheap suits in one place since I worked part-time at Robert Hall's. I'm hardly what you'd call a smart dresser, but I felt like *Esquire*'s man of the year compared with the rumpled group gathered in the GSD Winners Circle on Monday morning for an orientation brunch.

I should have been getting oriented with the amateurs in the clubhouse at noon, but Longshot Sam had pulled a few strings to get me in with the pros. I recognized most of the pickers from the bad photos in their junk-mail offers. Al and Sam identified the ones I didn't know.

I was glad to see that the new turnstile had withstood the test of Timmy Malkos, who was sitting at a table in the center of the room and savoring a private breakfast. Judging by the way the Greek was shoveling scrambled eggs and greasy sausage links into a mouth the size of a trash chute, I had a feeling he might not be so lucky getting through the turnstile on his way out.

The Greek looked a lot younger than the old-timer in his junk-mail mug shot, and I wondered if he had invested in a face lift. He had heavy, dark eyebrows that curled upward at the outside edges, but that was the only sign of hair on his round face. His cheeks were shiny and looked baby-bottom soft, and each one was about the size of a baby's bottom. Based on the sweet scent he was giving off, he must have splashed a gallon of cologne on his neck. This was no small accomplishment, since the Greek had no neck to speak of.

The guy I really wanted to get a look at was Toteboard

Tommy Stevens. After all, he was the only one in the bunch who had ever suckered me into buying a system.

Tommy was beefy, bald, and about fifty years old. His eyes were close together, possibly from too much squinting at the toteboard, but I suspected a congenital defect. He had thick eyebrows that merged to form a single awning and a nose that started near the brow, giving the impression that it was growing out of his forehead. It was a large nose, with nostrils wider than the Lincoln Tunnel and room for signs indicating inbound and outbound lanes. It was easy to understand why he didn't include a photo in his mailings. He probably couldn't find a camera that was willing to sit still long enough to take his picture.

Dr. Dave Higgins, the former racetrack vet, was sitting across from Tommy. He was about fifteen years older and wore thick bifocals that sat crookedly on a long, thin nose that rode all the way down to his upper lip. He had a small mouth, about the size of a buttonhole, and when he talked the nose seemed to drop down farther, giving the illusion that it had to unbutton the lips to speak. Like his friend, he seemed to have resigned himself that there was no Rx for baldness. The only hair he had left was some white fuzz that rimmed the sides of his perfectly round head like salt on a Margarita glass.

They were chatting with a bosomy redhead of about thirty-five who was standing at their booth. Even if she hadn't been the only female in the room, I would have known she was Serendipity McCall, the astrological handicapper.

Serendipity had dark-red lipstick on a tiny round mouth that looked like the top of a ketchup bottle in a household where mustard is the condiment of preference. She had a big face, but her peepers were small and set back deep in their sockets. The eyes were blue and she went heavy on the mascara and shadow, a shade of orange that made the roofs of HoJo's seem soft and subtle by comparison. Serendipity could barely contain her enthusiasm when she talked, and she wore a white sheer blouse that could barely contain a pair of zeppelins that left no doubt as to why she was nicknamed the Daily Double. She had on about twenty pounds of jewelry with a retail value of about fifty dollars. The centerpiece was a blue turquoise brooch about the size of a hockey puck that hung from her neck on a wide-link chain and rested on mother nature's shelf.

As I passed them on my way to the buffet table, I overheard Serendipity say she wished Longshot Sam wasn't in the contest.

"That goes for all of us," Toteboard Tommy said in a voice three octaves higher than the heavenly hosts. It was a disarming effect, like a meow emerging from the mouth of a bullfrog.

"Maybe you could do us a favor, Red, and knocker him off," Dr. Dave said. "Get it?"

"You mean you want that I should give him the old *one-two?*" She swung her hips so that her breasts jiggled on the count.

As luck would have it, she swiveled at the moment I went by. The races hadn't started and I had already hit the double. She winked at me, and I hurried on without breaking stride. I still wanted to be on her mailing list, but that was as close as I wanted to get.

Clocker Callaway was picking over the buffet when I got there. I recognized him from his junk-mail mug, even though he appeared thinner in person and twenty years older than his photo, where he looks about fifty. It probably helped that he had a stopwatch hanging from his belt loop and a see-through plastic pencil holder on his shirt pocket with three perfectly sharpened number 2s inside. His chin was sharper than the pencils, and its point formed the top of an inverted triangle, the base of which started at his cheekbones. His complexion was pasty and his cheeks were hollowed so deeply that it looked like someone was pulling on them from inside his mouth. Clocker's bony hands shook as he spooned potatoes onto his plate. Something told me his time was quickly running out.

Standing beside Clocker was a black guy about my age whose head almost touched the ceiling. It was a low ceiling, but he still had four inches on me.

"Looks like the Greek cleaned the place out already," he said to nobody in particular.

One glance at the offerings, and I decided to play it safe and stick with my usual black-and-white breakfast of coffee and cigarettes. "That might be lucky for us," I said.

"Man, you're not kidding. This looks like the same crap they feed to the horses."

"If you've seen the horses running at this place, you'll know better than to eat any of it."

He let out a laugh, then stuck out a paw the size of a baseball glove and wrapped my hand in a brother shake. "I didn't get your name, bro."

"Mark Renzler."

"Track Jack Jones."

"Yeah, I figured that."

"Process of elimination, right?" He grinned. "I don't remember you from last year. Are you from out this way?"

"I'm with the amateurs. I'm just here because I'm a friend of Al Phillips and Sam Natoli." I motioned toward Sam's booth.

"Oh, then you're in *bad* company, my man. This is Sam's track. He practically *owns* the place. Only way Sam can lose is if he drops dead. I don't think there's much hope of that."

"Let's hope *not*," I said. "Al tells me you're a pretty good handicapper yourself."

"Is that right? Al said that?" The grin spread across Jack Jones's face again. "Well I take that as a compliment, 'cause Al knows his business." He leaned in and lowered his voice. "I'm glad to see Al and Sam ironed out their differences and all."

I answered with a baffled look.

"Oh, I guess you didn't hear about that?"

I shook my head. "What happened?"

"I don't know exactly. But I heard there was some real bad blood between them after last year."

"Do you know why?" With all the clatter and chatter around us, I wasn't sure why I was whispering.

Track Jack shrugged. "I could sure take a guess."

I nodded, as if to say go ahead.

He tapped my shoulder with his finger. "Any time a couple of good buddies fight, you can bet it's about one of two things: money or a lady."

"Or both."

"Yeah, that's right." Jack laughed. "Well, I got to go sit down and eat these eggs before they get cold."

I didn't bother telling him I thought it was already too late. I returned to Sam's booth to find Lucky Lou Larson and Sulky Sol Epstein sitting with Al and Sam. I was sure they hadn't been invited. I knew Al didn't like them, and a few minutes earlier Sam had referred to them as Tweedle Dum and Tweedle Dumber.

Lucky Lou and Sulky Sol could have passed for brothers. They were short and squat, and between them they had about half a dozen chins and a dozen strands of hair, not counting the crop growing out of the matching moles on their chubby cheeks. The main difference between them was their method of coping with baldness. It looked like Lou polished his dome, while Sol opted to cover his with an ill-fitting hairpiece. They were nonstop talkers who didn't so much speak as blare. Their personalities were as loud as their sports jackets, which were plaid and double-breasted with wide lapels.

"Yeah, sure, I know this guy," Lou Larson said when Al introduced us. "He ain't no amateur. I seen him at Yonkers a million times."

Sulky Sol Epstein let out some exhaust fumes from a Dutch Masters. "We're starting up a pool on when Nixon resigns," he told me. "You in for a double sawbuck?"

"Sure thing." I pulled out a twenty and handed it to him. "I'll take Thursday."

"Aw, c'mon. You gotta be more precise than that," Sol said. "You gotta give me a time, too."

"Thursday night at nine o'clock. Is that precise enough?"

"It's just fine." Sol got up and I took my seat beside Al.

"So what do you do for a living, Renzler?" Lou Larson asked.

"I'm a private investigator."

"Is that right? Whaddaya know about that."

Just then a voice behind us wheezed, "Hey, Solly, put out that damn cigar! Can't you see I'm trying to eat my breakfast?" I turned to see Timmy the Greek glowering in our direction. He was twenty feet away, but I didn't doubt he could smell Sol Epstein's cigar. It was truly a stinker.

"Up yours, fat man," Sol replied.

At first I thought he was joking, then I realized his hostility was genuine. The Greek scowled and shook his head, then lowered it and began stuffing in more food. I heard a few snickers of laughter from Toteboard Tommy's booth.

"You *tell* him, Sol," Serendipity McCall said.

"Is it my imagination or is there some friction here?" I asked Al quietly.

Not quietly enough. Lou Larson overheard my question and answered for him. "Yeah, that's right, you ain't imagining anything," he said, glaring at Timmy Malkos as he lit his own cigar. I noted another difference between him and Sol—Lou was a White Owl guy. "We all hate each other's guts. Ain't that right, Sam?"

Sam replied with a deadpan look. "I hate yours, that's for sure."

Lou Larson snorted and Sulky Sol almost choked on his cigar. As they turned to leave, Serendipity waltzed up to our booth.

"Now here's somebody that everybody loves," Sol said, putting his arm around her shoulders.

Serendipity reciprocated with a kiss on the cheek that left a lipstick smear right over his mole. She placed her freckled hands on his buddy's dome. "Let me gaze into my crystal ball and see what I find."

"Be careful," Sam warned. "You'll go blind if you stare at that thing for too long."

Serendipity pressed her fingertips to her head. Excluding her thumbs, she had rings on all her fingers. "I sense a new presence," she said. Then she turned dramatically toward me. "Ah yes, here it is. And who do we have here?"

"Watch out, Red," Lou said as Sam introduced us. "The guy's a private eye."

"*Really?* You must be a Libra then. Libras are *very snoopy.*"

Suddenly it occurred to me that I could be looking at five very long days. If Al and I didn't walk away with some serious dough, I was going to be one unhappy chappy.

"Well, am I right?" she asked.

"I haven't the foggiest."

"You mean to tell me you don't know what your sign is!"

I confessed my sin by shaking my head. "Maybe I don't have one."

"Don't be silly. Everybody's got a sign. When's your birthday?"

"September fifteenth."

"Virgo. I knew it."

"I thought you said he was a Libra, Red." Sol slid his arm

around her waist. The top of his head came up to her shoulders, which put his eyes right at breast level.

"Virgo was my second choice." Serendipity winked at me, then smiled at Sam. "So, are you going to count my freckles again this year, Sammy Boy?"

I shot Al a puzzled look, but Serendipity intercepted it. "Last year Sam and Track Jack counted my freckles," she explained. "How many of them were there?"

"Five thousand, six hundred, forty-two."

Serendipity turned to face the emaciated figure of Clocker Callaway. "That's right!" she squealed. "And Clocker timed them. How long did it take? Do you remember?"

"Of course he remembers," Lou Larson said.

"One hour, two minutes, six seconds," Clocker said with authority if not conviction. Nobody challenged him on it.

"How about it, Sam?" Serendipity asked. "I think maybe you missed a few and might want to double-check your work."

"Sorry, sweetheart. I'm a married man again this year."

"Oh, I'm so sorry. What is this—your sixth or seventh?"

"Fifth." Sam looked at Clocker. "But who's counting?"

I shot another glance at Al, who nodded to confirm the information. I wondered if Sam's past wives were as good-looking as Michelle.

"What's this one's name?" Serendipity asked.

"Michelle."

"Wait a sec, Sam," Sol Epstein said. "I thought you was working your way through the alphabet."

Sam shrugged. "I changed my game plan. Time's running out."

"What were your other wives' names?" Serendipity asked.

"Ashley, Beverly, Candy, Daphne," Clocker said flatly.

"Maybe *you'd* like to count my freckles, Mr. Renzler."

I shook my head. "Math was never my strong subject."

Serendipity squealed again. "But if you're a private detective, I bet you like to uncover things."

"Private detective!" It was the first time Clocker had any inflection in his voice. "Are you here to investigate something?"

"Yeah," I said, doing my deadpan best to hold back a smile. "I'm looking into mail-order-fraud schemes."

Serendipity and Clocker looked like they had just swallowed

the cigars that Lucky Lou and Sulky Sol were smoking. Sam and Al started to laugh, then Lou and Sol followed their lead.

Things quieted down when a tall, middle-aged guy wearing a Detroit Tigers cap and wire-rimmed glasses stepped up to the bar and called for everyone's attention.

"Who's this?" Al asked quietly.

"That's Dave Gwynn." Sam grinned. "He's the PR director. And the racing secretary. *And* the track announcer."

"You're kidding. You mean this guy sets the odds *and* calls the races?"

"Not only that, Al," I said, "but he sells programs down at the door."

Al shook his head. "You were right, Renzler. This place really is small-time."

"Welcome to Garden State Downs," Dave Gwynn said, taking the words right out of my mouth. "I'm sure you're all going to have questions, but before you ask them, why don't you let me—"

"I want to say something first," Toteboard Tommy Stevens piped, rising to his feet.

I had a feeling Gwynn didn't like being interrupted, but he disguised his annoyance by mimicking Toteboard Tommy's voice. "And what might that be?" he asked in a lilting falsetto.

The room erupted with laughter, but Tommy continued undaunted. "I think the contest would be a lot fairer if you ordered Sam Natoli to drop dead."

That triggered some more laughs, but none from our booth.

Dave Gwynn smiled. "What do you think of that, Sam?"

Sam stood up and glared at Tommy Stevens. "I think that asshole better keep his mouth shut or he's going to end up watching the races from a hospital bed."

I searched Sam's face for a sign that he might be joking. I couldn't find any. As I looked around the room, I had trouble reading the reactions of the contestants. Some seemed amused, others surprised. Tommy Stevens looked downright terrified.

"I don't think your suggestion went over too well," Dave Gwynn said. In addition to his many roles at the track, the racing secretary seemed to have a gift for understatement.

9

After the brunch, Al and I ducked over to the bar at the Quality Motor Inn for a brief orientation session of our own. It had been years since we had seen each other, and we had some catching up to do. We also had to plan our strategy for Super Pick. And we couldn't resist the sign on the marquee that said: WELCOME SUPER DICKS.

Time had been kind to Al Phillips. He was aging gracefully for a guy who would hit sixty in four years. Al had always looked young for his age, and his small, pretty-boy face was still pretty much wrinkle-free. A few swatches of his blond hair had been replaced with patches of gray, and he had added a thin mustache that came in half and half. But it didn't cover the upward curl that turned what would have been a friendly smile into a sneer. It was a smile, he once told me, that had cost him several bloody noses and constant suspicion from teachers when he was a kid.

Al had studied the racing charts for the last three months at Garden State Downs and discovered a curious pattern. Although the favorite is likely to win a third of all races, at GSD the *second* favorite had also been winning at the same rate. By taking into account such other factors as post position and the records of drivers and trainers, Al had been able to raise the winning percentage to forty percent. At that rate, you could make a tidy profit. Probably enough of a profit to win the contest.

"Interesting, don't you think?" This time Al's smile was

intended to be a sneer. He was feeling smug and I didn't blame him.

"Yeah, very. And I might be able to explain why it's happening."

"I don't care *why* it's happening. I just hope it holds up."

"I'm afraid it might not," I said.

"Why's that?" Al's hands were shaking as he lit a cigarette.

I lit one of my own. "I think it might be your buddy Sam at work. Half the people at this track bet on his picks. They start out as longshots, but everybody bets them down. Those are probably the horses that are turning out to be the second and third favorites."

"So what's the problem?" Al asked.

"Without Sam's sheet to follow, the bettors won't know who to go with. The whole odds structure will be thrown off."

"And why won't they be able to follow his sheet?" Al was giving me the sneer again.

"You mean Sam's in the contest *and* publishing his picks?"

"Sure, why not? He makes two grand a day. He's not going to give that up for the contest."

That made sense, now that I thought about it. But it still seemed odd that Sam would be willing to tip off the competition by revealing the horses he was betting on. Then again, he might alter the picks on his sheet. Al had told me Sam was honest, but fifty grand can play some dirty tricks on any guy's set of values.

"Sam's got big balls," Al said in an admiring tone.

"He's also got quite a temper. What was going on with him and Toteboard Tommy?"

"Sam hates Tommy Stevens."

"He made that abundantly clear. But it seemed like there was more to it than that." I told Al about my chance meeting with Sam and Michelle.

Al nodded as I talked. "Apparently, Sam's gotten a few death threats over the phone the last couple of weeks. He doesn't think it's anything to worry about, but Michelle's been all upset."

"Maybe with good reason."

"Maybe. But Michelle's kind of high-strung."

Al had a point there. I recalled how upset she seemed when

I told them about my baseball injury. Still, I didn't think death threats should ever be taken lightly.

"Does Sam have any idea who's been calling him?" I asked.

"He says it sounded like Toteboard Tommy. Tommy's a big practical joker. He's also one very big pain in the ass."

I asked Al about Sam and Michelle. He said they'd been married six months after meeting at last year's contest. He chuckled. "It was love at first sight, just like the other four."

"Is that true about him working his way through the alphabet?"

"Not really. It just turned out that way. The first two were Ashley and Beverly, then the next one's real name was Marie but her nickname was Candy. She was cute as a button and had a brain about the same size. After her, I think he actually went looking for a girl whose name started with D. He found a real humdinger in Daphne."

"Is that good or bad?"

Al got a wistful look on his face. "She was a nympho. At least according to Sam. She ran the poor guy ragged. Sam told me she still lives around here. She's married to some horse owner with a funny name."

"Not Tony Lunaviva, by any chance."

"Yeah, I think that's the guy. He's the one who's having the big party for all the contestants on Wednesday night."

"I hadn't heard about it," I said.

"I'll bet you didn't even look in your registration packet."

As a matter of fact, I hadn't.

I told Al about enlisting my nephew as another partner in our venture. He was pleased with the idea, especially after I assured him that he'd still get half of our winnings off the top. "There might be one problem, though," I said.

"What's that?"

"Herbie's entered under the name of Nate Moore. Nate didn't want to come out here."

"Has Herbie ever been to the track before?" he asked.

"I'm afraid not."

"Well, I'd just make sure he doesn't ask any dumb questions in front of the other amateur contestants. The pros won't care." Al snorted. "Neither will the amateurs, now that I think about it. Why should they care if some young guy who doesn't know anything is entered? They'd probably like the idea."

I was tempted to ask Al about the dispute between him and Sam that Track Jack Jones had mentioned, but I figured it was none of my business. Besides, I had to pick up our partner in crime.

My sister and nephew were waiting on their front steps when I pulled into the driveway. I was late, as usual.

Herbie looked younger without a tie and jacket, but I still thought he could pass for eighteen. And I knew he'd look older when he wasn't holding a lunch box.

It was your basic silver cylindrical job. Not bad as lunch boxes go, but a lunch box just the same. At least it wasn't festooned with decals of his favorite cartoon heroes.

"I packed some sandwiches," Karen explained. "I thought that would be better than eating the junk they have at the track. They probably charge you an arm and a leg besides."

"Good idea," I lied. I told them about the contest and asked Herbie how he'd feel about spending five days at the track.

His eyes widened hopefully, but his crest fell fast. "I can't," he said.

My eyes widened, too. Unless Herbie could go all week, there wasn't much point in taking him at all.

"That's right," Karen said. "We're going to Pittsburgh tomorrow to visit Dick's parents."

"Lucky you."

Karen smiled. "I don't mind." She rubbed her son's head. "I just feel bad for Herb. He doesn't want to go. He's got practice on Thursday night."

"Practice for what—football?" I knew they were putting kids on a professional training schedule, but it still seemed a little early for tryouts.

"Oh no," Karen said, as Herbie shook his head. "Herb's the lead baritone in the school choir."

"Is that so?"

"He hates to miss practice, and now this racetrack thing is another reason to stay home."

And a curious mix of reasons, at that. "Well, why doesn't he?" I asked.

"There's nobody to stay with him."

"He's old enough to stay by himself." I gave him a man-sized pat on the shoulder. "Right, big guy?"

Herbie nodded, but it was a halfhearted effort. The idea of being alone in the suburbs seemed to frighten him. I had a similar feeling, with one major difference: He was afraid of what might happen to him; I was afraid of what I might do to myself.

"I don't think Dick would go for that," Karen said.

"I've got it!" Herbie blurted. "How about if Uncle Mark stays with me? He's a responsible grown-up."

The latter pronouncement sounded more like a question than a statement. I was sure my brother-in-law would dispute it. I wasn't real keen on playing *in loco parentis* myself.

"That's a wonderful solution!" Karen beamed at her only son. "You're so smart," she said proudly.

"Don't act so surprised, Mom. I got straight A's on my last report card."

It was hard to come up with an excuse under the glow of their expectant gazes. I was beginning to wonder what I *wouldn't* do for fifty grand. "Sounds great," I said with as much enthusiasm as I could muster.

Herbie rubbed his huge hands together and grinned. "Boy-oh-boy-oh-boy." That was one habit I'd have to break him of fast. I wondered how much damage I could do to a kid in five days.

Karen kissed her son as if she were sending him off to war and handed him a pair of army-issue binoculars. I gave her a hug before getting into the car. "You sell the idea to the Dicker and we'll get busy picking some winners," I said.

It was twelve-thirty when we pulled into the Quality Inn lot. Opening ceremonies started in half an hour, but post time wasn't until one-thirty. As we got out of the car, I told Herbie he should bring his binoculars but he could leave his lunch box on the backseat.

"What about if we get hungry?" I could tell he was hungry already.

"We'll grab a hot dog at the snack bar," I said.

"Really?"

"You bet."

Herbie grinned, but passed on the oh-boys. As I started to walk away from the car, he said, "Hey, Uncle Mark, you dropped your car keys on the floor."

"That's okay, Herb. I leave them there to make sure I don't lose them."

He frowned. "Aren't you afraid somebody might steal it?"

I shook my head. "Herb, I figure anybody who's desperate enough to steal this car is welcome to it."

That one puzzled him. I was sure it was the first of many times he'd be baffled by something I said or did.

Before going inside, we stopped by the fence at the edge of the parking lot and gazed down at the track.

"Boy, you can get a great view from up here," Herbie said. "If you wanted, you could watch the races from up here and not even have to pay to get in." That was the Dick Derkovich side of the kid talking.

"Yes, you could, Herb. But then you wouldn't be able to bet. And take my word for it: Harness races aren't much fun to watch if you don't have any money on them."

"Harness races? You mean it's those guys riding around in those funny little carriages?"

As if in answer to his question, two horses emerged from the paddock on the far end of the track. I could tell from his tone that he was disappointed.

"They're called sulkies, not carriages, Herb," I said. "Sometimes they're called bikes. These horses don't move as fast as the flats, but they're real graceful because they have to maintain their gait."

"What are flats?" he asked. I had a feeling it was going to be a long afternoon.

"Flats are thoroughbred horses, the ones that are ridden by jockeys. These are called standardbreds. You see the way they trot? That's called their gait, and it's actually bred into them to run like that. And the guys in the sulkies aren't just being pulled along. They're called drivers because they actually steer the horses with their reins. It takes a lot of skill, and it's a dangerous job."

Herbie nodded as he watched one of the horses pacing along the stretch down below. He seemed a little awed by it all. By the time we got inside he looked downright overwhelmed, surrounded as he was by cigar-smoking geezers spitting up their lungs and program-hawking vendors shouting out their lungs. I put my arm on his shoulder and steered him toward the card table that was set up for Super Pick registration.

"All right, Herb," I said. "You just go over there and tell that fat man your name is Nate Moore."

"I don't know, Uncle Mark. Are you sure that's okay?"

I took a deep breath, counted to three, and repeated the pitch I had given him while riding over in the car. "Now listen, Herb, I already paid the entry fee for Nate, but he can't be here. So all we're doing is giving his ticket to you. Do you understand?"

He nodded. "Sure, but why don't we just explain that to the man and maybe he'll let us switch the entry to my name?"

"We can't, Herb. You're not old enough."

"But that's not being honest, is it?"

I spoke in a calm voice, but it was the calm before the storm. We had already experienced some bad weather in the car. "I know exactly what you're thinking, Herb. And you're right. In the real world, this might not be completely honest." There were some dark clouds rising inside my head and I felt a hot wind blowing at my collar. "But this isn't the real world. It's the goddamn racetrack, for Chrissakes!" Oops. "Sorry, Herbie. I didn't mean to swear."

"That's okay. Mom swears all the time."

"Is that so?" Karen always was a gutter mouth. Of course her brother had been a good role model. "What about your dad?"

"No. He says 'shoot' sometimes, but that's about it."

"Okay, now listen," I said, my voice calm again. "I don't want to make you compromise your morals or ethics or whatever, but do you want to win twenty-five thousand dollars or not?"

"It would be awfully nice," he said.

"Damn right it would." I gave him a tough-guy pat on the shoulder. "I'm sure there's something you could spend it on."

"Oh there is, there definitely is. There's something I could really use it for."

"Sure there is. Now the thing to do—"

"We're trying to raise money to send our choir on a trip to the Vatican."

"That sounds like a fine idea for now. Your plans might change once you've actually got the clams in your hands. But you're not even going to have the opportunity to decide unless you go over to that table and say your name's Nate Moore." I stuck out my hand. "Okay?"

Herbie nodded and gave me the old knuckle cruncher. I lit a cigarette as I watched him walk slowly to the card table. It hadn't been easy, but we had managed to weather the first crisis of our partnership.

I bought a couple of programs and handed one to Herbie when he returned with his registration packet. Before going upstairs to the clubhouse, I took him down to the rail so he could see the track and the horses close up. I told him about the toteboard and the morning line, then showed him how to read the program. Or at least I tried to show him.

Figuring out how to read a racing program with all its numbers and symbols is about as easy as learning Chinese. Sometimes I'm amazed that I know how to do it. Herbie was studying Latin and Greek, so I knew he'd be able to pick it up eventually. But after five minutes of tutoring from Uncle Mark, the kid was thoroughly confused.

"Don't worry, Herb," I said. "You'll pick it up as we go along. But just be sure to remember what I told you in the car. If you have any questions, try to ask me about them when there's nobody around. Okay?"

He nodded, but I could tell his head was spinning from all the instructions he was getting. It was a good thing the kid was used to taking orders from Jesuits.

"Are you having a good time?" I asked as we walked up the apron to the grandstand.

"I will be," he said. "As soon as my headache goes away."

I spotted Al going over the program in a corner near the snack bar. "Good to meet you, Herbie," he said gruffly, wincing a bit as my nephew mangled his hand. "Everything's going to work out just fine, kid, as long as you remember one thing: Don't ask any dumb questions. Okay?"

"I already talked to him, Al," I said.

"Oh, sorry about that, kid. I didn't mean anything by it."

"That's all right," Herbie said. But I had a feeling he wished he still had a hold of Al's hand.

10

The sun disappeared behind the clouds as track owner Biff Bonnardo and his mother appeared down along the rail to open the Super Pick festivities. They were flanked by state senator Carmen Vitello, racing secretary Dave Gwynn, and the mayors of Pompton Plains and Pequannock. I couldn't figure out which one was which, but I did manage to get their names—Alton Selazny and Harry Spudder. I assumed the jobs were non-salaried positions.

We had a good view of the proceedings from a special section in the clubhouse, where about fifteen rows had been roped off for contestants. The first twelve were for amateurs, the last three for pros. A banner over our heads identified us as the SUPER PICKERS. It also said the contest was being sponsored by Holey Toledo Donuts.

I'd heard that Bonnardo was expecting people to turn out in unprecedented numbers to meet the celebrity pickers, but the crowd didn't look any bigger than Friday's. Except for Long-shot Sam's fans, none of the people who did show up seemed to notice us, except perhaps to wonder who those jerks were sitting behind the ropes.

Herbie and I sat in the last row of the amateur section. Because there were fewer amateur contestants than expected we had the row to ourselves, except for a middle-aged guy and his son. He didn't look much older than Herbie, which relieved any worry I had that my nephew might look out of place.

Other than a few stray platitudes from the guest speakers, I didn't catch much of the ceremony. For one thing, the public-address system was hardly state-of-the-art. For another, I wasn't paying attention.

I wasn't alone. The other contestants were hunched over their programs scribbling last-minute notes in the margins. They couldn't have cared less about the memory of Biff Bonnardo's father, though they did stand dutifully for a moment of silence. I don't think they cared whether it was a great day for Pompton Plains or Pequannock, as each mayor said. Or whether it was a great day for Jersey, as Carmen Vitello said. I don't think they even cared if it was a great day for racing, as Biff Bonnardo said. They simply hoped, as I did, that it was a good day for making some do-re-mi. And, like me, they were ready to get the show on the road.

The sighs of impatience became a steady murmur of groans by the time Vitello finished speaking. I doubted that most of the contestants were even registered to vote, but if they were, the senator had already lost some support in the upcoming election. When Biff Bonnardo took the mike and said, "And now—the moment you've all been waiting for," a burst of applause went up in our section.

"Yeah, that's right." I heard the unmistakable voice of Toteboard Tommy behind us. "Get on with the fucking races."

Bonnardo made a sweeping motion with his right arm as a young girl in a white dress with a sash and heels began inching down the steep gravel apron. The girl was wearing a crown that must have been on loan from the jewelry counter at Woolworth's. She was escorted by a stocky young guy in a blue uniform. I figured he was the highest-ranking Boy Scout in the area.

Biff held out his arms like Jerry Lewis urging a kid to throw away the crutches on the annual telethon. "And now," he said, "let's give a warm welcome to *Miss Garden State Downs!*"

The wolf whistles started as soon as the girl turned to face the crowd. Two rows behind us, I could hear the terrible tandem of Lucky Lou and Sulky Sol.

"Hey, girlie, what race are you running in?"

"A maiden race—what else?"

"If I was her boyfriend, I'd put her in a *claiming* race," Timmy the Greek said, eyeballing her through a pair of binoculars.

"What right do you guys have to talk?" Serendipity whined. "You haven't gotten laid since World War Two."

"World War One," Longshot Sam corrected.

"What's she talking about?" Dr. Dave muttered right behind me. "She's the one that diddled the Greek last year."

I shot a glance at Herbie, who was staring straight ahead. I had a feeling he was trying to block out impure thoughts.

Down along the rail, Miss Garden State Downs smiled and waved to the crowd just like the real beauty contestants do on TV. A few of the cigar puffers pushed forward for a closer look, but her escort was keeping them at arm's length by puffing out his chest. He was built like Mr. Universe—or at least Mr. Garden State Downs.

"Isn't she hot, folks?" Biff Bonnardo bellowed as the couple walked back toward the grandstand. Bert Parks he wasn't.

The crowd answered with a polite "yeah" that had all the enthusiasm of a maybe. You could almost hear people hoping the festivities were over.

They weren't. The DePaul High School Choir was about to sing "The Star-Spangled Banner."

"How long does this crap go on?" Toteboard Tommy groaned.

"It's been thirty-nine minutes," Clocker Callaway said.

I had witnessed some dreadful renditions of the national anthem over the years, and this one ranked right down there with them. It was so bad that halfway through, Herbie muttered, "They *stink*." I would have preferred "suck," but I was glad to see my nephew getting into the spirit of the occasion.

Despite the quality of the performance, the choir got the biggest round of applause all day. I suspected it had something to do with the toteboard lighting up behind them just as they finished singing. As they trudged to the grandstand, a drizzle began to fall. It was raining on Biff Bonnardo's parade.

The number 20 appeared in the "Minutes to Post" slot on the toteboard, and Dave Gwynn's voice came over the PA system. "The betting windows are now open. Super Pick is *underway*."

The contest rules were so simple, a child could understand them. Luckily, I had Herbie with me.

Everybody started with an imaginary bankroll of one thousand dollars, and the person with the most money left at the end was the winner. You could make as many bets as you wanted, but you had to wager at least two dollars on every race. The only restriction was on the final day, when you weren't allowed to wager more than you had during the first four days. This was to make sure nobody bet two dollars all along and then gambled everything on one race at the end. That wouldn't be handicapping, just dumb luck.

Instead of going to the windows, you simply marked your bets on a card and turned it in to one of the attendants stationed nearby. These were kids about Herbie's age who were dressed in Boy Scout uniforms. I wondered if they were being paid for their efforts or if they just earned badges.

It turned out that Herbie didn't even have to pretend his name was Nate Moore for the benefit of the attendants. Each amateur contestant was assigned a number, which was printed on the bet card. The kids gave the cards to a pair of old guys in moldy windbreakers, who posted the bets and results next to each contestant's name on two giant chalkboards outside the Winners Circle. One board was for the amateurs, the other for the pros.

All bets had to be turned in no later than four minutes to post time. This was to allow time for the pros' picks to be posted, so that the fans could see who they had bet on before each race. Amateur bets weren't posted until after each race was over, but we still had to turn in our cards by four minutes to post.

The time rule presented some logistical problems for us, because it wouldn't always be clear which horse was the second favorite until shortly before the race started. It was a bigger obstacle to Toteboard Tommy, since spotting overlays requires waiting until the last possible instant before betting.

There was an upside, however. Because we were playing with phony money, our wagers didn't drive down the odds. On a normal day at GSD, putting down two hundred bucks was almost like eating a billion hamburgers at McDonald's. They had to change the sign just to fill your order.

The first race was a $2500 claiming event, which meant every horse entered was for sale at that price. When I asked Herbie if he wanted to make a claim, he said he didn't know where he would keep it. The kid had quite a sense of humor.

Ten minutes before post time, the bugle sounded and the horses paced along the stretch in the post parade while Dave Gwynn announced the field. Herbie got a kick out of listening to the odd names of the horses. He got a bigger kick when I pointed out that the horses' names weren't nearly as funny as those of the pro pickers.

At six minutes to post, I told Herbie we'd probably be betting on the number 3 horse, Simple Pleasure, which had started at 8–1 on the morning line but was now going off at 3–1. Simple Pleasure was also the pick on Longshot Sam's sheet. I wondered which horse Sam would be betting on.

"Number three it is, Herb," I said, as the attendants lined up at the rows to collect our cards. "For fifty dollars."

"Fifty dollars! Wow, that's a lot of money, Uncle Mark."

"It's Monopoly money," I reminded him. He still looked nervous. I didn't blame him. I was feeling a little nervous myself.

"Do I go to the window and make a bet?" he asked.

"No. You just give the card to one of the Boy Scouts."

"Those aren't Boy Scouts. They're Holey Toledos."

"They're what?"

"The Holey Toledo Club."

I guess I looked a little puzzled.

"To-led-o," Herbie explained. "It's short for *To*morrow's *Lead*ers. They do good works and stuff."

I'll bet they did. And they probably worked cheap, too. I didn't need to inquire whether Tony Lunaviva was behind the idea. "Did you ever think about joining?" I asked.

Herbie shrugged. "I wanted to, but my dad wouldn't let me. He said they were a bunch of dagos."

We turned in our cards just as Dave Gwynn came over the PA system. "Four *min*utes. Four minutes to post. All Super Pick bets should now be in."

But they weren't. Tommy Stevens was waiting for one more odds flash, and Timmy the Greek didn't like it. He lifted himself out of his seat and pointed at Toteboard Tommy.

"This man should be disqualified," Timmy whined at the musclebound Toledo standing watch on his row.

"Shut up, Geek, you homo!" Tommy wailed.

"Two *min*utes," came Dave Gwynn's announcement as Tommy handed in his card.

"Next time I'll have to disqualify you," the kid warned. There was an officious edge in his tone that suggested he might be future attorney-general material. He even looked a little like a young John Mitchell.

"Who the hell are you?" Tommy demanded.

"I'm Matt Caldwell's brother."

Tommy snickered. "Am I supposed to know who that is?" I was wondering the same thing myself.

"You just better hope you don't have to find out, mister." The kid pointed a finger for effect.

Tommy ignored him and scowled at Timmy the Greek. "You get in my way this year, fatso, and I'm going to knock you right on your butt."

"You and what army?" the Greek wheezed back. He was out of breath just thinking up the clever response.

I could tell Herbie was holding back his laughter. Others nearby weren't doing as good a job. As I turned my attention to the track he asked, "What's that car doing down on the track, Uncle Mark?"

"That's the pace car," I said. "You see—the horses are all lining up behind the gate attached to it."

"This field is on gate," Dave Gwynn announced.

As the horses came around to our side, I lit a cigarette. I was good for a butt each race.

"This field is in motion," the track announcer said.

I had bet on more horse races than I could count, but this one was different. This time was the big time—the highest stakes I had ever played for. I gave my nephew a good-luck poke in the ribs. "This is it, Herbie."

He nodded, but I didn't think he appreciated how much was at stake. He was getting an interesting introduction to racing.

A familiar shiver went up my spine as the alarm bell rang and the betting windows locked shut. There was a momentary hush, followed by the roar of the crowd, then the voice of Dave Gwynn reciting the three most exciting words in the English language: "And they're off . . ."

11

Herbie cheered wildly as Simple Pleasure went right to the front, tucked in along the rail and held the lead through the first half mile. As the horses passed the grandstand, it looked like Simple Pleasure might tire and fade, as it had in its last race. But we got lucky at the three-quarter pole when the second horse, the favorite, went off stride, forcing the horses behind it to slow up.

Breaking stride is an oddity that makes some people think harness racing is about as authentic as Roller Derby. It occurs when a horse breaks out of its gait into a gallop. A horse that goes off stride isn't permitted to gain any ground on the rest of the field. The driver is required to restrain it and move to the outside. This is no easy task. A horse that breaks is usually finished for the race.

I could tell from the groan that went up in our section that most of the contestants had bet on the favorite or one of the horses stuck behind it. I didn't care one way or the other. I turned around and shot a glance at Al Phillips. He was sneering from ear to ear.

I elbowed my nephew. "Did you see that, Herb? The favorite went off stride."

"You mean that thing you told me that happens when they put an *x* next to the horse's name in the program?"

"Exactly." The kid was catching on. "That can only help our cause, Herb. We've got this one wrapped up."

Or at least we should have had it wrapped up. Simple Pleasure led by four lengths as he rounded the turn and hit the

66

top of the stretch. But two other horses were charging hard on the outside. They were closing the gap so fast, it looked like our guy was standing still. With a hundred yards to go, the lead was down to one length.

Next to me, Herbie had his fists clenched and eyes closed. His lips were moving, and I realized he was saying a prayer. I hoped he had better luck than I did when I used to pray.

All three horses were going at it neck and neck as they neared the finish line. But as they crossed under the wire, there was no doubt about the outcome. Through the din of the crowd, I could hear track announcer Dave Gwynn confirm what I already knew. "It's Simple Pleasure," he said. "*In front.*"

"We did it, Herbie!" I held out my hand and braced for a knuckle breaker, but he was too busy bouncing in place to notice.

A moment later, the INQUIRY sign began flashing on the toteboard. "What does that mean, Uncle Mark?"

"The judges are looking at the race again to see if one of the horses interfered with the others," I explained. "But we've got nothing to worry about. The questions will center on the horse that broke stride. It won't affect our horse, because he was in front of where it happened."

A few moments after, Dave Gwynn announced the official result and let Herbie know how smart his uncle was.

I could tell from the grumbling around us as we went to check the standings that most of the pros had taken a pass on the first pick in Longshot Sam's tout sheet. All of them, in fact, except Al and Sam.

Most of the contestants were gathered around the chalk-boards, where the geezers were totaling up the results. A cheer went up from a small crowd of fans off to the side when Longshot Sam's bet was tallied. Although we had gone with the same horse as Sam, he had bet $100 to our $50. On a $7.60 payoff, that put his bankroll at $1280. Ours was at $1140.

I looked at Al and watched his sneer turn into a frown. We had won, but we were already trailing Longshot Sam.

"What an asshole," I overheard Toteboard Tommy mutter to Dr. Dave. "I can't believe he's got the nerve to bet on the same horse he picked on his sheet."

"What's wrong with that?" Dr. Dave asked.

"Are you kidding?" Tommy snapped. "I don't believe the balls on the guy."

Tommy was more steamed after the second race, when Sam really did the unthinkable: He bet $100 on a *different* horse from the one on his sheet and won the race. Tommy went with Sam's pick. He wasn't alone. We played it, too.

A couple of Sam's fans were also a little miffed. "Hey, Longshot," one of them whined. "Where do you get off playing a different pick?"

"I play longshots," Sam said. "That horse went off at three to two. A longshot ain't a longshot when it's bet that low."

"Yeah, but I blew four bucks on your sheet. I expect you to play the horses you got listed."

The smile on Sam's face didn't cover his contempt as he pulled a fiver out of his pocket. "Here," he said, "I'll buy it back from you. You can keep the change." Sam looked up at the crowd that had gathered around him and waved a wad of bills. "Any of you others want to sell me back their sheets?"

No, they certainly did not.

Our horse put on a strong closing move in the third race, but not strong enough to catch the leader. It was the first time we played a horse that wasn't on Sam's sheet. As luck would have it—his, not ours—he elected to stick with his pick.

We didn't make any money in the fourth race, but Herbie had the good fortune of making some new friends. He was studying Greek in school, so he asked Timmy Malkos if he knew any. It turned out he did. Despite the twenty-century linguistic gulf, he managed to persuade Herbie to get him a Polish with everything on it and a diet soda. Then Clocker Callaway gave him a tutorial on speed rating in return for a cup of coffee and a report on the contest standings.

"The next race will be really interesting, Herb," I said. "It's for trotters."

"Isn't that what we've been watching?"

"No, what we've seen so far are pacers. They run with their front and hind legs in perfect step. Trotters have a more elegant gait. Their front legs move in a kind of a rolling motion that's out of step with their hind legs."

He seemed to enjoy watching, which was a good thing. The horse we played didn't provide too much in the way of entertainment, unless you were into self-abuse. I'm sure Herbie wasn't. But I could tell he was getting restless.

I didn't blame him. After the initial excitement of winning the first race, dropping four straight was a letdown. For me, as well as Herbie. So far, Al's system didn't seem to be working.

"I think we should continue with it," he said, while we conferred behind a post near the stairway. I doubted anyone was paying attention to us, but we were still making an effort to be discreet about our collaboration. "But I think we should start looking for prospects for side bets."

"Karen's Choice might be worth looking at," I said. "It won a qualifier last week."

"What's a qualifier?" Herbie asked.

"A qualifying race," I said. "It's a race without betting for horses that have been breaking stride or haven't run in a while. A lot of people ignore horses coming off qualifiers, so they usually go off at long odds."

Al rolled his eyes. "Herbie, why don't you just read the program and hold your questions for a while. Okay?"

"Why don't you call me Herb like I asked you to?"

I looked at Al, then at my nephew. This I didn't need. "Here, Herb," I said, pulling a ten out of my pocket. "Why don't you go to the window and make a bet of your own."

"You mean a real one?" he said hopefully.

"Sure. Just tell the clerk the number you want and say you want to put two dollars on it to win."

"Thanks, Uncle Mark."

"Don't mention it, Herb. And while you're at it, get yourself another dog if you want." As Herbie walked away, I told Al, "Try to be more patient with the kid. It's his first time at the track."

"Okay, I'm sorry. You know how I am."

"The trainer of Karen's Choice won with another horse coming off a qualifier on Friday," I said, looking back at the program. "I think we should keep an eye on it."

"You keep an eye on it. I've got better things to watch."

I followed Al's gaze to a tall, slim woman who was turning heads all the way down the clubhouse as she walked toward us. I didn't recognize Michelle Natoli until she took off her sunglasses and waved.

"Isn't she a sight to behold?" Al said as he waved back.

"She is indeed. But I don't think she'd be held by the likes of us."

"I wouldn't be so sure of that."

It was a pleasant surprise to see Michelle because Sam had told me she wouldn't be there. She was staying home to make dinner for us. "Lasagna!" he had said. "My favorite. Michelle makes better lasagna than my mother used to make." Sam looked like the kind of guy whose mother knew how to make lasagna.

"I'm just stopping by for a minute to give Sam a good-luck kiss," Michelle explained.

"He doesn't need it," Al said. "But I sure could use one."

Michelle let out a laugh and gave him a hug.

"Uh, while you're at it," I added, "if it's not too much trouble . . ."

She smiled and made a mock threat to slap my face before kissing me on the cheek. It seemed like innocent stuff, but Al's comment made me wonder just how serious a flirt Michelle could be. I can be pretty serious about it, but I like to think I'm not a heel. I didn't know Sam Natoli very well, but well enough not to take shots at his wife—even if they were longshots.

Michelle surprised us again when she turned to Al and said, "Would you mind letting me talk to Mr. Renzler alone for a moment?"

"It's Mark," I reminded her. "Or just Renzler, if you'd like. This 'mister' stuff makes me feel old enough to be your father." I wondered if I was for an instant, but a quick calculation convinced me that it would only be possible in rural counties in Georgia.

"I'm sorry for being so strange on Friday," Michelle said. "I know I made you uncomfortable."

I didn't see any gain in telling her it was Sam who had made me uncomfortable. "There's nothing to apologize for," I said. "And by the way, I spoke to Al this morning. He told me about the calls Sam's been getting."

"He did?"

"I asked him what was wrong," I explained. "You did manage to arouse my curiosity." I refrained from adding that it wasn't the only thing she had aroused.

Michelle smiled but it was a worried smile. "Sam thinks I'm being ridiculous. He doesn't want to make a big deal out of it."

"Well, he's wrong, at least about the first part. I'll keep an eye on him for you—without making a big deal of it."

Relief washed over Michelle's face. "Thank you so much," she said, pressing my hand. "I wouldn't want anything to happen to him."

"Don't worry," I said, squeezing back. "Nothing will."

But as I listened to the words spill out of my mouth, I felt a thud of dread knocking around in the back of my head. That was the sort of promise I had learned the hard way never to make. At least I thought I'd learned. I hoped I wasn't due for another lesson.

12

I pointed Michelle Natoli toward our section, then took a look around the clubhouse for my nephew. Herbie stepped out from behind a post a moment after Michelle walked away.

"Hey, Uncle Mark, who was that lady you were talking to?"

"That was Longshot Sam's wife."

"She sure is pretty."

"She is indeed." I was relieved that Herbie had noticed. I had nothing against the kid becoming a priest, but the celibacy vow seemed like an awful tough nut to crack.

"So who'd you bet on?" I asked.

Herbie held out his ticket. "Number four—Karen's Choice."

"We'll be putting something down on that one for the contest," I said.

"Well, we should. It *is* Mom's name."

I hadn't made that association. Now that he had pointed it out I felt certain we were doomed. But at 20–1, it was worth a small bet. With a thousand-dollar bankroll, that meant twenty bucks.

We got back in time to turn in our cards without raising the ire of Timmy the Greek or one of Tomorrow's Leaders. Our main choice got boxed in along the rail, but Karen's Choice mounted a late charge that brought Herbie and me out of our seats. Behind us, Serendipity McCall urged Karen's Choice on. Apparently, the moon and stars were on our side as well. That didn't make me feel too good.

It was a photo finish with the number-1 horse, an odds-on

favorite named Zhivago. Herbie coped with the suspense by closing his eyes and praying. I looked at Al.

"Close call," he said, shaking his head.

"It was the one horse, no doubt about it," Dr. Dave said.

I turned and eyed him skeptically.

"Just ask Tommy," he said.

I didn't bother to ask Mr. Toteboard, but Dr. Dave's referral for a second opinion reminded me of a junk-mail offer in which he had included an "audit deposition" certifying that he had earned a hundred thousand dollars the year before. Instead of a firm like Arthur Andersen or Coopers & Lybrand, the statement was done by his personal CPA. The thinking, I guess, was that even if you didn't trust a "doctor" named Dave Higgins, surely you wouldn't question the word of an accountant named Harvey Schwartz.

I was about to ask Dr. Dave how that offer had done when the winning number was posted on the toteboard. I didn't think he'd be in any mood to answer my question.

Serendipity let out a shriek of delight so loud that it frightened some of the horses down on the track. I turned to see Track Jack Jones shaking his head beside her. He looked like he wanted to hide, but that's a tall order when you're six foot six.

"I won! I won!" she squealed.

"No kidding, Red," Dr. Dave muttered.

I walked Herbie to the cashier's window to collect his payoff. He got $43.20 from his two-dollar bet and insisted on returning the ten bucks I had given him and treating me to a beer. It was an offer I couldn't refuse.

As we headed back to our seats, Herbie spotted Michelle Natoli and Al Phillips chatting behind a post near the stairway. They seemed startled as we approached, and I had a feeling we were interrupting a private conversation.

I put some distance between Herbie and the priesthood by introducing him to Michelle. He blushed when she shook his hand, and I hoped he had the good sense not to give her the crusher. Evidently not, because she invited him to dinner. With his parents leaving the next day, he had to turn her down. But he did get to see her negotiate the stairs in high heels on her way out. That would give him something to think about during his next spiritual retreat.

Although the rain had stopped by the eighth race, the great drainage system at GSD made it necessary to downgrade the track condition from "fast" to "good." If it got any worse, it would have to be further downgraded to "sloppy."

I showed Herbie how to check the program for horses that raced well on off tracks. It's a simple trick that's often overlooked, but it didn't elude the bettors at GSD. Quite a few of them noticed that a longshot named Hello Dolly had won on a sloppy track a month before. They made Dolly the odds-on favorite, ignoring the likely favorite, Tea for Two.

Just because Tea for Two hadn't raced in bad conditions didn't mean he couldn't. Al and I decided to go against the flow. We put down a fifty, and Tea for Two went wire to wire, leading Dolly by a length until the final turn, then saying good-bye in the stretch. We were feeling pretty smug until we looked at the standings board and saw that Longshot Sam had done the same thing. There was one difference: He had bet a C-note.

Although Al's system wasn't holding up, we were getting by okay on pluck and luck. With three wins in eight races, Al was in third place behind Longshot Sam and Clocker Callaway. The amateur board told a happier story. The leader was a guy named Sheriff Maszursky, but there was a tie for second between Nate Moore and Dark Penzler.

"I still don't understand why you used that funny name, Uncle Mark."

"It's an inside joke, Herb." To our left I overheard Toteboard Tommy talking to Dr. Dave.

"Hey, look," he whispered, pointing at the amateur board. "There's that guy."

"What guy?"

"The guy with the weird name—Dark Penzler."

"Yeah, you're right," Dr. Dave said. "If I was you, Tommy, I'd watch out. Don't you still owe the guy a refund?"

Toteboard Tommy looked worried as he glanced around. "I wonder which guy he is."

I wasn't about to tell him.

While looking over the entries for the ninth race, I noticed a filly named Glazed Donut. I also noticed that Longshot Sam had ignored her on his sheet. I wondered if it was a deliberate oversight. Despite Al's contention that Sam was honest, I didn't think it was a coincidence that his picks weren't doing as well as they had on Friday.

Based on Glazed Donut's record, it made sense that Dave Gwynn had set the horse's morning line odds at 30–1. But after what I had seen of Tony Lunaviva's other horse, I figured anything was possible. With the odds on Glazed Donut increasing to 40–1, Al and I decided to put down a twenty.

We were chatting with Sam near the Winners Circle when I noticed a wiry greaser in a cheap leather jacket standing near the stairs about twenty feet away. He was waving his fingers to get Sam's attention while trying to avoid attracting mine.

I was acquainted with Dino LaRussa from my work at the harness trial. Dino had been a groom at Rockingham Park in New Hampshire until a few years back, when he got banned for life after being caught injecting a horse with illegal drugs. A small-time hood who had bounced around the circuit, he had turned up in the Superfix case as a ten-percenter—a gofer who cashed winning tickets to help the big guys dodge their tax bullets.

Somewhere along the line, Dino had been a mob errand boy. The feds dropped an assault charge against him in return for his testimony, which of course turned out to be of no value. After the trial ended, I heard through the grapevine that Dino had pissed off somebody important. The word was that he had a contract out on his life, but nobody would take it because the price was too small. By now I figured he had taken up permanent residence in the Meadowlands.

It took Dino a moment to catch Sam's eye. You had to be watching closely to notice, but he nodded his head as Sam glanced in his direction. I was watching very closely.

"Excuse me," Sam said. "I'll be back in a minute."

I thought he was going to talk to Dino. Instead he walked quickly to the betting area, where he marked his race card and handed it in. Meanwhile Dino moved farther away and hid his mug in a racing program. I had a feeling he was afraid I would see him, but he seemed to be waiting for something.

I had no interest in getting a better look at Dino LaRussa's face, but I did relish the thought of confirming one of his fears. I excused myself and took a stroll of my own, starting out in the opposite direction from Dino, then circling back around the stairway and coming up on him from behind.

"Long time, no see, Dino." He wasn't the kind of guy you wanted to waste any of your A-material on.

I startled him enough that he challenged Bob Beamon's Olympic long-jump record. "What the fuck are you doing here, Renzler?" he asked, craning his neck to look up. Not only was Dino a weasel; he was a little weasel.

"I'm a friend of Longshot Sam's. What's your excuse?"

"Same as yours."

"That's probably the only thing we'll ever have in common." Dino turned away and sneered as Sam Natoli sauntered over.

"Hey, you guys know each other?" Sam asked.

Dino nodded sullenly, but I was more enthusiastic. "We go way back," I said. "We're practically from the same patch."

Sam looked puzzled. "You from Clifton, Danny?"

Dino shook his head.

Danny? I gave it to him with both eyeballs, even though one was just for effect. "Did you change the last name, too?"

Longshot Sam looked a little more puzzled. "I thought you knew each other," he said to me. "This is Danny Moreno."

I did my best imitation of an Al Phillips smile. Danny/Dino looked like he wanted to crawl under a rock. He'd feel right at home there. Maybe it sounds like I'm being too rough on him, but his assault charge had been on a sixteen-year-old girl.

"I gotta talk to you, Sam," Dino said. "*Alone.*"

"Yeah, sure." By now Sam was totally bewildered. He held out his hands with palms turned upward. "Will you excuse us?"

As I watched them start down the stairs, my promise to Michelle Natoli flashed in my mind. I didn't think Dino LaRussa posed a threat. I was more curious to know why a supposedly honest guy like Sam would associate with a slime-ball. But I decided to play it safe just in case.

"Hey, *Danny,*" I called. "You're not packing, are you?"

He stopped and turned around ever so slowly. "No, I'm not."

"Mind if I check?"

As I walked toward him, he realized he didn't have any choice. "Be my guest, asshole," he said, lifting his arms. "What are you—his bodyguard?"

"Something like that."

"Hey, what are you doing, Renzler?" Sam demanded, as I gave Dino a quick but thorough frisk. "This guy's a friend of mine."

I was tempted to tell Sam what I thought of his taste in friends, but it wasn't any of my business. "Just a precaution, Sam," I said.

"Michelle put you up to this."

"She just wants to make sure nothing happens to you, Sam."

Sam rolled his eyes. I had a feeling dinner at the Natoli house might not be too pleasant.

"C'mon, let's go, Sam," Dino urged.

I didn't notice the crowd that had gathered to watch my shakedown of Dino until I started back up the steps. As I did, I almost bumped into Toteboard Tommy and Dr. Dave, who hurried past without saying anything.

Herbie more than made up for their silence. "Hey, Uncle Mark, you really frisked that guy!"

I answered with a sheepish smile. At least I was feeling pretty sheepish.

"What was that about?" Al asked.

"I wouldn't be too sure your friend Sam is so honest."

"What makes you say that?"

"Something about the company he keeps." I gave Al a capsule sketch of Dino.

He whistled softly. "That doesn't sound like Sam."

I suggested we might be able to capitalize on Sam's relationship with unsavory types by increasing our bet on Glazed Donut. I don't usually rely on hunches, but I had a sneaking suspicion Dino's tip-off to Sam had something to do with Tony Lunaviva's horse. It turned out to be a very good hunch.

For the first half mile, Glazed Donut stayed right where the past-performance chart indicated she should be—at the back of the pack. After that I didn't pay much attention to the race.

As the horses passed the grandstand, I spotted Dino LaRussa down the rail about twenty yards before the finish line. Longshot Sam was standing beside Dino to his right. Even with their backs turned to me, I could see they weren't doing anything suspicious. In fact, they didn't even appear to be talking to each other. All they were doing was watching the race.

For some reason, I couldn't stop watching them. I asked Herbie for the binoculars and kept them trained on Dino and Sam. Call it intuition, call it premonition. Call it anxiety or paranoia. Whatever you want to call it, I couldn't shake the feeling that something was about to happen to Sam Natoli.

As I watched him standing in the sunlight that had just popped through the clouds, I realized what was making me so nervous. It was the memory of the fear I had seen in his wife's eyes a few days before. It was the knowledge that I had promised her nothing would happen to him. Now, with him so far away, it was clearly a promise I couldn't keep.

I tried to dismiss it as superstition, as a train of thought worthy of Serendipity McCall. While the horses thundered down the stretch, I tried to keep my mind on Dave Gwynn's call of the race. But I couldn't keep my eyes off the pair of guys along the rail.

As Glazed Donut put on a closing move and glided past the lead horse about twenty-five lengths from the wire, I saw Longshot Sam clench his fist by his side in jubilation. It was a subtle gesture, but I was watching closely. Suddenly, I felt foolish for worrying about a guy who was about to cash another big winner. I should have been glad that I was about to cash the same big winner myself.

Beside me, Herbie was cheering deliriously. Down along the rail, I saw Dino turn toward Sam and say something. Sam nodded in response, then turned and looked up the hill toward the parking lot. He had a stogie in his mouth and a smile on his face. What the hell was I worried about?

It happened fast, very fast.

To the left of Sam, I saw Dino move a few steps over and out of the scope of the binoculars. I moved with him and watched as he looked up the track apron toward the parking lot. Just as Dave Gwynn said, "Glazed Donut—*in front*," I looked back at Sam.

Longshot's expression had taken a sharp turn—a turn for the worse. His hands clutched at his chest. Blood spurted from under the hands like a fountain and flooded over his white knit shirt like a rampaging river. Sam's arms flailed as he fell back and slumped against the rail. And all the while the stogie was still in his mouth.

Whoever shot Longshot Sam was a good shot. But from what I knew of Sam, somebody had a pretty big target to aim at. He shot the poor guy right through the heart.

13

I screamed and cursed as Dino LaRussa slipped away through the crowd down near the rail. I almost knocked Herbie over as I bolted out of our row. The kid had no idea what hit him. He only knew that his uncle was going berserk.

The future of one of Tomorrow's Leaders looked bleak as I barreled over him on my way up the aisle. I knocked down a few more people as I pushed my way down the clubhouse stairs. When I hit the ground floor, I took a right and headed straight for the parking lot at the far end of the grandstand.

I could see Dino LaRussa far ahead of me. He was setting a brisk pace, but he was walking to avoid attracting attention. He had a fifty-yard lead on me, but I thought I might be able to catch him if he didn't catch sight of me.

No such luck. Dino shot a glance over his shoulder and spotted me. From that moment on, it was a footrace to the parking lot. If I'd been handicapping the event, I would have given the edge to Dino.

I've got a natural reservoir of speed left over from my glory days as a jock, but a pack of Camels a day for the last twenty years has pretty much dried it up. I managed to cut Dino's lead in half with a solid stretch move, but by the time I reached the parking lot, he was already climbing into the passenger side of an old-model white Mustang convertible.

Dino turned on the charm as he got in, raising his hand in a good-bye gesture. Needless to say, it wasn't a peace sign. His hesitation enabled me to get a few steps closer. With the top up, I couldn't see the driver, but I did get a look at the license plate:

BC 658, from the Show Me State. If I had paid more attention—paid any attention—during license-plate games on car trips as a kid, I would have known which one it was. But I drew the line at memorizing state capitals.

The rear wheels of the Mustang sprayed damp gravel at me as the car screeched away. Just then I saw Track Jack Jones emerge from behind an orange Volkswagen van that was festooned with the signs of the zodiac. The van was parked perpendicular to where the Mustang had been waiting.

"Did you get a look at the driver of that car?" I blurted, gasping for breath.

"Hey, slow down, bro, what's going on?" Track Jack raised his hands, wary that my momentum would carry me into him.

"Did you see the driver?" I repeated.

He looked at me like I was from another planet. "It was a broad."

"Are you sure?"

"Sure I'm sure."

"What did she look like?"

"Red hair, down to here." Jack rested a hand on his shoulder. "Not bad-looking, if you like white meat." He didn't say whether he did, and I didn't ask.

"How old?"

"I dunno. Late twenties maybe. She was wearing shades. I wasn't really looking at her." Jack motioned toward the track. "I was watching the race."

I nodded, still trying to get my breath.

"What's going on, bro?" Track Jack asked again.

"Somebody shot Longshot Sam."

"You're shittin' me."

"I wish I was. Did you hear any gunshots?"

"Now that you mention it, I guess maybe I did hear something that sounded like a shot. But I didn't think anything of it. I'm kinda used to it. You know, being from Detroit and all."

I did know, sort of, being from New York and all, but I was dubious that he wouldn't have noticed a gunshot. I was also curious what he was doing in the parking lot. But I figured there'd be time to ask those questions later.

I ran back into the grandstand with Jack on my heels, against the first wave of bettors on their way out. By the time we got down to the rail, a throng of people was gathered around Sam Natoli. A muscle-bound guy in a uniform was shouting at people to stand back. I recognized him as the escort for Miss Garden State Downs, but I didn't know if he was official track security or a senior member of the Holey Toledo Club. The crowd seemed to be ignoring him. I did the same and pushed my way to the front.

A shudder went through me when I saw Al Phillips on his knees, weeping beside the body of his friend. My nephew stood over them, whispering prayers in Latin and making the sign of the cross. That made me shudder even more.

Al looked up at me. "He's gone," he said, choking back tears. "Sam's gone."

I nodded. I pretty much knew that the instant I saw him go down.

Al had thrown his sports jacket over Sam's bloody chest, but his face was uncovered and his eyes were still open. He had died a sudden, violent death, but with the afternoon sunlight shining on his face, he was a picture of peace.

I leaned down to take a look just as a pair of first-aid guys arrived with a stretcher. I helped Al to his feet, and he buried his head against my shoulder and continued to sob. I touched Herbie's elbow with my free arm and steered him out of the way. As our eyes locked, I could see he was starting to cry.

I've seen quite a few dead bodies over the years, but I'll never get used to the feeling of total emptiness that sweeps over you. It was Herbie's first time, but I knew the feeling was the same for him as it was for me. This time, for me, there was the added sense of helpless rage.

I thought of Michelle Natoli and the promise I had made, the promise I hadn't kept. It was hard enough seeing Al and Herbie. I didn't know how I would be able to face Sam's wife.

Serendipity McCall came over to comfort Al, but he waved her off. "Get the hell away from me!" he snarled.

"I was just trying to *help*!" she wailed.

Al ignored her and turned to me. "You've got the catch the asshole who did this, Renzler."

"If it's the last thing I do."

As I watched one of the first-aid guys look at his partner and shake his head, I heard a woman behind me shriek, "There he is! There he is!"

I wheeled to see a middle-aged lady in a wheelchair pointing at a startled Track Jack Jones. A young black woman in a nurse's uniform stood behind her and gripped the handles of the wheelchair.

"Get him, Matt!" the wheelchair lady screamed at Mr. Garden State Downs. "*That* guy! He's the one that shot Sam!"

"What?" Track Jack glared at the woman. "Lady, you are *crazy*." I felt certain the nurse would have agreed.

Unfortunately for Jack, Matt had a different opinion. Or perhaps Matt was a little crazy himself. "Okay, hands in the air, spook," he shouted.

"Who the hell are you?" Track Jack put his hands on his hips and glowered at Matt. I had a feeling he was making a big mistake. Mr. Garden State Downs was almost a foot shorter, but he was built like a dump truck. I figured he had a brain to match.

"I'm Matt Caldwell, head of security."

"Two-fifty an hour and all the pride you can swallow," Al muttered beside me.

And, on a good day, all the ass you could kick.

"Who the fuck are *you?*" Caldwell demanded. He didn't wait for an answer.

Mr. Garden State Downs charged at Track Jack with fists flying. The big guy didn't have a chance. He raised his hands to shield his face, but Caldwell hit him with a pair of body blows that would have knocked the wind out of a horse. Track Jack let out a sick groan, crumpled, and slumped to the ground. He was finished, but the security guard was just getting started.

Caldwell grabbed Jack by the shirt and yanked him to his feet, tearing open his pocket and causing the stub of a hand-rolled cigarette to fall out. I thought that might answer my question about what Jack had been doing in the parking lot. But it didn't explain why he was so vague about hearing the gunshot.

"It's marijuana!" I heard someone say.

"Be careful, Matt!" the wheelchair lady warned. "He's high on dope!"

Caldwell pushed Jack back against the rail and lined him up

for more battering practice. In the absence of professionally trained law-enforcement officials, I felt some responsibility to help restore order—or at least to save Track Jack's life. My nephew had the same idea, only he acted on it a little faster.

"Hey, that's enough, leave him alone," Herbie said, grabbing one of Matt's meaty arms. In doing so, he made several major mistakes. Two come quickly to mind. The first was thinking he could reason with a jerk like Matt, the second was trying to.

Caldwell shook him off, wheeled and took a roundhouse swing. The bad news was that it landed on Herbie's cheek. The good news was that it left Mr. Garden State Downs in perfect position for Herbie's uncle to land the sucker punch of a lifetime.

"Who do you think you are?" Caldwell screamed at my fallen nephew.

I answered the question by drilling him with a right that landed full force on his temple. A blow like that can cause brain damage, but I didn't think that was a concern in Matt's case. It drove him sideways and down the apron about ten feet. He would have gone ten more if the rail hadn't been in his way. He used it to pull himself up to his knees, but a moment later he slumped down again and collapsed in a heap.

When he woke up, his first question would be, "Who hit me?" I had no intention of telling him. The last thing I wanted was a rematch. This was clearly one strong, mean son of a bitch.

I rushed over to my nephew and helped him to his feet. "Are you okay, Herb?"

He nodded as I looked at his face. Fortunately, Caldwell had hit him with a glancing blow. The main damage was a sprained ego, but he would have a nasty shiner to go with it.

"It was a sucker punch," Herbie said, rubbing his eye.

"It sure was. That's the best kind to throw."

The woman in the wheelchair began to shriek again as Track Jack Jones stood up slowly, clutching his ribs and shaking his head. With track security temporarily out of the way, I didn't think there would be any more problems. Just to make sure, I walked over to Matt Caldwell and checked inside his blazer. Sure enough, he had a small revolver in a shoulder holster.

Count our blessings that Matt preferred hands-on law enforcement.

I pulled out the gun and slipped it into my jacket pocket just as someone in the crowd yelled, "Here comes Mr. Bonnardo!"

The throng parted, and the owner of Garden State Downs strode through the gapers' tunnel, followed by Dave Gwynn and the mayors of Pompton Plains and Pequannock, Harry Spudder and Alton Selazny. I wouldn't have recognized them if they hadn't been wearing ID tags. That spoke well for their name recognition.

It seemed like it had taken them a long time to get there, but I realized it had only been a few minutes. In the distance, I could hear sirens wailing. The law was on the way to restore order, but I had a feeling the confusion was just beginning.

14

"**O**kay, what happened?" Biff Bonnardo demanded. "Oh my God!"

One look at Longshot Sam answered Bonnardo's question, but fifty onlookers began offering explanations just the same. Matt Caldwell picked that moment to wobble back to his feet. "Who hit me?" he asked.

I moved away from the fray and stood beside Al Phillips.

"I'm going with Sam," he said, nodding toward the first-aid guys, who were carrying away the covered body of his friend. For a moment, I considered telling them to wait for the cops so they could mark the scene, but I didn't think that was going to be much help anyway. Better to get him away from the sightseers.

"And I've got to get to a phone and call Michelle," Al said.

That was a chore I didn't envy. "Do you want me to come with you?" I asked.

"No. I think it makes more sense for you to stay here and try to figure out what the hell's going on."

Another unenviable task, but it made more sense to me, too. "Is there anything I can do for you?" I asked.

Al shook his head sadly. "I'll be okay. But I'm not sure it's such a good idea for you to stay at Sam's tonight. I mean, I'm not sure how Michelle's going to feel . . ."

My lodging was near the bottom of my list of concerns, so there was no reason for it to be near the top of Al's. But I knew from experience that some people can get preoccupied with minor details in moments of grief.

"Don't worry about me, Al. You just look after Michelle. I'll call you later."

I felt a bit lonely as I watched him leave, but there were plenty of other people to keep me company. Biff Bonnardo had gotten most of them to quiet down, with the exception of the woman in the wheelchair, who was still babbling away.

Dave Gwynn stood beside her, holding her hand and stroking her head. "Calm down, sweetheart," he urged, "calm down."

It took me a moment to realize that she was no ordinary nut. She was the nut who was married to the track announcer. If I had any feelings left in me, my heart would have gone out to the guy.

"Who *did* hit him?" Bonnardo asked, gesturing toward his groggy security guard.

He singled out the tattered Track Jack as the most likely suspect, but fifty fingers pointed him in another direction. "Who are you?" he asked me.

"He's a private detective," someone behind me said. I thought it was Sulky Sol Epstein. The revelation sent a murmur through the crowd. Apparently most of these people had only seen one of me on TV.

"Watch out, he took his gun, too," someone else added.

I thought it was time to make my own introduction. "Mark Renzler," I said, extending my hand. "I'm a contestant in Super Pick."

The track owner shook with some reluctance, offering me a paw that felt like a slice of soggy Wonder Bread. His face was soft too and a bit on the pasty side. He had gone a little heavy on the cologne that morning. This isn't my area of expertise, but I think it was a brand called Hai Karate.

"Your security guard went berserk," I said as I pulled out my ID. "He would have killed *him*." I pointed at Track Jack. "He also slugged *him*." I pointed at Herbie.

Bonnardo nodded, as if he weren't surprised to hear that Matt Caldwell had been less than gracious. He gave Herbie and Jack a passing glance, saving most of his attention for my ID. He studied it carefully then handed it to the mayor of Pompton Plains, who looked at it with a combination of curiosity and awe before giving it to his counterpart from Pequannock. I hoped he wasn't planning on passing it through the crowd to let everyone have a look.

"Did you take his gun?" Bonnardo asked.

I nodded and pulled it out of my pocket. "I don't think it's a good idea to let a guy like that carry one of these."

"He's the head of security here," Bonnardo said.

Oh, that explained it. "From what I've seen, I don't think that's such a good idea either," I said.

The track owner glared at me as he took the revolver. I had a sneaking suspicion he didn't care much what I thought. But at least he had the sense not to return the gun to Matt Caldwell.

"Does anybody know where the shots were fired from?" Bonnardo asked.

"*The parking lot*," came the answer in a chorus that sounded like a studio audience being prompted by a game-show host. Bonnardo had sounded a little like a game-show host when he posed the question.

I followed the track owner's gaze up to the edge of the lot, near the corner of the grandstand where the barbed-wire fence met the track apron. It was about seventy-five yards from where Sam had been standing. Based on the angle Sam had been looking at right before he got shot, that seemed like the likely spot to me as well. I figured the shooter had been crouched behind a car. I didn't see any gain in challenging Bonnardo's assumption that more than one shot had been fired. I figured I'd stay out of the whole mess until somebody with at least some vague legal affiliation arrived.

"Did anybody actually see what happened?" Bonnardo asked.

"I did! I saw the whole thing!" said Mrs. Dave Gwynn.

"Mrs. Gwynn did!" Matt Caldwell was back on his toes but still a stride off the pace.

It was my first chance to get a good look at the security chief. His head was almost a perfect square, with straight, well-defined lines at the chin and forehead. The distance from his lower lip to his chin took up about half his face, and the forehead accounted for about another third. I'm kind of lazy when it comes to converting fractions to common denominators, so let's just say that barely left room for one tiny nose and two beady eyes. The eyes were too close together for any parent's comfort, suggesting that Matt had spent too much time trying to get a peek at the nose. More than likely, it had been the time when he should have been studying.

"Why don't you tell us about it, Carol," Bonnardo said.

"Calmly," her husband cautioned.

Carol Gwynn took a deep breath, nodded, then pointed at Track Jack Jones. "*He* did it! I saw him!"

"You're nuts, lady." Track Jack shook his head.

"And he was high on dope, too!"

To support her claim, a geezer in a Mets cap stepped forward and held out his hand. "This fell out of his pocket, Mr. B." "Thank you, George," Bonnardo said as he took the joint.

I wondered what had become of Track Jack's reefer. I also wondered if Biff Bonnardo was on a first-name basis with every bettor at his racetrack. Attendance couldn't have been that bad.

"I saw him go out to the parking lot before the start of the ninth race," Toteboard Tommy Stevens said.

"So did I." Count on Dr. Dave Higgins for a second opinion.

A murmur went up in the crowd. Track Jack looked downright terrified as he stepped over and stood next to me.

"I think it would be a good idea to wait until the Pompton Plains police get here," Alton Selazny said. Guess which town he was the mayor of.

"I think the Pequannock Township police should handle it," Harry Spudder countered.

"Isn't this the jurisdiction of the *county?*" someone asked. Probably a lawyer with no clients.

"That's right!" Matt Caldwell was feeling feisty again. Not to mention officious. He pulled a badge from his shirt pocket and puffed out his chest. Taking a step toward Track Jack, he said, "As deputy sheriff of Morris County, I hereby place you under arrest for the murder of Longshot Sam."

"Aw, shit!" Track Jack planted his feet, but he looked like he wasn't sure if he should put up his hands or put up his dukes.

"But he didn't do anything," Serendipity McCall pleaded. I wondered whether she was just saying that or if she actually knew something. Either way, it wouldn't have mattered to Matt Caldwell.

I was afraid I might have to step in again until I heard a voice behind me boom, "Leave him alone, Caldwell!" That stopped the deputy in his tracks.

I turned to see a giant of a man pushing through the crowd. He was about the same height as Track Jack and about the same width as Timmy the Greek. His head looked smaller than it should have been for a body that size, but that may have been an optical illusion created by his ears. They were large enough to hang umbrellas on.

"Sorry it took me so long to get down here," the giant man said to Bonnardo. "I was up drinking in the Winners Circle and didn't hear a thing about it until someone came up and got me." He smiled a big wide grin. "I had myself a pretty good day."

"No problem, Sheriff Maszursky," the track owner replied.

Herbie shot me a glance, and I nodded in response. That solved the mystery of who our main competition in the contest was. But the only mystery I was interested in solving was who shot Longshot Sam.

15

It took more than an hour to sort everything out. A major step in that effort occurred when Anton Selazny and Harry Spudder agreed to make the investigation a cooperative undertaking between their two towns. The battle for local supremacy would have to be fought by their respective high school football squads. For now they shook hands and agreed to be "players on the same team," as Harry Spudder put it.

The quarterback of the operation was the Pequannock police chief, a ruddy-faced guy named Tom McReynolds, who I later learned had made second-team all-state at that position twenty-five years back. After getting hit with a barrage of advice from Biff Bonnardo and the local political hierarchy, McReynolds called as his first play a search of the parking lot, carried out by the entire police forces of both towns. This was hardly a cast of thousands. There were barely enough guys for a pickup game of touch. But they had that one ingredient that many people think is essential to good investigative work—enthusiasm. It was partly for lack of this ingredient that I elected to go into private practice.

The search turned up a high-powered rifle with a telescopic sight, but no shells. The rifle was found under the Volkswagen van where I had first seen Track Jack Jones. The van turned out to be owned by Serendipity McCall. It was conceivable that the woman in the Mustang had stashed the rifle there, but I was puzzled that Track Jack hadn't noticed her. I've heard of people getting so high on pot that they hallucinate, but I've never heard of a person being too stoned to see someone next to him.

In all likelihood, there wouldn't be any fingerprints on the rifle, but McReynolds turned out to be a stickler for detail, at least compared with other small-town cops I've encountered. He ordered it sent to the lab.

It seemed strange to me that the killer would have left the rifle but taken along the shells. McReynolds must have thought so too, because he ordered the team to continue searching until they found something. They didn't, but it kept them occupied while he was busy asking questions.

Once the search was underway, McReynolds began interviewing the person Biff Bonnardo was touting as the only witness to the shooting—Carol Gwynn. Before he started, I managed to strong-arm my way into the huddle and advise him to issue a radio bulletin for a white Mustang with out-of-state plates.

"Who are you?" McReynolds asked.

"He's a private eye." Sulky Sol did the honors for me again. Or maybe it was Lucky Lou.

This time I didn't bother with ID. "I didn't recognize the plate, but it was from the Show Me State," I said.

"Missouri," Herbie blurted. If it had been a quiz show, they would have let him advance to the bonus round.

"I think he's right," I heard Timmy the Greek say behind him.

"Of course he's right," said Clocker Callaway.

"I have reason to believe that the person who did the shooting drove away in that car," I said.

"No, he didn't!" Carol Gwynn pointed at Track Jack. "He's standing right over there!"

Track Jack shook his head in disbelief as Dave Gwynn took his wife's hand. "Calm down, sweetheart," he said, a blank expression on his thin face. His voice was soothing, but I had a feeling he was seething inside.

McReynolds frowned, and his freckles formed straight lines above the creases on his forehead. "Did you see the shooting?" he asked me.

"No, I didn't. You can go ahead and ask all the questions of everybody that you want and I'll wait my turn. In the meantime, I think you should put out a call for that car."

McReynolds shrugged. "Okay. It can't hurt."

Under the police chief's prompting, Carol Gwynn's story spilled out slowly. From down near the rail, she had seen a tall black man up in the parking lot a few minutes before the ninth race began. It didn't take a big leap of her imagination to identify Jack as the guy. But it took a quantum leap to put the rifle in his hands.

"So you didn't actually see a gun and you didn't actually see him with it," McReynolds said, with disappointment in his voice. Biff Bonnardo had given her a big buildup.

"Well, what would *you* assume?" she snapped.

McReynolds' eyes did a full rotation in their sockets. Carol Gwynn's looked like they were about to pop out.

"What's so bad about that?" She looked to her husband. "Did I say something wrong?"

Gwynn shook his head. "No, it's all right. You did just fine." He spoke to the nurse. "Val, why don't you take Carol up to the grandstand."

"No, you don't," Carol snapped. "I'm staying *right* here."

"You see—what'd I tell you?" Track Jack threw up his arms and addressed his remarks to anybody who wanted to listen. It was hard not to listen, because he was shouting. "I'd have to be *crazy* to come out here and shoot somebody in broad daylight! This is Honkeyville, man!"

That sounded plausible to me, but the police chief didn't seem to think so. "What *were* you doing up in the lot?" he asked.

"I wanted to get some fresh air."

"Fresh air!" Matt Caldwell snorted. "Smoking marijuana's more like it."

"What's that?" McReynolds asked.

"Yeah, that's right," Bonnardo said, handing over the confiscated joint. I suspected the track owner would just as soon have let that one pass. His security guard had already battered two contestants. Another had been murdered. Smoking a little grass seemed a minor infraction by comparison. Plus it wouldn't have surprised me if Biff had occasion to puff on a spliff himself once in a while.

"Fresh air, huh?" McReynolds held the joint and sneered.

Track Jack answered with a sheepish grin. "Shi-it," he said, shaking his head.

"Did you hear any shots?" McReynolds asked.

"Yeah, I heard one. Except I didn't know it was actually a shot until Renzler told me about Sam and all."

"Where did it come from?"

"Over near the grandstand, I guess."

"What do you mean—you 'guess'? You mean to tell me you heard a gunshot and you didn't notice where it came from?"

Jack glanced in my direction. I thought he wanted me to jump in and help him until I realized his appeal was directed at Serendipity, who was standing to my left.

"I let him borrow the keys to Zodiac," she said.

"To what?"

"That's the name of my van—Zodiac. I told him I had the new O'Jays tape and he wanted to listen to it."

"That's right, man," Track Jack said. "She's got quad in that thing. It's pretty nice."

That answered my question about why he hadn't noticed someone stashing the rifle under the van. I didn't know who the O'Jays were, but I had a feeling they were best appreciated when you listened at high volume.

"Of course I didn't know he'd be smoking marijuana," she added. Of course not. I wondered why Serendipity hadn't gone out to the van with him.

"I can confirm that there was only one shot fired," Dave Gwynn said. "It came from the parking lot, right next to the grandstand." He pointed to the announcer's booth, which was on the clubhouse level, adjacent to the lot. "It startled me so much that I flubbed the call of the race."

Now that he mentioned it, I had noticed that Gwynn had first called the winning horse *Sugar* Donut instead of Glazed Donut.

"Did you see anything?" McReynolds asked Gwynn.

He shook his head. "I was watching the race. I have to watch the race. I didn't even realize it was a gunshot until I saw everybody gathering around Sam. I thought it was a kid setting off a cherry bomb or something."

"What about you?" McReynolds asked Track Jack.

Jack shrugged. "Just the car Renzler told you about. That chick almost ran over me."

"What chick?"

"The one that was driving the damn car," Jack replied, as if the answer should have been perfectly obvious.

"What did she look like?"

"*Good*-looking lady. Red hair, down to here." Jack held his hand to his shoulder.

"Like mine?" Serendipity asked.

"Nah." Jack wrinkled his nose. "Yours is orange. This was more like reddish brown. And it was silky smooth. Not all ratty like yours is, if you know what I mean."

I think she knew exactly what he meant. So did the rest of the crowd, judging by the laughter. I had a feeling that would be the last time Track Jack got the keys to Serendipity's van.

"Okay, now tell me your story," McReynolds said, turning to me. He had saved the best for last, if I do say so myself.

I told him about the threats on Sam's life, admitting right off that I had gotten the information third-hand. Then I told him about Dino LaRussa taking Sam down to the rail before the ninth race.

"It's clear Dino was in on it," I said. "His job was to bring Sam down into the line of fire for the hit man. Or, I should say, hit *woman*."

"So you think the lady driving the car also did the shooting," McReynolds said.

"It looks that way. There could have been a third person, who was hiding in the backseat when they pulled away. Another possibility is that the shooting was done by a third person who didn't leave in the car at all. A person who maybe hasn't left yet."

That prospect sent a murmur rippling through the crowd.

"I don't think that's too likely," McReynolds said.

I refrained from asking him why, in that case, he had wasted so much time talking to Carol Gwynn and Track Jack.

"If what he says about LaRussa is true, then maybe somebody was trying to kill *him*," suggested a young blond cop from Pompton Plains. "Maybe they just missed."

"Good point," said the mayor of Pompton Plains.

I tried to let them down gently. "The victims of hits don't usually have getaway cars waiting for them."

"How do you know so much about this Dino LaRussa?" Sheriff Maszursky was getting into the act on behalf of the county. I wouldn't have been surprised if a representative from the Holey Toledo Club asked the next question.

I gave him a brief report on my work at the Superfix trial and Dino LaRussa's rise from sleazy groom to small-time gangster. "But he's changed his name since then," I said. "Around here he seems to be known as Danny Moreno."

"Isn't that the new guy who works for Tony Lunaviva?" Dave Gwynn asked Biff Bonnardo.

"Yeah, I think so," he said.

"What does he do?" I asked.

"He's a groom or something," Bonnardo said. "I think him and Natoli were kind of chummy. I saw them here together a couple times."

"He manages the Holey Toledo on Valley Road." That information was provided by the club member who had taken Toteboard Tommy to task for turning in his bet late. Now that he was standing next to Matt Caldwell, I could see the family resemblance. "I know because he's a counselor for our club."

"Doesn't Tony Lunaviva collect Ford Mustangs?" asked George, the guy who had turned over Track Jack's joint to Bonnardo.

"Yeah, I think you're right," said a fat guy next to him.

"I think it would be a good idea to talk to Mr. Lunaviva," I said.

"I don't think he was here today," Gwynn said.

"That seems kind of odd," I said. "He had an entry."

"Now hold your horses," Biff Bonnardo said. That admonition sounded particularly stupid coming from the owner of a racetrack.

Bonnardo began attacking the space between us with his index finger. Excluding his thumb, it was the only finger on his right hand that didn't have a ring. "I know Tony Lunaviva," he said. "He's done more work for good causes than you could possibly know. So don't go off accusing him until you've got your facts straight, mister. I don't care *what* line of work you're in."

"I didn't accuse him of anything," I replied. "And I don't like guys sticking their fingers at me to make stupid points."

"Hey, take it easy," McReynolds said. "Don't worry—we'll talk to him."

I didn't bother to tell him that I intended to have a word with the donut king myself.

The police chief suggested that it might be a good idea for all the bystanders to clear out.

"Does that mean I'm free to go?" Track Jack asked.

"No, I'm going to want you to sit down with a police artist and do a sketch of this lady you saw," McReynolds said.

"*And* you're gonna book him for possession of marijuana," Matt Caldwell added.

"After he's done charging you with assault," I said. I smiled for effect.

"You wanna see an assault, asshole?" Caldwell raised his fists and took a step toward me.

Sheriff Maszursky stepped between us. "Keep your shirt on, Matt," he ordered.

McReynolds turned toward me. "I think it might be a good idea if you were on your way."

"That's a *damn* good idea," Bonnardo added.

I couldn't have agreed more. But I also thought Track Jack might need a little support. "Do you want me to stick around?" I asked.

He shook his head. "If I was you, I'd get out while the gettin's good."

McReynolds escorted Herbie and me up the track apron on his way to check out the progress of business up in the lot. "Are you from around here, Renzler?" he asked.

"I grew up out here. I'm in New York now."

"You didn't play football for Clifton High School, did you?"

Baseball was my primary sport, but like most other jocks, I put in my time on the gridiron and the basketball court. I nodded and watched a sheepish smile spread across McReynolds' boyish face.

"You're the jerk that intercepted a pass against me and ran it back for a touchdown."

I confessed my guilt by returning his smile. I refrained from telling him it was the only pass I ever intercepted.

"I hope you're not going to be a pain in my ass again," he said.

"Not to worry, Chief," I replied, invoking the honorable mayor of Pequannock. "We're on the same team this time."

16

Under the pretense of getting ice to put on Herbie's eye before taking him home to face Daddy Doom, I pulled into the first joint we came to that served booze. It was a restaurant half a mile down Route 23 called the Triangle Hofbrau, which Longshot Sam had told me was the best place in twenty miles to get a decent meal.

When an Italian recommends a German restaurant, that either means the chow there is exceptionally good or the chow everywhere else is exceptionally bad. At that moment, I couldn't have cared less about food. All I wanted was five or six martinis. Dry, neat, and in a beer stein.

It turned out Herbie knew the Hofbrau, too. Dick and Karen ate there on their bowling night, and it had been the scene of his birthday dinner on Friday.

One of the waitresses rushed right over to him when we entered. "My God, what happened to you? Don't tell me you're still celebrating."

"Hi, Lucille," he said sheepishly. "I got sucker-punched."

"I'll say you did. But I'll bet the other guy looks worse."

"Nope." Herbie just didn't have it in him to tell a lie. "But my uncle knocked him *senseless*," he added, his expression brightening a bit.

"There wasn't much sense in that guy to start with, Herb," I said. That made him chuckle a bit.

"Where were you—down at the racetrack?" she asked.

I nodded. "We had a little run-in with the security guard."

"Not Matt Caldwell."

"Yup, that's the guy. *Matt Caldwell*." Herbie repeated the name slowly, with a notable absence of Christian charity in his tone.

"No wonder. You're lucky he didn't kill you."

"You're familiar with Mr. Caldwell," I said.

"Oh yeah, a real troublemaker." Lucille nodding knowingly. "Let me get some ice to put on that shiner."

We went into the bar and I got some gin to put on my headache. I asked Herbie if he wanted a beer. The management wouldn't like it, but I thought I might be able to sneak him one.

"I can't," he said. "I'm not eighteen yet."

"I won't tell anyone if you don't."

"Really?"

I nodded as he thought it over. Apparently, it was a big decision. "I don't know," he said at last. "I don't think my dad would like the idea."

The kid was showing better judgment than his uncle there. I'd be in enough trouble with my brother-in-law for bringing his son home looking like a punching bag. If I brought him home half in the bag, he'd probably have me brought up on morals charges.

"Good thinking," I said. "We'll do it later in the week."

Lucille arrived with some ice wrapped in a cloth. "Somebody was in here a little while ago saying there was a shooting over at the track today."

"There was," Herbie said. "Somebody killed Longshot Sam."

"Oh my God!" Lucille put her hand to her mouth and closed her eyes. "I don't believe it! He was just in here yesterday."

"It was really sad, Lucille."

I didn't think she needed Herbie to tell her. She took a deep breath and seemed to be holding back tears. "Did you hear that, Dieter?" she called to the bartender. "Somebody killed Sam Natoli."

Dieter rushed over, spilling half of my second martini. "Do they know who did it?"

"No, but my uncle's going to find out. He's a private detective."

The three other patrons in the bar began firing questions at us. I decided to let Herbie tell the story. I lit a cigarette, grabbed my drink and slipped away to the phone booth. It was time to call for some help.

Nate's usually slow in responding to intrusions like the telephone, but this time he answered on the first ring. I figured he must have been expecting an important call, but it turned out he was just in an exceptionally good mood. It didn't take me long to change it.

"Sure, I'll accept the charges," he told the operator. "I'll pay my bill on time this month if you like, too. If Ma Bell was around, I'd even plant a wet one right on her kisser."

"I'm sure that won't be necessary, sir."

"Did you hear?" he asked excitedly when she put me through.

"Hear what?"

"Three of the tapes Nixon had to turn over show he ordered a halt to the investigation six days after the Watergate break-in. This is it, for Chrissakes! The final nail in the coffin. I'll bet the old Commie basher's seeing red tonight."

And I'd be willing to bet Nate had started drinking pretty early in the day. A day earlier, and I would have shared his enthusiasm.

"What's the matter, Renz? You don't sound too pleased."

"It's great news, Nate. The best I've heard all day. Matter of fact, it's the only good news I've heard all day."

"What's wrong? Did you guys get skunked?"

"Don't I wish. No, I'm afraid it's worse than that."

"What could be worse than losing all your money?"

"Watching Longshot Sam get shot."

"Jesus Christ!" I could almost hear the color drain out of his face. "Is he dead?"

"Very."

"What happened? Did somebody go crazy or was it a hit?"

"Looks like a professional job all the way. Or at least a lot of planning went into it."

"I'll be damned. So his wife had reason to be worried, after all."

"I'm afraid so."

"How's she doing? Was she there when it happened?"

"Luckily, no. She was home making dinner for us." I took a mouthful of gin. "Lasagna. Sam's favorite."

"Small consolation that it freezes well." I knew Nate was concerned, but he has a dark sense of humor.

"Or that it tastes better on the second day," I said. I have a dark sense of humor myself. It's a defense mechanism, according to a psychologist I dated briefly. I gave Nate a quick summary of the day's events.

"Do you think one of the contestants was behind it?" he asked when I finished.

"Could be. From what I've seen so far, these guys don't like each other. But most of them are from out of town. I don't know how they'd be working with a local guy like Dino LaRussa. It's possible that whoever killed Sam did it during the contest just to create that suspicion."

"Dino *did* drive away in a car with Missouri plates," he said.

Good point. I took another mouthful of gin, leaving myself with the only kind of martini that was more dry than I liked. "I don't know what to think," I said. "I'll have a better idea once I talk to Michelle and get some details about the threats Sam was receiving."

"That should be lots of laughs. When are you planning on doing it?"

"Tonight—if she's in any shape to talk."

"Speaking of the beautiful Michelle," Nate said. "I know you're not going to like this, but based on the description you got, do you think there's any chance she might have been the woman in the Mustang?"

"You're right, I don't like it. But it did cross my mind. Only for a moment, though. When Michelle spoke to me last week, she was one frightened lady."

"Woman," he corrected. Nate had recently fallen in with a group of feminists. "Well, you're the one who saw her, partner. That's enough for me." He paused to light a cigarette. "Do you want me to come out there tonight?"

"I'm not sure I'll be able to pick you up." Nate had a driver's license, but the idea of him actually using it was a pretty chilling thought.

"Don't worry about coming to get me," he said. "I'll take a bus."

"You—a bus?"

"Don't act so surprised. I've been on a bus before. It's one of those long smelly things, right? A rolling plague unit. If I hop on one right now, I could be out there in, what—a few days?"

"More like an hour."

"But it would probably be the longest hour of my life."

"You might learn something from the experience," I said, "but I'll spare you the agony. Just be ready at the crack of dawn tomorrow."

"Do you have a breakfast appointment lined up?"

"Something like that. Tony Lunaviva's having us over for coffee."

"Does he know we're coming?"

"Not if I can help it."

"Good. Maybe he'll run out of donuts before we get there."

Herbie was alone when I got back to the bar. His eye was swollen shut and was beginning to take on the colors of sunset over Secaucus. I was tempted to wash down another drink, but I figured it was time to take him home.

As we were on our way out, Lucille came over to us. "I hope you find the guy who killed Longshot Sam," she said.

"I'll do my best."

"By the way, Sam was in the bar here day before yesterday with Tony Lunaviva. Do you know who that is?"

I nodded.

"They seemed to be having some kind of argument. I don't know what it was about, but Sam's ex-wife was with them, too."

"That would be Daphne," I said.

"No, that was the odd part. Daphne's married to Tony Lunaviva, but the woman with him was Candy Miller. She used to be married to Sam, too. I don't know if that means anything to you or not."

"Thanks, Lucille," I said. "You never know. It just might."

As we were getting into the car, Herbie said, "Uncle Mark, do you think it was inappropriate for me to deliver the last rites to Mr. Natoli?"

I hadn't realized Herbie had been administering an actual sacrament. To me it was just a hocus-pocus prayer.

"No, Herb," I said. "I thought it was a very wise and thoughtful thing for you to do."

"Oh, good. I was afraid you thought it was weird because you had such a strange look on your face."

"No. I was just sad about Sam dying. And thanks to you, Sam is probably already in heaven by now."

"I sure hope so. You do know that a lay person is allowed to administer last rites when there's not a priest around."

I didn't. "Sure I do, Herb."

"How many people have you seen die, Uncle Mark?"

"Too many, Herb."

"Is it always as sad as this?"

"Not all the time, Herb. It's only this sad when good people die."

Herbie nodded. I hoped he wasn't going to ask me how I could judge the good people from the bad. He didn't.

"I've only seen one other person die," he said. "Grandpa. I was only a kid then, but it was still really sad. I remember you were crying at the funeral, and I didn't think you would. That was the only time I ever saw you cry, Uncle Mark."

"We all cry sometimes, Herb. There's never any shame in crying."

"I know," he said. "Do you miss Grandpa a lot, Uncle Mark?"

"Yeah, I do, Herb."

"I think Mom does, too."

As we pulled up to the house, I asked Herbie whether he'd mind if I didn't come inside with him.

"No, that's all right," he said, pointing to his swollen eye. "You don't want to have to explain things to Mom, do you?"

"No, Herb, I sure don't." But that wasn't the only reason.

"I don't blame you," he said. "Neither do I."

I waited until he got to the door before driving away. When I got around the corner, I pulled over to the curb and thought about my father for a moment. Then I thought about my mother being all alone and how much she missed him sometimes. Then I started to cry.

17

I checked into Howard Johnson's, grabbed a take-out drink from the lounge, and headed for my room. I turned on the box just in time to catch the evening news. The new Watergate revelations took center stage on the network report, but the top local story was the shooting at Garden State Downs.

The report was obviously thrown together quickly, and the facts were sketchy. But in TV news you don't necessarily need facts to make a good story. I learned this from my friend Carol Robertson, a rising young star at WNBC. What you need, she told me, is film. The station I watched, her station, had some very good film—a replay of the race, complete with Dave Gwynn's stretch call.

Needless to say, it wasn't the action on the track that made the story so riveting. It was the activity at the lower right corner of the screen as the horses crossed the finish line. You had to look carefully to see it the first time, and just in case you didn't, they ran it again in slow motion. They even put a circle around the central attraction and froze the frame at a critical moment—a very critical moment from Longshot Sam's point of view. It was the moment when his expression changed from casual mirth to abject terror, the moment when the fatal bullet entered his body.

It had been shocking enough when it had happened, but it was sheer agony to see it again. I hoped Michelle Natoli wasn't watching the evening news.

The information I had supplied about Dino LaRussa/Danny Moreno was featured prominently, probably because Dino had a cameo role in the film. Apparently, there hadn't been time to interview McReynolds, Bonnardo, or any other prominent local figures. I knew of at least two mayors who would have been tickled to show their mugs on TV. I figured they would turn up on the late broadcast.

The report said Dino had escaped in a car driven by a woman, and a rifle had been found in the parking lot. I wasn't surprised that Dino's employer, Tony Lunaviva, managed to escape mention, but I was irritated to learn that the police were still entertaining the ridiculous notion that Dino, not Sam, had been the target of the hit.

I had another drink and a sandwich that did nothing to enhance HoJo's reputation, then called Michelle's house. I was relieved when Al Phillips answered the phone.

"How's Michelle doing?" I asked.

"She's been better, that's for sure. All things considered, I'd say she's holding up pretty well. Plus she took enough Valium to put a horse to sleep."

"Is she sleeping now?"

"Oh no, she's awake. Sam's lawyer is over here, and they're going over the will."

"I see." That seemed a little sudden to me, but I wasn't about to say anything. "Did you watch the news?"

"Yeah, we saw it all right. What a bunch of bloodsuckers. Sam's lawyer thinks we might be able to sue."

Evidently, Sam's lawyer wasn't familiar with the First Amendment. I wasn't going to be the one to tell him about it. Nor was I going to get into a discussion with Al or Michelle. They had a right to be pissed, but there was nothing they could do. Not unless Judge Hoffman was appointed to the Supreme Court, and that didn't seem too likely.

"If Michelle's up to it, I'd like to ask her a few questions," I said.

"I'm sure she is. She said she wanted to talk to you. Why don't you stop by?"

Al gave me directions, and ten minutes later I pulled up to a huge two-story house on Lake Drive West with a sign on the front lawn that said "The Natoli's." In the dark, I couldn't see the lake, which I took to be Packanack, but I was willing to believe it was there.

I could tell from her eyes that Michelle had been crying, but she was calm and poised when she came to the door.

We looked at each other for a long moment after I stepped inside. "I'm sorry," I said in a faltering voice.

"I know, I know," she said softly. She held out her hand and I squeezed it.

"I'm sorry I let you down," I said.

"No, you didn't. There was nothing you could have done."

It made me feel better to hear her say it, but I felt like a cad knowing I needed to hear it, knowing I had made her say it. Sam was gone, but at least I was off the hook.

"I'd like you to find out who did it."

"Of course. I intend to."

"I don't care how much it costs, Mr. Renzler. I can pay you."

"You wouldn't dare." I was a bit chagrined that she thought I'd want money, but this wasn't the time to be thin-skinned. "And drop the *mister*," I added.

She forced a smile and wiped at a tear that had trickled down her cheek. "What should I call you? Just Renzler?"

"It was good enough for my mother."

That made her chuckle a little.

Michelle led me into the living room, where Al was sitting with a short, chunky guy in a rumpled jacket.

"This is Sam's lawyer, Bernie Rich," Michelle said.

"And lifelong friend," Bernie added.

We shook hands and stood awkwardly for a moment while we agreed how terrible it all was, then sat down as Al went to mix me a drink.

"There's not going to be any funeral," Michelle said. "Sam was Catholic, but he didn't believe in them. He thought they were ghoulish."

I nodded. A man after my own soul.

"Sam didn't believe in a lot of things," Bernie said. "Take his will, for example." He held up a white envelope. "He insisted on writing it himself. Of course I went over it with him and made sure it met all the legal prerequisites. Given Sam's, uh—shall we say, for lack of a better word—*predilection* to matrimony, it was essential that it be done with the utmost care and attention to detail."

Judging by the expression on Michelle's face, I thought she

might have felt better if Bernie had been able to come up with a better word.

"I mean, given the number of prior spouses and the short duration, relatively speaking, of Sam and Michelle's marriage, one might expect that this could be a contestable situation. Which is why I rushed right over when I heard the news. Being Sam's lifelong friend, I felt a personal obligation to assure Michelle that she would be well taken care of."

"I don't really care about the money, Bernie."

"I know you don't, sweetheart. But nonetheless—oh, thank you," Bernie said to Al as he handed him a drink. "I was about to leave, but I guess I'll stay for one more." Bernie chuckled. "I mean—if you insist."

It was probably my imagination, but I thought Al pulled the glass back for a split second as Bernie reached for it. But the damage was already done.

"The official reading of the last will and testament will be done at the ceremony," Bernie explained to me. I could tell from their expressions that this was familiar terrain for Al and Michelle.

"I thought there wasn't going to be any ceremony," I said.

"No *funeral*," Bernie said, smiling and holding up his index finger. "There's a difference between a funeral and a ceremony." I stifled the urge to tell him I knew that ceremony was something you stood on when you stopped yourself from slugging another guest at somebody's house.

"I don't think we need to go over this again," Al said impatiently.

"Oh, I'm sorry." Bernie's self-awareness light went on. "I guess I'm overdoing it again." I had a feeling his status as Sam's attorney was more attributable to lifelong friendship than to superior legal skills.

"That's okay, Bernie," Michelle said, patting his leg. This was one extraordinary lady. Woman, I mean.

"Sam wanted to be cremated and have his ashes scattered at the nearest racetrack," she said to me.

I managed to keep my eyes from popping, but I couldn't stop my eyebrows from lifting.

"I know, it's weird," Michelle said. "But Sam was weird, too. Like the will. He told *everyone* what was in it. All his ex-wives

are in it. He let all of them know, and he let me know, too."
Michelle let out a throaty chuckle. "Once, when we were at a
party, Sam was telling everybody about the will. And this guy
Dave Gwynn, who announces the races, asked Sam if he could
marry him just for the weekend so he could get into the will."
Michelle laughed, then shook her head and sighed. "I just wish
I didn't have to make all these crazy arrangements."

"And you don't, my dear," Bernie said, standing up with a
courtroom flourish that had probably earned his clients countless continuances over the years. "I'll take care of everything.
You just let old Bernie handle it."

He took Michelle's hand and kissed it, then turned to me. "If
I can be of any help in any way with your investigation, don't
hesitate to let me know."

Despite Bernie's protestations, Michelle escorted him to the
foyer, where I suspect he tried to kiss more than her hand.
When she returned, I asked, "Are you ready to answer some
questions?"

She smiled. "After Bernie, I can handle anything."

I asked about the handicappers. Al and Michelle both
thought all the Super Pick contestants were above suspicion,
with one exception.

"Toteboard Tommy Stevens," Michelle said. "He's the one I
wonder about. And that's because of the phone calls."

"Tell me about the calls," I said. "How many were there?"

Michelle counted on her fingers. "Four, I think. Maybe five.
I don't really know, because I was only here for a couple of
them. There may have been more that Sam didn't tell me
about. One time I answered. That's how I found out it was
happening to begin with."

"What did the voice sound like?"

"Sam thought it sounded like Toteboard Tommy. He was
convinced it was him. I told him he should say something about
it, but he just wanted to let it drop. He didn't want Tommy to
know it was bothering him."

"Did you think the voice sounded like Tommy?"

"I'm not sure. I guess so, but maybe that's because of what
Sam thought. It was a high-pitched voice, but I thought it
might be somebody trying to disguise their voice."

"And what did the voice say?"

"I don't remember exactly. Something about if Sam entered the contest, they were going to kill him." Michelle took a deep breath and shook her head. "Oh God. I can't believe this is all happening."

"Are you okay?" I asked. "We can do this another time."

She bit at her lower lip. "No. I want to help."

"So the caller specifically mentioned the contest."

"Yes. That part I'm sure of. Is that important?"

"It probably means someone in the contest killed Sam," Al said.

"Probably. It could mean somebody wanted it to look that way."

"It's a little like handicapping a race, isn't it?" Al said.

"It's exactly like handicapping a race. Let's go over the field. Is there anything else that makes you think Tommy might be involved?" I asked Michelle.

"Not really. It was just that he was so weird last year."

"How so?"

"Tommy's one of those guys who look you up and down, like they're sizing you up. Like . . . I don't know." She shivered. "He just gives me the creeps. Do you know what I mean?"

"I know exactly what you mean." I hoped I didn't give her the creeps. But I figured as long as there were guys like Tommy Stevens around, I probably wouldn't have to worry about it.

"He's a lech," Al said.

"I had the impression they were all leches," I said.

"Oh no," Michelle said. "Not Timmy the Greek or Clocker Callaway."

"Well, those guys can hardly stand up," I said. "Clocker looks like he's about to croak any second."

"He looks a lot better than he did last year," Al said.

"I'll have to take your word for it." I spoke to Michelle. "Who else didn't Sam like?"

"He didn't like any of them really." She smiled at Al. "Except you, of course."

"What about Dr. Dave?"

"Oh, Sam *hated* him. He and Tommy Stevens are like *this*." Michelle crossed her fingers. "If Tommy's involved, they're probably in on it together."

"That makes sense to me, too," Al said.

"It makes more sense when you consider that Tommy and Dr. Dave followed Sam and Dino LaRussa down the stairs at the track."

"Really? I hadn't noticed that," Al said.

"Did you happen to notice who was in the section when the race started?"

Al shook his head. "I don't know. It was cleared out by then. I remember seeing the Greek and Clocker. They were talking to the Daily Double."

"Who's that?" Michelle asked. "Sulky Sol and Lucky Lou?"

"Uh . . . no," Al said sheepishly. "That's our nickname for Serendipity."

"What about Sol and Lou?" I asked him.

"I think they were there. But I wouldn't swear to it. I was talking to your nephew."

"Are you sure you weren't staring at the Daily Double?" Michelle asked sarcastically. I sensed a bit of irritation in her voice, but she could have been joking.

Time to change the subject just in case. "What do you know about Dino LaRussa?" I asked Michelle. She looked momentarily baffled. "Danny Moreno," I prompted.

"Nothing really." She curled her nose in disgust. "I only met him once or twice. He seemed kind of cheap and oily. I couldn't understand why Sam was so nice to him."

"Because Dino—or Danny, if you prefer—was giving Sam tips on Tony Lunaviva's horses." I was a bit wary of offending Michelle, but there was no point beating around the bush.

"Do you think so?" She sounded hopeful, as if a dishonest reason was better than none at all.

"I *know* so. Did Sam ever say anything to you about something fishy going on with Lunaviva's horses?"

"Sam didn't talk to me much about his work. And I guess I didn't listen very well when he did. He used to sit in that chair"—she pointed to the worn La-Z-Boy lounger Al was sitting in—"and talk to himself. He used to say the names of the horses and the jockeys—I'm sorry, I mean *drivers*." Michelle let out a quiet laugh. "I should've at least learned *that*. God knows Sam told me enough times." She smiled sadly as she stared at the chair, looking right through Al, who vacated the sacred spot and went to get more drinks.

I watched Michelle, and her eyes narrowed. "But he *did* say something about Tony Lunaviva," she said suddenly.

"Do you recall what it was?"

"No, but I remember he said he was going to talk to Dave Gwynn about it. He's the racing treasurer."

"Secretary," Al corrected. He stroked her head gently as he walked past. Michelle looked up at him and smiled.

"How long ago was that?"

"Let's see." Michelle tilted her head back and shook it slightly, tousling her hair in the process. She seemed unaware of how pretty she was. "A couple of months ago, at least."

"Do you know if he talked to Gwynn?"

"No, I'm sorry, I don't."

I paused to take a mouthful of my drink and light my last cigarette. "Did Sam keep his old racing programs and sheets?" I asked.

"Are you kidding?" Michelle got up and walked to a row of drab gray filing cabinets that looked like they had been purchased at a used-office-furniture closeout. "These things are filled with them," she said. "It's amazing. There's twelve rooms in this house. Sam even had a study upstairs. But he liked to do all his work right here in the living room."

"What are you thinking?" Al asked me.

"I'm thinking it would be a good idea if you went through the programs to see if you can figure out what was going on with Lunaviva's horses."

"Sure thing. I'll get right on it."

"Good luck trying to figure out Sam's filing system," Michelle said. She started to chuckle, then her chuckle turned into a laugh. She laughed long and hard, then started to cry.

I figured that was my signal to leave. Besides, I was out of cigarettes.

18

Tuesday morning got off to a slower start than I had hoped. I could have blamed it on the HoJo's desk clerk for being late with my wake-up call, but when I charged down to the lobby to let the old biddy have it, I discovered instead a cute young blonde who was being "trained" by the day manager, a twerp in an orange sports coat with a bad case of acne and a worse case of halitosis. I had to duck for cover when I got within ten feet, so I figured she was having a bad-enough day already.

As I headed toward the snack shop to fill my tank with coffee, I saw Track Jack Jones loading luggage into a car outside.

"Hey, Jack," I called as I ran out into the parking lot.

He winced as he turned. It would be a few days before the bruises inflicted by Matt Caldwell would heal. "What's happening, bro?" he said.

"What's happening with *you?* It looks like you're on your way out of town."

"You bet your ass I am. It's bye-bye burbs for this boy."

"What about the contest?"

"Screw the contest. I'm getting out of this honkey burg and back to Motown, where it's safe."

All things considered, I couldn't say that I blamed him. "What about the entry fee?"

"I cut a deal with that Bonnardo jerk. I told him, 'You give me back my fee, and I won't sue your ass.'" He grinned. "He was happy to reciprocate. I think he kind of liked the idea of getting rid of me. Having me around was bad for business."

"Well, I might want to ask you a few questions," I said. "I'm investigating the murder of Longshot Sam."

Jack pulled a business card out of his wallet. "I'll be happy to answer all the questions you want. But I got a plane to catch, so you're gonna have to do it telephonically."

I took out one of my cards and wrote down my sister's phone number. "After your head clears out, if you think of anything that might be useful, try calling me here."

"I will do that, Renzler. Thanks for your help yesterday. If I ever see that motherfucker again, I will kick his ass so hard he'll be shitting out his mouth." Jack put out his hand. "If you ever get out to Detroit, be sure and look me up. I'll show you a good time."

I waved as he drove off. Now there were eight pros left in the contest. Al Phillips' chances of winning were looking better all the time. And so were everyone else's, for that matter.

I went inside and got a coffee to go, then raced over to my sister's house. I figured Nate and I would be too busy with our investigation to compete in the contest, so we needed Herbie on hand to salvage at least one of our entries. Although the murder of Longshot Sam had dampened my enthusiasm for Super Pick, I wasn't ready to throw away the chance of winning a bundle of dough.

Needless to say, it took some smooth talking to convince Herbie's parents to leave their only son with good old Uncle Mark while they were away. Dick hadn't been keen on the idea to start with, and bringing the kid home with a shiner hadn't helped my case. I started off shakily, making a wisecrack about Herbie's resemblance to Cyclops that failed to amuse anyone, then waited patiently while my brother-in-law labored with a little sarcasm of his own.

"So what have you got planned for today, Uncle Mark? A broken arm?"

"It's not that bad, Dad," Herbie insisted. "I kind of like it, in fact."

In some ways I thought it would be better if my nephew went with his parents. I wasn't sure how much time I'd be able to spend with him. But I knew he wanted to stay home. He even started to cry when it looked like things wouldn't go his way. I think that was what finally tipped the scales in my favor.

"It was just for effect," he explained as we pulled away and headed toward Hoboken, where we were supposed to pick up Nate. "It works all the time."

"You're sixteen now, Herb. You ought to find a better way to be persuasive." Did I really say that? In less than five minutes, I was already sounding like a goddamn parent.

If there was any doubt it was going to be a bad day, a massive traffic jam at the junction of Route 46 and Route 3 removed it. The fuse for the radio had burned out again, but Herbie managed to get it working with a piece of aluminum foil off a hamburger wrapper that somebody had left on the floor of the Pinto. The delay was due to an overturned tractor trailer in Lyndhurst. The traffic reporter advised motorists to use alternate routes, but he didn't offer any help in finding them. It was the first time I ever thought there was a shortage of roads in Jersey.

We pulled into Hoboken two hours late. Nate was standing outside the train station drinking a beer wrapped in a brown bag. I was glad to see he was setting a good example for my nephew.

"What took you so long?" he asked as Herbie squeezed into the backseat. "This is the most time I've ever spent in New Jersey by myself. And let me tell you, it hasn't been a pleasant experience."

Nate kept up a steady stream of chatter asking Herbie about the minor seminary while I searched out an alternative route back to Garden State Downs. I sensed that Herbie was a little pressed, so I changed the subject by filling them in on what I had learned from Michelle last night.

It was pushing noon by the time we pulled into the Quality Inn lot. I was disappointed to see that they had changed their sign from SUPER DICKS to SUPER PIKS. But what really caught my attention was the parking lot itself. It was almost full. In view of the sparse crowd at yesterday's opening, the sudden surge of interest could only be attributable to one thing—the shooting of Longshot Sam.

"Ah, yes, Garden State Downs," Nate said as we approached the grandstand. "Herbie, I hope you realize that you're about to enter one of the true architectural wonders of the world."

Nate waited until he had Herbie's full skepticism. "It's a

wonder anybody had the bad taste to build it," he said. "Take a good look, pal. If horse racing ever makes it to Albania, this is exactly what it will look like."

Herbie looked at Nate as if he were from Albania. "By the way, Uncle Nate," he said. "I like to be called Herb now."

Al Phillips was coming out of the Winners Circle when we got to the clubhouse. "Yeah, sure, I remember you," he said after I introduced him to Nate. "You're a painter or something."

Nate nodded diffidently. "Or something."

"There was talk this morning that Biff Bonnardo was going to cancel the day's card out of respect to Sam," Al said. "But people started showing up three hours early. This is the biggest crowd they've had since the place opened. So Dave Gwynn suggested that they postpone the contest for the day."

"Did they?" I asked.

Al shook his head. "We took a vote on it. Sam lost, five to three."

"I'd be curious to know how people voted," I said.

"It was a secret ballot—Dr. Dave's idea."

"That should tell you where one of the five votes came from," Nate said.

I asked Al if he had been able to determine anything about Tony Lunaviva's horses from studying Sam's old racing programs.

"No, not yet. I haven't had a chance to go over them. I barely had time to handicap today's program." I thought his priorities were odd, but I didn't want to comment in front of Nate and Herbie. "I promise I'll get to them today," he said.

"The sooner the better."

"Yeah, I know."

The handicappers looked a little subdued as they filed out of the Winners Circle. I figured most of them were still in shock over the death of Sam, but I was sure a few of them were making a concerted effort to conceal their glee. Regardless of whether any of them were involved in Sam's killing, they were all a whole lot closer to winning fifty grand.

I pointed the pickers out to Nate and gave him a little background on each one.

"It's a great-looking bunch of guys," he said. "Send them on a publicity tour, and I bet they'd really enhance the reputation of the racing industry." He raised his eyebrows as Serendipity McCall stepped out, followed by Biff Bonnardo and Dave Gwynn. "And just who may I ask is *that?*"

"That's the track owner and the racing secretary," I said.

"What's the racing secretary's name?"

"Dave Gwynn."

"Very funny." Nate frowned. "I mean the woman, Renzler." Nate has a soft spot for redheads. And he likes his women big.

"That's Serendipity McCall," Herbie said. He giggled. "They call her the Daily Double."

Nate nodded and gave him a wink. "If the bra fits, wear it."

Al sounded contemptuous as he told Nate about Serendipity's handicapping method, not realizing that my friend couldn't have cared less. "She's a real dingbat," he said.

"All the same, I like her freckles."

"If you're nice, she might let you count them," I said.

"Oh yeah?"

Serendipity's jewelry jingled as she came over to chat. "Who's your new friend, Al?"

Instead of introducing us, Al gave her a sneer and stalked away. Serendipity pretended not to notice as I did the introductions, but it was obvious Al had hurt her feelings.

"Your friend Al's a real charmer, Renzler," Nate said.

"He's a stuck-up male chauvinist pig is what he is," Serendipity said.

I left Nate and Herbie with Ms. McCall and ventured over to talk to Dave Gwynn and Biff Bonnardo. I didn't need their permission to question the pickers, but I thought it would be good to let them know Michelle had asked me to investigate.

"No problem," Bonnardo said. He seemed a lot friendlier than he had been the day before. "There's nobody that wants to find the killer more than I do. Believe me. When something like this happens, it's bad publicity."

I refrained from pointing out that the publicity hadn't done Bonnardo any damage so far. "I just wanted to make sure I don't have any more trouble with Matt Caldwell," I said.

"No, I promise, you won't. I'll be sure and talk to him. I told him to take the day off today. And by the way, I thought you'd be glad to know: I did take away his gun."

"That's a fine idea."

"Matt's a good kid," Bonnardo said. "He's just a little excitable, that's all. I'm sure you understand."

I'm sure I didn't.

Bonnardo glanced at his Rolex. "Well, I've got to be going. If we can help in any way, just talk to Dave or myself."

"Mr. Bonnardo's right," Gwynn said as we watched the track owner stroll away. "Matt is a good kid. He's just had a lot of problems. He served in the same unit with my son in Vietnam. They were buddies since childhood. They were in the Green Berets together."

I nodded. That explained a lot about Matt Caldwell right there. Gwynn told me a little more.

"They were captured by the Viet Cong." He took a breath but spoke in a measured tone. "They were humiliated, tortured. God only knows what they did to them—well, Matt could tell you."

I didn't need to hear any more, but it was clear that Gwynn wanted to tell it. "Fortunately, Matt managed to escape. He was out wandering around the jungle alone for a week before our guys found him. That was after Davey—that was my son's name—well, the bastards killed him."

"I'm sorry," I said.

Gwynn nodded. He took off his glasses and rubbed his eyes, but there was no evidence of sadness in them. "I didn't tell you this for sympathy, Mr. Renzler. I just wanted you to try and understand where Matt was coming from yesterday."

I said I understood even though I didn't.

"I guess I should apologize for my wife, too."

"There's no need for that."

"Carol's been, well, I guess you could say she's been crazy ever since it happened. You see, Davey was our only son. She was depressed and then she started drinking and then she had the car accident—drove right into a telephone pole down here on Twenty-three." Gwynn pointed in the direction of the highway. "The doctors said it was a miracle that she lived, but—I don't want this to sound the wrong way—I'm not sure she really wanted to, if you know what I mean."

I knew exactly what he meant. A kid had been sent to fight in a stupid war, and three people's lives had been ruined. Of course, I'm not sure Dave Gwynn would have seen it that way.

"Well, I don't know why I'm going on like this," he said. "I just wanted you to know that I considered Sam Natoli to be a friend of mine. If I can be of any help, don't hesitate to ask."

I thought about inquiring if Longshot Sam had talked to him about Tony Lunaviva's horses, but Tommy Stevens wandered over to ask him a question about the contest. I figured it might be better to wait until Al figured out exactly what was going on before I broached the subject.

Sulky Sol Epstein and Lucky Lou Larson were talking with Nate, Herbie, and Serendipity when I got back.

"Hey, Mr. Private Eye," Lou said. "You want to get in on another pool?"

"What's this one about?"

"You're supposed to guess when that Danny Moreno guy's going to turn up," Sol explained.

"What makes you so sure he's going to?"

"Oh, he'll turn up all right," Lou said. "And when he does, he'll be wearing a cement overcoat."

I shook my head. "I think I'll take a pass on this one."

"What's a cement overcoat?" Herbie asked as we walked away.

"It's an expression he learned from watching too much TV," Nate said. "What I want to know is how you tell those two guys apart."

"Lucky Lou's the one with the rug," I said.

"No, Uncle Mark. That's Sulky Sol."

"I think you might be right, Herb."

When we got to the contestants section, I told Herbie that Nate and I had to leave.

"Can't I go with you?"

"No, you stay here and put in the bets Al tells you to."

"But I'd like to help you investigate." It suddenly dawned on me why Herbie had wanted to stay home. Betting on harness races had nothing to do with it.

"You *can* help," I said. "You can be a big help. I want you to keep your ears open and listen for anything that anybody says about Longshot Sam. Okay?"

"All right." Herbie stared at the floor. "But do I have to stay with Al?"

"He's the one who's going to tell you who to bet on. Do you

have a problem with that?" I was afraid Herbie was having another ethical crisis.

"Not really. It's just that"—he shook his head—"I just don't like him."

"Spoken like a true Jesuit," Nate said. "That makes two of us, Herb. I guess you'll just have to offer it up."

As we walked across the parking lot, I asked Nate what he had against Al.

"Nothing, except that I think he's a two-bit hustler and a get-rich-quick schemer."

"That sounds a little like me," I said.

"It sounds a *lot* like you," he corrected. "But you're my friend. I can't do anything about it."

19

"**I** hope Mr. Lunaviva doesn't mind that we're coming for lunch instead of breakfast," Nate said as we cruised up Route 46 toward Parsippany.

"I don't think he will. You know the Holey Toledo slogan."

"Yeah, that's right." Nate proved he had stayed up late watching "Joe Franklin" too many times by singing the tune to "Old MacDonald Had a Farm" in a booming baritone: "WE MAY DOZE, BUT WE NEVER CLOSE. HO-LEY TO-LE-DO."

"Very good," I said. "Maybe he'll let you do a commercial with him."

"I don't think so. Tony strikes me as kind of an insecure guy."

I didn't know exactly where Lunaviva's place was located, but we didn't have any trouble finding it. When we came over the crest of the hill near the Boonton Reservoir, we could see the world's largest donut through the trees to our right. Since I had last seen the famous donut tower—on one of those deadly TV news features that run late on Saturday afternoons—Lunaviva had added a cup and saucer.

"I wonder if it's the world's biggest," Nate mused.

"I no longer wonder why they get so many UFO reports around here. It gives new meaning to the concept of flying saucers."

"Not to mention the concept of flour power."

We had a clear view of the tower once we got off the highway, but it took a few minutes to find the entrance to the estate. There was a gate marked with the Holey Toledo logo, a vertical donut with a halo shimmering above it. "I think this could be the place," Nate said. Nobody was standing guard, so he got out and opened the gate himself, waving to a video camera that was mounted on a cement ledge.

The drive leading down to Lunaviva's house was set on a steep hill and formed a circle that must have been a quarter mile in circumference. The Holey Toledo logo was splattered all over it. The donut tower was next to the house at the bottom of the circle.

"This just might be the world's biggest driveway," I said.

"Tony just might be the world's biggest asshole."

As we began our descent, we could see two horses grazing in a pasture behind the house. In the distance to the left, a man was putting another horse through its paces on a racing oval. Two other people were standing outside a barn about fifty yards from the track. I figured that was the stable. To the right of the house was a huge round patio with a round swimming pool in the center of it. A woman in a bikini was sunbathing on the patio.

"Who does this guy think he is?" Nate said. "The Lord of the Rings?"

I parked at the bottom of the driveway, in front of a circular walk leading to the house. Needless to say, it was a big house. But it wasn't shaped like a circle. That would have been impractical.

Nate gazed up at the tower as we got out of the car. "Tony showed admirable restraint putting it down here. If it was up on the hill, you'd be able to see the damn thing all the way from New York."

"He's a circumspect guy," I said.

We resisted the temptation to cut across the perfectly manicured lawn and followed the walk instead. When I pressed the doorbell, the Holey Toledo jingle blared out of a speaker mounted above the door, next to another camera.

"Oh, I like that," Nate said, pushing the button. "Let's do it again."

Before the first jingle finished, a fat, freckle-faced kid in a Holey Toledo Club uniform opened the door. Either he was very quick or he had been watching us through a monitor. I figured the latter. I wondered whether working for Tony was a benefit of membership or a salaried position.

I told him who we were and said we were looking for the man of the house.

"He's not home." The kid had a bad lisp.

"When do you expect him?"

"I don't know. Maybe you should ask Mrs. Lunaviva."

That sounded like a fine idea. "And where is she?" I asked.

"Out by the pool. I'll take you there."

"Don't bother, we'll find it," Nate said. "Should we take a cab or walk?" he asked me.

"Oh, no, I have to take you," the kid said, bounding through the doorway faster than I would have thought possible. "Nobody's allowed on the grounds alone. It's the rules."

"Well, we wouldn't want to break any rules," Nate said.

We followed him down a path to the patio, where Longshot Sam's ex was lying on her stomach on a lounger. She was wearing the world's smallest bikini. Or at least half of it. The string to the top was untied to permit maximum tanning. She had a nice tan. She had a nice body.

Daphne Lunaviva leaned on her elbows and cradled her chin in her hands as she watched our approach through mirrored sunglasses. She was balancing a drink on the edge of the lounger and sipping through a straw. It was a neat trick. She held that pose while the kid told her who we were. He botched the names, but she got the general idea. Just to be sure, I showed her my ID. As she looked at it, she licked a few drops of her drink off her lips.

Daphne had long, thick blond hair that fell over her bare shoulders, but not long or thick enough to prevent our getting a full report on the progress of her tan in front. It was coming along quite nicely. I could see almost to her nipples without sighting a tan line. I had a feeling I wouldn't find one if I looked all day. But I wouldn't have minded trying.

"My husband will be home in a few minutes," she said in a bored voice.

"Do you want me to stay with you until he gets back, Mrs. Lunaviva?" the kid asked.

"No, that's okay, you can go, Jimmy. They look civilized."

Jimmy looked disappointed. I didn't blame him. As he turned away, Daphne said, "Before you do, you could give them a drink."

Jimmy walked to a table and poured screwdrivers from a glass pitcher. I thought he looked a little envious as he handed me my glass. Some guys have all the luck.

Daphne invited us to sit down, but we chose to remain standing and enjoy the view from the mezzanine. She didn't seem to mind. In fact, I had a feeling she enjoyed the attention.

"It was a terrible tragedy," she said when I told her why we were there. "I don't know if you know this or not, but Sam and I used to be married."

"Yeah, I do know that."

She let out a short laugh. "I was number four. For some reason, it didn't take. I guess we were both too independent. But of course, none of Sam's marriages ever take." She shook her head, and her hair danced on her shoulders. "We used to fight all the time. Boy, did we fight. But I'll tell you something: I still loved the guy. Sam was a good friend to me."

I nodded. I thought Daphne might be starting to cry, but it was hard to tell through her shades. Not only were they mirrored, but the lenses were bigger than the cups on her bikini top. It was hard to tell what she looked like.

"We're trying to find Danny Moreno," I said.

She let out another laugh. "Well, he sure ain't around here."

"We figured that. Do you have any idea where he might have gone?"

"Are you kidding? On the TV, they said there's a contract out on him. He's probably in Bora Bora by now." Daphne took off the shades for a moment to reveal blue eyes and a prom-queen face that was a good match for the body. I figured she was old enough for her tenth high school reunion. "I hope they find that creep," she said.

"How long did he work here?" Nate asked.

"Too long."

Just then, the world's biggest limousine swung through the gate at the top of the hill. "My husband will be here in ten minutes," Daphne said sarcastically. Apparently, we weren't the only ones amused by the size of Tony Lunaviva's driveway. "He can tell you all about Danny Boy. He's the one who hired him."

We watched as Daphne reached behind her back and fastened the clasp on her bathing-suit top. On a scale of ten, I would have given her a 9.9. She did it with one hand. She made another nice maneuver when she lifted herself up with her elbows and wiggled her breasts into their parking spaces. Even a Soviet judge would have had a tough time taking points off for that one.

"If I tell you guys something, can I trust you not to say anything to Tony about it?"

"Absolutely," Nate said. "Talking to us is like confessing your sins to a priest."

Daphne giggled. I figured she had plenty of sins to confess. "I'm *serious*. Tony will kill me if he finds out I told you this."

"We're serious, too," I said.

"Okay." Daphne shot a look toward the front of the house, where her husband was getting out of his limo. Jimmy was there to meet him, and he pointed toward the pool. "Last week I saw Sam out here real early one morning talking to Danny," she said hurriedly. "When I told Tony about it, he hit the roof."

"Do you know what they were talking about?" I asked.

"No." Daphne glanced down the walk. Her husband was still a hundred feet away, but she lowered her voice to a whisper. "I think Sam was paying Dino to give him tips on Tony's horses. You won't say anything to him about it, right?"

"Of course not."

"Who are you?" Tony Lunaviva demanded, quickening his pace as he reached the patio. "And what are you doing bothering my wife?"

"They're private detectives, darling," Daphne chirped from her perch on the lounger. "Michelle Natoli hired them to look into Sam's death."

"And what do they want from me?" Lunaviva strode right past us and leaned down to kiss his wife. He was thinner than he looked on TV but just as short. Even with a lift from the heels on his alligator shoes, he couldn't have cleared five-seven.

"We'd like to ask you a few questions," I said.

"I already talked to the police. I've answered enough questions."

"They want to know where Danny Moreno is," Daphne said in her bored voice.

"How the hell am I supposed to know?" Lunaviva went to the pitcher to pour himself a drink. He frowned as he came up with less than half a glass. I'm sure it didn't make him any happier that we were the ones who had tapped out his supply. "The kid's hiding out from the mob. They say there's a contract out on him."

"We thought you might have some idea where he went," I said, offering my ID.

He barely gave it a glance, choosing instead to glare at me. "Well, you thought wrong."

I glared back. "When's the last time you talked to Danny?"

"Yesterday morning." Lunaviva downed his drink. "For Chrissakes," he muttered. "You do a kid a favor and give him a job, and the next thing you know everybody's giving you the third degree. How the hell was I supposed to know the guy's a mobster?"

I refrained from telling him that it wouldn't have taken much imagination. "Did you check his background?"

"You kidding? I met the guy in a bar. He knew who I was, so he came up and started talking to me. He said he used to work in racing and gave me a sob story about being down on his luck, so I helped him out and gave him a job. No big deal. All I wanted him to do was water down horses and shovel shit. I'm supposed to do a background check? You guys are giving me a headache."

"Maybe it was something you ate for breakfast," Nate said.

As Lunaviva glared at him, I noticed that he had a perfectly round face. "Didn't he manage one of your donut shops?" I asked.

"He just liked to tell people he was the manager. It made him feel important. Besides, that's none of your business."

"We understand you collect Mustangs," I said.

"Yeah, that's right. What about it?"

"Danny Moreno drove away in a Mustang," Nate said.

"I collect them. That doesn't mean I own every Mustang in the state of New Jersey. Besides, I heard that one had out-of-state plates." He waved with a fat hand as if he were shooing away a cat. "Now why don't you guys just be on your way."

"After you're done answering our questions," Nate said.

"Hey, I know the law, buddy. I don't have to tell you a damn thing."

Lunaviva walked to the table and pressed a button on an electronic gizmo that was hooked up to the telephone. The phone had the world's longest cord. He might have been calling for backup, but I figured he just wanted more booze.

"Calm down, darling," Daphne said. "They're not accusing you of anything. They're just doing their job. Why don't you come over here and put some lotion on my back like a good boy."

That turned out to be a good idea, at least for the time being.

"You had a big winner in the ninth race yesterday," I said.

Lunaviva grinned, revealing the face that we knew and loved from TV. He seemed to take my comment as a compliment. Or maybe the backrub was doing the trick. "Yeah, we've been bringing that horse along real slow," he said. "It finally paid off."

"It's too bad you weren't at the track to see it. Of course, that was right when Sam Natoli got shot."

"What the hell are you inferring?"

"Implying," Nate corrected.

Tony's fat hand came to a halt on the middle of his wife's back. "Ooh, don't stop, honey," she said. "It feels good."

"You almost had a big winner on Friday, too," I said. "It's interesting how these horses of yours are suddenly coming in. You'd never expect it from looking at their past performances."

"Okay, that's it. I've talked to you jerks long enough. Time to go." Lunaviva stood up and looked toward the house. Jimmy was on his way with a tray. A heavyset dark-haired guy was with him.

"But Longshot Sam expected it," I said, ignoring his invitation to leave. "He made Sugar Donut his Slam of the Day on Friday. Is that what the two of you were arguing about at the Hofbrau restaurant a couple of days ago?"

That one made even Daphne sit up and take notice. It seemed like she hadn't been listening, but I had a feeling she was tuned in loud and clear. Her reaction would have been more interesting if I had mentioned that Sam's third wife, Candy Miller, had been there, too.

"What!" Lunaviva exploded. "Who says I was?"

"This is the part where you're supposed to remind him that you're the one asking the questions," Nate said to me.

Daphne snickered slightly, but the donut king wasn't amused. "Listen, buddy, that's slander," he said, pointing his finger at me. "You better watch what you say, or I'll sue you for defamation of character."

"To do that, I think you need to have a reputation to damage," Nate said. "Between you and me, I don't think a guy who puts his head through a jelly donut on TV is going to be able to meet the minimum criteria."

"Fuck you, asshole."

"It's a cream donut," Daphne added.

Jimmy arrived on the patio with a big guy in an ill-fitting suit. Unless there was a senior chapter, he was too old for the Holey Toledo Club.

"What took you so long?" Lunaviva barked.

"Ed was on the can," Jimmy said.

Ed failed to confirm or deny the allegation. He seemed to be the silent type. But I could tell by the bulge under his jacket that he was prepared to make a lot of noise.

"I guess maybe it is time to go," I said to Nate.

20

"Tony's not as friendly in person as he is on TV," Nate said as we drove away. "But I did like his wife. How do you figure a guy like that gets a girl like that?"

"Maybe she views him as a father figure."

"Thank you, Dr. Freud. I think maybe she likes viewing the figures in his bank account."

"I have a feeling old Tony might be having some trouble keeping the young lady satisfied," I said. "From what Al told me about her marriage to Sam, Daphne has an insatiable appetite."

"Is that so? Well, I sure wouldn't throw her out of bed for eating donuts."

"I was talking about her sexual appetite."

"Well, I wouldn't throw her out of bed for eating long johns, either."

Nate said talking about sex made him hungry, so we stopped at a charbroil joint called the Lantern on Route 46. While Nate was finishing off his second order of onion rings, I went to the phone and called Tom McReynolds. I wanted to let him know I was working for Michelle Natoli. More than that, I wanted to find out if he had learned anything.

As I suspected, McReynolds hadn't turned up any trace of Dino LaRussa or the car he had driven away in. But he had managed to find something.

"You should've stayed around," he said. "We located the shell from the rifle."

I didn't bother to remind him that he was the one who had told me to leave. "Where was it?"

"Right next to the grandstand, just like the track announcer said. There's a doorway in the corner where the building juts in."

"Did you find any footprints?"

"Oh yeah, lots. Too many, in fact. It was all stamped down. You could see they did it intentionally. I'll tell you one thing, though: The guy had big feet. So much for your theory that a woman did the shooting."

"Unless she was wearing men's shoes," I said.

"Ha! Men's shoes. That's pretty funny. I hadn't thought of that." I had a feeling he didn't think much of it.

"There could have been somebody in the backseat of the car," I said.

"Yeah, that's what I'm figuring too. By the way, we talked to Tony Lunaviva this morning. I interviewed him myself. He's a pretty nice guy. And funny, too. I love those TV ads of his." McReynolds must have taken my silence as a sign of ignorance, because he started to tell me about the Holey Toledo commercials.

"I've seen them," I said, cutting him off in mid-sentence. He probably thought I didn't have any sense of humor. "Did you ask him about his car collection?"

"Yes, I did. As a matter of fact, he even let me have a look at them. Not just Mustangs. Fairlanes, too. The car we're looking for wasn't there."

Surprise, surprise. "So I take it you don't think Lunaviva had anything to do with it."

"Off the record?"

I told him it was. McReynolds wasn't much smarter than most of the small-town cops I had dealt with, but he was a lot nicer.

"I doubt it. All he did was hire the guy. You can't blame him for that."

And you couldn't blame Nixon for Watergate. I asked him to let me know if he turned up anything, then assured him I'd do the same.

"You know, Renzler, it's just like high school again," McReynolds said. "Only now we're on the same team." Now there was an original thought.

"Well, you're still the quarterback, Tom," I replied. I think that made his day.

The eighth race had just ended when we got back to Garden State Downs. Before going in, we checked out the doorway where McReynolds said the shot had been fired from. It was just around the corner from the main entrance, on the side of the grandstand that faced the track and overlooked the infield. It was only a few steps in from the end of the building near the parking lot, a little nook hidden from the view of the lot and the apron. There was a rust-colored steel door leading inside. I tried the handle, but it wouldn't budge.

I took a few steps back to the fence and looked up to the announcer's booth, where Dave Gwynn was sitting in a swivel chair. He looked down and saw me, then got up, leaned out the window at the corner of the booth, and pointed down. "That's where the police think the shooting came from," he called.

"Where does the door lead to?" I said. With the large crowd on hand, I had to yell to be heard.

"Into the office area. Do you want me to come down and open it up so you can have a look inside?"

I could tell that Gwynn was pressed for time. I told him it wouldn't be necessary.

"He seems like a helpful sort," Nate said as we went around the corner and into the grandstand through the main entrance.

"So far he has been," I said. "I think he's trying to compensate for his loony wife. He gave me an earful this morning about their son dying in Nam. He was in a POW camp with Matt Caldwell, our buddy from security. Caldwell managed to escape."

"From what you've told me about Caldwell, I get the feeling he's still missing in action."

"He's missing something, that's for sure."

My nephew seemed to be missing when we got to the clubhouse. "I see him," Nate said after we wandered through the crowd for a few minutes. "He's over there chewing the fat with Timmy the Greek."

"That's Toteboard Tommy," I said.

"Forgive me. I don't know how in the world I could get these guys confused."

Tommy was giving Herbie a free introductory lesson on using his toteboard computer. I hoped it wasn't too late to stop the sale. They were talking so intently that they didn't notice us approach.

"If I understand you correctly," Herbie said, furiously scribbling numbers on a sheet of paper, "what you're saying is: If x sub one over x sub two (where x sub one is the amount of money bet on horse A to win and x sub two is the total amount of money in the win pool) *divided by* y sub one over y sub two (where y sub one is the amount of money bet on horse A to show and y sub two is the total amount of money in the show pool) is greater than one, an overlay exists and the percentage of the overlay is the amount of the fraction that exceeds one."

"Exactly! Exactly!"

"Would you mind repeating that, young man?" I said, afraid after I did that Herbie might take me literally.

He shrugged. "It's a simple algebraic proportion, Uncle Mark."

I knew the kid was being humble, not dismissive, but I felt like smacking him in the chops just the same.

"What I don't understand is"—Herbie held Tommy's pride and joy aloft—"what do you need *this* thing for?"

Tommy's chin dropped about a foot. He paused, then said hopefully, "To figure in the tax takeout, of course."

"The state of New Jersey takes fifteen percent off the top," I explained. I had a feeling taxes were one of life's many horrors that Herbie hadn't been exposed to yet.

He shrugged again. "Then all you have to do is multiply by point-eight-five. I don't see why you need this thing."

Nate pulled me aside and whispered, "It looks like Herbie isn't the nerd Tommy hoped he'd be."

"No. He's an even bigger one."

"I hope I didn't hurt his feelings," Herbie said as we watched Toteboard Tommy stalk away.

"Don't worry, he'll get over it," I said.

I suggested we go find Al so Herbie could turn in his bet.

"I have kind of a confession to make, Uncle Mark."

"What's that?"

Herbie stared at his feet. "I haven't been betting on all the horses Al says to."

I tried not to sound alarmed. "Which horses *have* you been betting on?"

"Well, I'm kind of using my own system now."

"Uh, I think I'll go get a beer," Nate said.

"Better get one for me, too."

"But it's working!" Herbie said in response to my skeptical look. "You just bet fifty dollars on number two. We won three out of the last four races."

"And how did you come to decide on number two?"

"That's my birthday—the second of August. And Mom's birthday is on the second, too."

That sounded like a foolproof system. "Do me a favor, Herb," I said as Nate returned with the beers. "Let's stick with Al's picks, okay?"

Herbie nodded, but he didn't look convinced. Nate wrapped his arm around the kid's shoulders. "Some things you've just got to accept on faith, Herb," he explained.

We found Al alone outside the Winners Circle. "It's been a rough day," he said, shaking his head.

"Yeah, Herbie told us."

"Not just at the track," he said. "Michelle was here looking for you. The cops came to see her. It sounds like they were giving her a hard time."

"What do you mean?"

"They told her she fit the description of the woman who drove away in the car yesterday. Can you believe those pricks?"

"Was it McReynolds?"

"Who's that?"

"He's the chief of police."

"I don't know. She didn't tell me the name. She just asked if you'd stop by the house later on."

In the background, I heard Dave Gwynn's voice. "Four minutes to post."

"Okay, let's go, Herb," Al said. "We're betting on number five. Fifty bucks again." He winked at Nate and me. "Unless of course you see something better."

"I kind of like the number-two horse," Herbie said without hesitation.

Al seemed a little taken aback. That's what he got for asking. He glanced at the program, then shook his head slowly. "I don't think so, kid."

Nate and I went to the chalkboard and checked the contest standings while Herbie and Al turned in their bets. Timmy the Greek had taken over first place from Al, who still held a small lead over Clocker Callaway for second. I was surprised to see that Serendipity was in fourth, followed by Toteboard Tommy, Dr. Dave, Sulky Sol, and Lucky Lou. I was even more surprised to learn that Dark Penzler and Nate Moore were still right behind Sheriff Maszursky in the amateur standings.

While we were watching the ninth race, I asked Herbie how he had been able to play two entries in the contest.

"Easy," he said. "I just slipped a sawbuck to one of the Holey Toledos."

It was comforting to know that the kids Tony Lunaviva was grooming to be tomorrow's leaders already had a grasp of how the world worked. To say nothing of the progress my nephew was making. A few more days at the track, and I figured he'd be ready to bag the whole priesthood thing.

Down on the track, our horse was ahead by three lengths at the top of the stretch. But as the horses charged for home, old number five ran out of gas. Three horses were fighting for the lead at the wire, and I couldn't see which one pulled it out.

Somewhere inside me, I knew there was never any doubt.

"Number two," Dave Gwynn said. "In front."

Herbie gave me a look, but didn't say anything.

21

Nate opted for Howard Johnson's over the couch at my sister's, but once he checked in and got a look at his spacious room he decided to watch the evening news back at the house. "Might as well drink your brother-in-law's booze," he said.

Herbie shook his head. "Dad locked the liquor cabinet. He said he didn't want Uncle Mark sitting around getting plastered."

"But he didn't say anything about Uncle Nate, did he?"

"Only because he didn't know you were coming," I said.

"It's okay," Herbie said. "I know where he put the key."

Nate made himself right at home, three feet from the TV set.

"Doesn't he know it's bad for your eyes to sit that close?" Herbie whispered.

"He thinks they can hear him better when he talks back."

"Huh?"

Just then, Dick Nixon's press secretary, Ron Ziegler, came on with some reassuring words for the American public. "Go find a real job, you sorry sack of shit," Nate yelled. "Oh, sorry for the vulgarity, Herb," he added at normal volume.

"Don't worry about it," I said. "His mother swears all the time."

"Yeah, but not like *that*." Herbie got up off the couch. "I'm going up to my room to say the rosary."

"Be sure to put in a good word for me, Herb."

"I'll try, Uncle Nate. But I'm not sure it will do any good."

While they were working on their hobbies, I called Michelle

Natoli to find out when I could stop by. She wanted all of us to come for dinner. I told her that sounded like a lot of trouble.

"Don't be silly," she said. "I made lasagna. It helped keep my mind off things."

Either Michelle had been making a lot of lasagna lately, or she hadn't gotten around to it yesterday. I didn't bother to ask. Instead, I asked about her visit from the police.

"This guy really gave me the creeps," she said. "I thought he wanted my help, but then it was like *I* was on trial. He wanted to know where I was yesterday and everything."

"Was his name McReynolds?" I asked.

"No. Sergeant Quinn. He was really ugly. He said he was a friend of Matt Caldwell's."

· "Then he's probably dumb, too. I wouldn't worry about it."

"No, I'm not worried. I'm just mad. I called Bernie, and he said if they ask any more questions, he wants to be there."

"That's probably a good idea," I said. I didn't add that it might be a good idea to find a better lawyer than Bernie.

We all watched the local news before leaving for Michelle's house. The report on the killing of Longshot Sam didn't have anything new, but it did provide an excuse to roll the film one more time.

"You know, there was something odd about that report," Nate said as we got into the car. "I don't think I heard a gunshot."

Now that he mentioned it, I wasn't sure I'd heard one either.

"They probably recorded it through an internal microphone," Herbie said. "You get better sound reproduction that way."

"There's your answer," Nate said. "All you've got to do is ask Mr. Science here."

Maybe so. But this time I had a feeling my nephew might be wrong about something for a change. For that reason alone, it was worth looking into.

When Michelle Natoli answered the door, she proved without trying that black could be a sexy color. "Oh my God!" she gasped, when she saw my nephew's black eye.

Herbie blushed as she planted a kiss on his cheek. If that didn't make the pain go away, nothing would.

"It's almost worth going out and getting socked in the puss for," Nate whispered to me.

"I'm sorry about what happened to Mr. Natoli," Herbie said. "I said a rosary for him tonight."

"Thank you, Herb. That's very sweet of you." Michelle looked like she was about to burst into tears, but she held her poise while I introduced her to Nate.

We moved into the living room, where Al was sitting in Sam's lounger and poring over a stack of racing programs. "You were right about Tony Lunaviva," he said to me. "He was holding back his horses to build up the odds, then bringing in longshots out of nowhere. Look at *this*."

Al thrust a sheet of paper at me that had a list of dates, race numbers, horses' names, and payoffs he had recorded. "And Sam was on to it," he said, pulling a pile of LONGSHOT SLAMS out of a battered ring binder. "He made notes on all his programs. He knew what Lunaviva was doing, but it took him a while to figure out when his horses were going and when they were just out for a Sunday drive. But he finally did, and then he started picking them on his sheet."

"And each time he did, he drove down the odds," I said, more for Herbie's and Nate's benefit than Al's.

"Exactly." Al pointed to one of the columns on the list he had compiled. "Look at these measly payoffs. That's when Sam started picking them on his sheet." He picked up another program. "And a week before that, he made a notation."

I leaned in to read the scrawl in the margin. Longshot Sam had apparently left the Palmer Method behind him when he had left the Catholic Church.

"Michelle had to decipher it for me," Al said. "It says: 'Talked to Gwynn.' Interesting, huh?"

"Very." I was interested to know what Gwynn had to say.

"This proves Lunaviva had Sam killed," Al said.

"Not necessarily. But it sure makes it look that way."

I had seen enough of the evidence, but Al kept pulling out more. Fortunately Michelle announced that dinner was ready.

"Boy, does it ever smell good," Herbie said.

It probably tasted good, too, but I didn't get a chance to find out. Nate did. He took the liberty of digging in before Herbie started to say grace. The telephone rang before he finished the part that I knew.

I could tell from the startled expression on Michelle's face that something was wrong the instant she answered the phone. She nodded for a moment, then said in a shaky voice, "Yes, I understand. Yes, I know where it is. Half an hour."

Michelle covered the mouthpiece with her hand. "It's Danny Moreno," she whispered. "He's at a motel down on Route 46. He wants a thousand dollars to tell who killed Sam."

Al pointed me to the extension in the living room. I got on in time to hear Moreno say, "I'd ask for more, Mrs. Natoli, but I know it'd be kinda hard for you to get it on such short notice."

"You've always been such a considerate guy, Dino," I said.

"Who the fuck is this?"

"It's your buddy Renzler."

"Holy Christ! Just the asshole I wanted to talk to."

"Mutual, I'm sure, scumbag."

"I don't got much time, Renzler, so what do you say we cut with the bullshit."

"I'll say you're short on time. I figure your time's just about up."

"Fuck you, too. Just bring the money and then we'll talk."

"Not so fast. I've got a couple of questions first."

"*After* I get the money."

"No, I think now."

"I don't care about the money!" Michelle said. I could see her in the dining room. Al was standing beside her. I motioned to him to calm her down. Al put his hand on her shoulder and whispered something in her ear. She nodded and hung up.

"Good thinkin', Mrs. Natoli," Dino said. "You're a lot smarter than the idiot you got workin' for you."

"You've got bad timing, Dino," I said. "The lady hung up before she could hear your compliment. But I'll be glad to pass it along."

"Aw shit."

"That's right. You're negotiating with me now. And the way I see it, you're in no position to bargain. I figure you got double-crossed and didn't get paid for your work. Now you need the dough to get out of town. You need the dough a whole lot more than I need your info."

"I could hang up the fuckin' phone right now."

"And I could call the cops. Or"—I paused for dramatic effect—"I could call Tony Lunaviva."

"Don't you dare, asshole."

I chuckled. "By the way, it was nice of you to let us know where you are. You couldn't shake down a Christmas tree."

"Yeah, who says I'm there? Maybe I'm somewhere else."

"Maybe you're too dumb to live."

"Fuck you." Dino let out a long sigh. I figured he'd had a long day.

"You're just a small-timer in this—as always. You'll get your money, Dino. But first, you have to give me something, so I know I'm not wasting my time. And it better be something good."

Dino sighed again. "I should know better than to trust an asshole like you."

"You should know better about a lot of things."

"Okay. I'll give you something," he said at last. "One of Sam's wives is involved. How's that?"

"Sam had a lot of wives. I think you can do better."

"Goddammit! If you hadn't showed up at the track, Renzler, everything would have worked out fine and I wouldn't be in this fuckin' mess in the first place."

"Well, I'm glad I could make your life a little harder. Now try to make mine a little easier. No info, no dough."

"Okay, okay. What would you say if I told you Sam wasn't shot from the parking lot?"

"You mean he was shot from inside the track?" That was an intriguing possibility. It was also possible Dino was lying through his crooked teeth.

"I told you enough already. Just bring the money, and I'll tell you everything. And don't try pullin' any funny stuff."

Cliché la vie. "All right, Dino, I'm on my way."

"I don't think I have a thousand dollars in the house," Michelle said worriedly when I came back into the dining room.

"Forget the money," I said. "I wasn't planning on bringing any. You just tell us how to get there."

"But how are you going to get him to talk if you don't have the money?"

"Don't worry," Nate said, wiping tomato sauce from his mouth onto his shirt sleeve. "We'll get him to talk."

"Can I go with you, Uncle Mark?" That sounded like a very bad idea.

"Of course you can, Herb," I said. "As long as you don't tell your mother."

22

We were supposed to meet Dino LaRussa in room 6 of the Hi-Way Motel in Fairfield, a desolate stretch of prime swampland along Route 46 between Wayne and Parsippany that was populated with squat office buildings, flat-roofed furniture warehouses, and sprawling auto junkyards. To avoid the inevitable crush of shoppers at the Willowbrook Mall, Michelle had told us to take a shortcut leading from scenic Mountain View across Two Bridges, where the Passaic and Pompton rivers conspire to flood out local residents every spring.

"Some shortcut," Nate muttered as we came to an orange sign that said DETOUR: BRIDGE CLOSED. "From now on, let's stick to roads that somebody has taken the trouble to name."

Luckily, Herbie knew an alternate route that ran along the river past a mud-encrusted trailer park and a ramshackle row of bungalows on stilts. But we still lost some time. It was after eight o'clock when we got to the Hi-Way Motel.

"Hey, we're in luck," Nate said. "I think there might still be some rooms available." I didn't know if he was referring to the deserted gravel parking lot or the dimly lit neon sign with both A's burned out of VACANCY.

The Hi-Way was one of those dingy single-story joints with about a dozen rooms—more than enough to serve a clientele that probably ranged from motorists in distress to lowlifes on nooners. The only thing it needed more than some customers was a few coats of paint. Unless you wanted to include the weeds growing up out of the parking lot, the only sign of life in the place was the light of a TV coming from behind a door marked OFFICE.

We didn't bother to stop there before going to Dino's room. Herbie was disappointed when I told him to stay in the car and stay down, but he didn't put up any protest. I had a feeling he was a little scared.

"No car," Nate said, as we threaded our way through the weeds. "Do you think Dino took off?"

I shook my head. "He probably parked it in back."

There was no answer when I knocked on the door to room 6. I pounded one more time, then tried the knob. The door was open, so we stepped inside. I went first, with my gun ready, in the unlikely event that Dino had any bright ideas. He didn't.

"Great air freshener they use around here," Nate said. He hit the light switch, and a bare bulb went on overhead.

"Kind of makes you appreciate the homey quality of HoJo's, doesn't it?"

He nodded. "Looks like nobody's home. Maybe Dino isn't here yet."

That was a possibility, but I thought it more likely that he was waiting in another room and planning on taking us by surprise. I guess you could say I was half right.

Dino was waiting for us all right, but he was in the bathroom, or at least the squalid little cubicle that passed for a bathroom in room 6. And he did manage to surprise us, but not in a way he would have planned.

"Well, well, *arrivederci*, sleazebag," Nate said when I pushed open the door. I couldn't have put it any better myself.

Somebody had shot the little weasel right through the center of his thick head. Not a spot where you would have thought he was vulnerable, but even guys like Dino need what few brains they have to survive. It was only a matter of time before it happened, and I could tell by the warmth of his hand that it was only a matter of minutes since he had been killed.

"I wonder how many other people knew Dino was here," Nate said.

"I wouldn't think too many."

"Does that trouble you a little?"

"It troubles me a lot."

"Yeah, me too."

Herbie joined us as we went to the office. I rapped on the door five times before I was able to startle a frail old guy in a white T-shirt and checkered shorts away from a black-and-white TV.

"Sorry, I thought it was open," he yelled as he opened the door. As we stepped inside, "Adam 12" committed assault and battery on my eardrums. "What can I do you for?"

"Did you see anybody come in or out of here in the last few minutes?" I asked.

"Huh?" He smiled as he fiddled with a hearing aid that covered his right ear. "Sorry, I'm a little hard of hearing."

More than a little, judging by the volume of the TV set. I repeated the question at about twenty decibels. That did the trick, but I figured it wouldn't do any good. I didn't think this guy would notice if a bomb went off in the parking lot. I was wrong. It happens sometimes.

He scratched at the few white hairs on his head. "They just left a couple of minutes ago."

"Who did?"

"A red-haired lady in a white Mustang. Out-of-state plates. She must've been visiting the fella in room six."

"You said 'they.' Was anybody with her?"

He shook his head. "No, I just call people they. I didn't mean anything by it, mister." He looked a little frightened. I didn't blame him. He was an easy target for a robbery. The only thing saving him was the absence of anything worth stealing.

He forced a nervous chuckle as he took a step back and leaned on a counter. I hesitate to call it a registration desk.

"Funny thing, you know. That fella usually got a blonde with him when he comes here. First time I ever seen him with a redhead."

"How many times has he been here before?"

"Oh, I don't know. Two, three times maybe. I ain't seen him for a while until he showed up this evening. Just checked in a little while ago. A real smart aleck. Last time he was here, he tried to duck out on me without paying. And then he left the room a god-awful mess."

"Where did he park his car?" Nate asked.

The old guy hooked his thumb in the air over his shoulder. "In the back."

"Did that strike you as odd?"

"Mister, nothing strikes me as odd around this place."

"Well, how about this one," I said. "You've got a dead body in room six."

"Holy mackerel! Are you shittin' me?"

I phoned the Pequannock police station and told the guy on the desk to call Tom McReynolds at home. While waiting for him to arrive, we went back to Dino's room to have a look around. I let Herbie come in, but I made him stay out of the bathroom. One dead body was plenty for the kid to see.

"Boy, it sure smells funny in here," Herbie said.

"It's not the place to come for fresh air," Nate replied.

"You know what it smells like, Uncle Mark? It smells kind of like Mrs. Natoli."

I shot a glance at Nate as we both sniffed the dank air.

"I think he's right," Nate said.

"What does that mean?" Herbie asked.

"Probably just a coincidence," I replied. I hoped it was a coincidence.

Nate gave me a knowing look but didn't say anything. "What's that?" he asked as I bent down and plucked a shiny red pin out of the snotty shag carpeting.

"I think it's an earring."

Herbie leaned in close to have a look. "No, it's not. It's a Holey Toledo pin. Like those guys at the racetrack wear. See? It's shaped like two donuts."

In fact, it was shaped like the Holey Toledo logo. I didn't chide my nephew for failing to recognize a halo. Leave that to the headmaster at his school. He'd already been as helpful as an angel in lifting a weight off my mind. I didn't think it was too likely that Michelle was a member of the Holey Toledo Club.

The Fairfield cops got there first, so there was a minor jurisdictional dispute when McReynolds arrived ten minutes later. He settled it with the poise of a veteran quarterback. He went easy on the motel clerk, who seemed more nervous when he repeated his story. His anxiety might have been due to being questioned by a cop, but I had a feeling he was holding something back. When McReynolds was done with the old guy, he tore into me like a middle linebacker on amphetamines.

"Why the hell didn't you call me?" he demanded.

"I did call you."

"I mean before you got here."

"There wasn't enough time. I planned to call you as soon as we arrived."

"You took the law into your own hands," he shouted. "And look where it got us—another dead body."

I didn't bother telling him I viewed Dino LaRussa's loss as the world's gain. My only concern was that he had passed on without passing along the info I wanted. I just stood there and took my lumps like a good citizen should.

"Were you able to get anything out of him over the phone?" McReynolds asked.

"He told me Longshot Sam wasn't shot from the parking lot."

"He's full of crap. Anything else?"

"Yeah. He was scared of Tony Lunaviva."

"I already talked to Mr. Lunaviva."

"If I were you, I'd talk to him again."

"Well, you're not me. So don't you go out there badgering him anymore."

I wondered how he knew we had talked to Lunaviva, but didn't bother to ask. Nor did I pass along Dino's tip that one of Sam's wives had been involved in his murder. I was afraid he'd go right for Michelle. I didn't even want to consider the possibility that she killed Sam, but I had seen enough over the years to know you can't trust anybody. But I wasn't about to share my doubts with the cops.

"What do you make of the pin?" Nate asked.

McReynolds shrugged. "A lot of people wear those things. They give them out to anybody that buys a dozen donuts. It could've been Moreno's, but it probably fell off the broad that killed him. One thing seems sure: The lady that killed him was the same one you saw drive away in that car yesterday afternoon."

"Did you get a line on that car yet?" I asked.

He shook his head. "So far, the Nebraska state police haven't turned anything up."

"And they won't," Nate said.

"Why not?"

"Because the car was registered in Missouri," I said.

McReynolds' face turned a curious shade of red. "Okay, you

three can get out of here," he snapped. "But next time you hear something, I want to know about it. And not tomorrow or next week. I mean right away. Is that clear?"

Yessir, and loud too.

"Boy, he sure was mad," Herbie said when we got outside.

"Probably because he missed the end of 'Adam 12,'" I said.

"And 'Hawaii Five-O' is already half over," Nate added.

Before leaving we took a look behind the motel.

"Where did his car go?" Herbie asked.

Good question. I went into the office and tried it out on the clerk.

"Holy mackerel! You mean to tell me it ain't there?"

I told him that was exactly what I meant. "What kind of car was it?" I asked.

He frowned and scratched his chin. "To be honest with you, mister, I didn't see it."

"What kind of car did he usually drive?" Nate asked.

"I don't know. I'm not sure I ever noticed."

"But you did manage to notice that the Mustang had out-of-state plates," I said. "How do you explain that?"

His brow furrowed as he pursed his lips and shook his head back and forth. "I don't know. I guess I just did. Listen, mister, I don't want any trouble."

And I wasn't about to give him any. Especially when there were cops on the premises.

"What do you think happened to the car?" Herbie asked as we walked to ours.

"Most likely, it was driven away by the person who helped the lady kill Dino," Nate replied.

"Aren't you going to tell the police chief about it, Uncle Mark?"

I shook my head. "Don't worry, Herb. He'll find out soon enough."

23

The lights were out when we got back to the Natoli house shortly before ten o'clock.

"That's odd," Nate said as we pulled into the driveway. "I thought they'd be waiting for us."

"So did I," Herbie said.

And Uncle made three. I'd been hoping to get a helping of that lasagna.

"Another coincidence?" Nate asked me as Herbie ran ahead of us to the door.

This time I wasn't so sure. "Maybe they got tired and went to bed."

As usual, Herbie came up with the answer. "They left a note," he said, waving a piece of paper from the steps. "They had to go to the airport and pick up Mrs. Natoli's sister. She's coming in from Kansas City." Herbie bounded down the walk carrying a small brown bag. "She left some chocolate-chip cookies for us."

"Well, isn't she a sweetheart." I looked at Nate.

"I guess there's an explanation for everything," he said.

"And a good one at that. I wonder if Michelle's sister is married."

"What difference does that make? I just wonder if she's as good-looking."

We got the answers to both our questions the next morning. Nate and I agreed that Melanie Wyatt was only half as beautiful as her older sister. That still made her a knockout—at least in my book. Her marital status was single, but there was a large asterisk next to it in the form of a small nerd standing next to her. His name was Cove, which was short for Covington. Melanie introduced him as her "boyfriend," but Cove made it clear that he preferred "fiancé."

While they bickered over the point, I turned to Nate. "He reminds me of Steven Weed," I said, a reference to Patty Hearst's jilted fiancé.

"Yeah, only not as interesting," he replied.

I thought he was being a little quick to condemn, but Cove quickly proved worthy of scorn. When I asked what time they got in, he provided a full report on their itinerary, complete with flight number, scheduled versus actual departure and arrival times, and such scintillating details as when they had left their house in "KC," which lot they had parked in, and the distance from the check-in terminal to the gate. The only thing he didn't tell us, Nate later pointed out, was what they had eaten on the plane. Cove said it had been an "exhausting" trip, but it couldn't have been as exhausting as listening to him talk about it.

"We were scheduled to get in at nine-oh-eight, but we didn't touch down until nine-seventeen," he said. "By the time we got to the gate, it was nine twenty-three. And then, wouldn't you know it, we had to wait another fifteen minutes before her sister got there to pick us up."

"Oh, don't be such a whiner," Melanie said.

"I'm not whining. I just think we would've been better off renting a car like I said we should've done in the first place."

Melanie ignored him. "I'm just sorry we have to meet under these circumstances," she said to us.

"So are we." Nate's reference was to the hovering presence of Cove, hers to the ceremony that was about to begin.

I had seen some strange pre-race activities at the track over the years, but nothing to match the spectacle at Garden State Downs that day. About two hundred people were huddled together on the muddy track apron, clothes soggy from high humidity and light drizzle. All the contestants were there, along with an assortment of Sam's friends, GSD personnel, racetrack regulars, and the usual array of local political leaders.

A few cops were also on hand, and we wandered over to where Tom McReynolds was talking with Sheriff Maszursky.

"Somebody else must've been there last night," McReynolds said to me. "Danny Moreno's car was gone."

I pretended to be surprised. "Is that so?"

"Yeah. And another thing—we found the white Mustang."

I didn't have to feign surprise about that one. "Where?"

"A couple miles down Route 46 from the Hi-Way Motel. In the parking lot of a Holey Toledo in Totowa. Somebody torched it."

"Were there any witnesses?"

He shook his head. "The place was closed."

"Closed?" Nate said. "I thought they barely even dozed."

Sheriff Maszursky let out a husky laugh. "Not at this one. They shut the place down over a month ago."

"Board of Health violations?" Nate asked.

The sheriff shook his head. "Lack of customers."

That was another surprise. I had the impression Tony Lunaviva's donut business was thriving. "So you don't know what time it happened," I said to McReynolds.

"Yeah, we do. A little after eight. Somebody spotted it from the highway and called the fire department."

"Have you talked to Lunaviva?" I nodded toward the donut king, who was standing with his wife about fifty feet away.

"Don't worry. I'll talk to him. But this isn't the time or place. And I don't need you pushing me."

Maszursky shot me a knowing look. "I'd say he's definitely worth talking to, Tom. There's a lot of funny business going on with his horses."

"Oh, you noticed that," I said.

"Noticed it! How could you miss it? If only I could figure out when he was doing it. Then I'd be able to retire."

"The way you're going in that contest, you might be able to retire anyway," Nate said.

A grin spread over the sheriff's face. "It ain't over till it's over," he said, quoting the philosopher Yogi Berra.

The crowd quieted down as another philosopher of sorts spoke from a platform that had been set up along the rail. Michelle Natoli stood at his side. We moved over next to Al Phillips.

"I'm Bernie Rich, Sam Natoli's personal attorney and lifelong friend," he began. "Now I'm going to make this brief, because it's raining and all, and besides, that's the way Sam wanted it—short and sweet. If he told me once, he must've told me a thousand times. He said, 'Bernie, when I go, I want you to make it short and sweet.' And that, friends, is exactly what I plan to do today. Because that's the way Sam wanted it."

I had a feeling we were in for a long one.

"Now a lot of you here today knew Sam well, but probably none of you knew him as well as I did. I knew Sam Natoli since elementary school down in Nutley, which is where I still live. When we were kids, Sam and I used to do everything together—and I do mean *everything*. Sam used to say the reason I became a lawyer was because we got to know the law so well from getting in so much trouble together as kids. And, of course, being *his* lawyer, I got to become intimately familiar with all the details of Sam's personal affairs. Let me tell you—some of them were pretty darn juicy."

Bernie let out a chuckle. A few people joined in, but not many. "I mean, when you handle four divorces for a guy, you really get to know what makes him tick."

"Who the hell is this guy?" Lou Larson muttered to my left.

"He's the kind of guy that gives Jews a bad name," Sol Epstein said.

"Now I know this is a sad occasion for all of us," Bernie continued. "When you lose a friend like Sam, you can't help but be sad, especially under the circumstances. I mean, it's not every day your best friend gets shot, right? But Sam told me he didn't want people dwelling on the negative side of things when he died. So that's exactly what we're going to do today, because that's how Sam wanted it."

"I think he covered that part already," Nate whispered.

"Bernie has a tendency to repeat himself a little."

"A lot," Al corrected. "For Chrissakes, get on with it."

"Now it was Sam's wish that we do things exactly the way he wanted, so I'd like for all the ladies here who were married to him at one time or another to come down here along the rail," Bernie said.

I watched as a petite young redhead stepped gingerly down the infield under the direction of Biff Bonnardo. "Who's that?" I asked Al.

"Candy. She was number three."

She was number one in the race to the rail. Daphne Lunaviva came in a close second, and a pair of fading blond bombshells were involved in a photo finish for show.

"That's Ashley on the left and Beverly on the right," Al said.

"Unbelievable," Nate whispered.

Indeed it was. Next to me, I could sense Herbie's faith being put to the test.

Longshot Sam's ex-wives all wore black dresses. If they had been competing for prizes, Daphne, with a neckline that plunged almost to her navel, would have won the award for slinkiest, but Candy gave her a run for her money with the shortest. Ashley, with the biggest chest of the four, took the title for tightest, but Beverly cleaned up with most jewelry honors.

It soon became clear to everyone that they *were* giving away prizes.

"Now I will read the last will and testament exactly as Sam wrote it," Bernie said. A hush fell over the crowd as he started to read.

"It is my sincere wish that my house, my possessions, and half my cash assets be left to my current wife at the time of my death, whoever that happens to be. The other half is to be divided equally among my previous wives and my dearest friend, Al Phillips."

Bernie paused for a moment, then said, "And I think you'll all be glad to know that Sam's liquid assets are worth approximately one-point-six million dollars."

The crowd let out a collective gasp, and Sam's ex-wives began blubbering in unison. Next to us, Al shook his head. "Damn, I didn't know he was worth that much."

"Ah, come on," Nate said. "You must've had an inkling."

Al glared at him. "What's that supposed to mean?"

"Take it easy, Al," I said. "He's just kidding."

"You've got some weird friends, Renzler," Al said.

"I'll say," Nate replied as Al stalked away.

Sam Natoli's ex-wives were making a good show of how upset they were, but their sobs were drowned out by the wailing of Serendipity McCall about twenty-five feet to our left.

"What's eating Red?" Lucky Lou said.

"She's probably upset she got left out of the will," Sulky Sol replied. Whatever it was, Timmy the Greek lumbered over and tried to comfort her by putting his arm around her shoulders.

"Oh, get out of here, you faggot," Serendipity sobbed. It was no laughing matter to her, but she provided a few chuckles for Toteboard Tommy and Dr. Dave.

"Please be quiet, there's a little more," Bernie said. He waited a moment for the murmurs to die out before continuing.

"So long, my friends, it's been good to know you. My only regret is that I won't be around to spend the loot with you. But as the saying goes"—Bernie's voice began to crack—"them's the breaks."

Michelle looked dazed as Bernie turned and handed her a small urn. "And now, in keeping with Sam's wishes, his ashes will be scattered on the track by his last wife, Michelle," Bernie said with his customary tact.

If Longshot Sam had been hoping for wide distribution, he would have been sorely disappointed. Michelle lifted the urn over her shoulder, turned her face away and emptied the contents in one spot. Her husband may not have believed in formal funerals, but he had made certain that his was a goddamn circus. If I had been Michelle, that would have been reason enough to kill the guy.

"Good-bye, Sam," Bernie bellowed. "We'll see you again someday at that fifty-dollar window in the sky."

"Thank you all for coming," Michelle blurted. She waved off Bernie's assistance as she stepped down from the platform. Al was waiting to put his arm around her.

"Boy, was that ever weird," Herbie said.

"You've got a gift for understatement, young man," Nate replied.

There was a ripple in the crowd as Longshot Sam's ex-wives made their way up the apron of the track. Candy was escorted by Biff Bonnardo, and Daphne walked arm in arm with her charming husband.

"Looks like Ashley and Beverly might be available, partner," Nate said. He smiled as they walked past, and Ashley gave him a wink.

"I think I'll hold out for Michelle's sister."

We fell into step behind them, overtaking the despondent

figure of Timmy Malkos, who had stopped to catch his breath about halfway to the grandstand.

"Are you okay, Greek?" I asked.

"Oh sure," he lied. "Couldn't be better. I won fifty bucks in the pool on when that Moreno guy would turn up. I knew he didn't have long to live."

I nodded. "I thought maybe you were having a little trouble with Red over there."

"Oh, you saw that, huh? Ah, that's nothing. It's just, now that Sam's gone, except for Al, I don't have any friends left in the group."

"I'll be your friend, Greek," Herbie said.

"You're a good kid, kid. Will you get me another Polish this afternoon?"

"Sure I will." Herbie nodded. "Hey, Uncle Mark, did you notice the perfume those ladies were wearing?"

Now that he mentioned it, I realized I did. "It was the same as Mrs. Natoli's, wasn't it?"

"Yeah, that's right," the Greek said. "Sam made all his wives wear the same perfume. Chanel Number Five." He sniffed at the air and winked at Herbie. "Kind of nice, isn't it? I'm even thinking about getting a little for myself."

Herbie laughed, but as Timmy the Greek walked away, he asked, "Do you think he's serious?"

That was another question for the headmaster to answer. It also gave me another question to ponder: Which one of Sam's wives had been at the Hi-Way Motel?

Based on the description the clerk had given us, I was starting to lean a little toward Candy. But the odds could change at any time.

24

I thought about having a word with Candy Miller, but she and Daphne Lunaviva dashed into the ladies' room to powder their noses or perhaps ponder their plans on spending their windfall. Biff Bonnardo and Tony Lunaviva lurked outside.

"There's a gruesome twosome," Nate said. "I wonder if they're into swapping."

They became a loathsome threesome when Matt Caldwell, looking fit and rested after his day off, wandered over to join them. He glared at us from across the way, and I gave him a friendly wave just to make sure his disposition didn't improve. That was as close as I wanted to get. Even if Candy had been at the Hi-Way Motel, it wasn't too likely she'd tell us about it.

I didn't think we'd learn much from talking to the pickers, but I did have a few questions for Toteboard Tommy and Dr. Dave. They were only so happy to answer them.

"Can't you see we're trying to work on our programs?" Tommy griped.

"Yeah, I can. I also saw both of you follow Sam downstairs right before he was killed. And you seemed a little quick to accuse Track Jack."

"You're crazy." Dr. Dave waved his program, and a few pages of notes flew out of his hand. Herbie bent down to pick them up. I was going to have to teach him to be less polite.

"We didn't follow anybody," Tommy said. "There's no crime in going down to the grandstand. Is there?"

I ignored his question and asked one of my own. "You didn't make any phone calls to Sam before the contest, did you?"

"No, why would I do that?"

"A guy with a voice like yours made some death threats. Sam thought it was you."

"Well, it wasn't."

"Maybe you'd like to give us your phone number and we could check with Ma Bell," Nate suggested.

"Maybe I wouldn't," Tommy retorted.

"Maybe you'd like a shiner like his," Nate said, nodding at Herbie. His voice was quiet, but he sounded like he meant it.

"Why don't you give it to him and then maybe they'll leave us alone." I couldn't tell whether Dr. Dave was motivated by cowardice or good sense.

Tommy scowled. "Okay," he said at last, scrawling the number on a scrap of paper with a BIC pen that had been chewed off at the top. "Here—you satisfied?"

I glanced at the paper and shook my head. "That one's been disconnected." I wasn't sure it was the same number Tommy gave out in his money-back guarantee, but I figured it was a pretty good bet. I turned out to be right.

Tommy glanced nervously at Dr. Dave. He probably figured I was clairvoyant. I didn't say anything to suggest otherwise.

"Here," he said indignantly. "That's my home phone. It's not listed, so don't give it out."

"Don't worry," Nate assured him. "I hardly think it's the most-sought-after number in America."

"That depends on how many suckers are trying to return his stupid calculator," I said.

The dawn of recognition swept slowly over the horizon of Toteboard Tommy's brow. "Mark Renzler . . . Dark Penzler," he said softly, enunciating like a tourist practicing the local idiom for "Where is the American Express office?"

I smiled my charming smile. "You're not as dumb as you look, Mr. Stevens."

"Yeah, well, if you're so smart, why don't you talk to Al Phillips?" Dr. Dave said. "He's the one that was diddling Sam's wife before Sam was."

"Is that a fact?" Nate asked.

"Yeah, it is." Tommy nodded.

I sent my nephew to get a hot dog. When he was out of earshot, I said, "Well, then, by all means, let's have the details."

Dr. Dave snorted. "What details?"

"You made an allegation, now back it up."

He decided to back off. "I dunno. I thought they were together last year." He looked to Tommy for a second opinion.

Tommy shrugged. "Yeah, that's right. Everybody knew it." He looked at his watch. "Now why don't you just leave us alone."

"What do you think?" Nate asked as we walked over to meet Herbie.

"I don't know. I hope it's just gossip." But I had a feeling there was something to their accusation. Track Jack Jones had said there was bad blood between Sam and Al at last year's contest, and Al and Michelle did seem pretty close.

"All the same, I think you should talk to him," Nate said.

"Yeah, I intend to."

My intention was to do it later in the day, but the opportunity came up sooner than I expected. While Nate and Herbie were eating lunch, I spotted Al studying the racing program outside the Winners Circle. He was working so intently that he didn't notice me until it was too late to cover up three pages of notes that he was referring to.

"Aren't those Sam's notations?" I asked.

Al spun around, startled. "Oh, Jesus. I was afraid you were one of the other handicappers."

"You didn't answer my question, Al."

He chuckled anxiously. "Hey, don't be so serious." He held the sheets out. "This stuff is going to make us rich, partner."

"Thanks to Sam, you're already rich, partner."

Al chuckled again. "Well, as Sam used to say, you can never be rich enough."

"I don't think you should be using that stuff, Al."

Al gave me the sneer. "It's part of his estate." When he saw I wasn't smirking along with him, he added, "I asked Michelle. She said it was okay."

I nodded. "You didn't tell me you knew Michelle before Sam did."

"And you didn't ask me. Who the hell have you been talking to—that nosy bitch, Serendipity?"

"It doesn't matter who I heard it from, Al. Is it true?"

This time Al gave me a real sneer. "Am I being interrogated?"

"You could say that."

"It sure feels like it, Renzler. And I sure don't like it."

"I don't blame you. What's the answer to my question?"

"I don't believe it. You think I killed Sam, don't you?"

I shook my head. "No, Al. I just think you're not being honest with me."

"Oh, Jesus!" Al buried his head in his hands for a moment. "Okay, here's how it was. I did know Michelle before Sam did—for about one hour." He held up a finger for emphasis. "I met her through a friend who told me I should look her up when I got to Omaha. I did, and she came to the track with me. We hit it off fine, but she and Sam hit it off better. That's all there was to it. If you don't believe me, you can ask her."

"Did you and Sam fight about it?" I asked.

"Hell no! But all these jerks would sure like to think we did. They're always looking to stir up shit. They're a bunch of parasites." Al shook his head. "Sam Natoli was my best friend, Renzler. If you think I killed him, you're sadly mistaken."

"I think you're overreacting, Al. I didn't say you killed Sam."

"No, but you thought it."

He had a point there. I told him I was sorry for pressing him. As I turned away, Al handed me Sam's notes. "Here, take them. I thought I was helping both of us. But if it eases your conscience, I'll work without them."

I folded the sheets and put them in my pocket. "You probably memorized them anyway," I said.

The sneer was back. "You bet your ass I did."

25

I found Nate leaning on the bar, clucking over stories in the *New York Times* about Richard Nixon's imminent demise. The Republican rats reportedly were deserting the sinking ship, but Barry Goldwater had delivered a tirade on the Senate floor denouncing the press as "a rotten bunch" for quoting him as saying old Captain Queeg had made up his mind to jump overboard. Vice-President Gerald Ford was keeping mum, but rumors were flying that he'd be steering the ship of state by the end of the week. My Thursday night bet was looking pretty good.

Herbie was standing next to Nate and studying the racing program. "Hey, Uncle Mark," he said. "What do these little circles next to the quarter times along the past-performance line mean?"

"Those tell you that the horse was running on the outside. A horse that isn't along the rail has to make up extra ground and it's very taxing. One circle means he was one width from the rail, two means he was two wide, and three means he was parked on the outside."

Nate glanced up from the paper at Herbie's baffled expression. "He told me those circles stood for how many times the jockey made hay with the horse." I wasn't sure my nephew got that one, either.

"They're not called jockeys in harness racing," I said. "They're called drivers."

"Until last year, I couldn't get your uncle to understand the difference between a painting and a picture, Herb."

"For each circle and each quarter mile, a horse loses approximately two-fifths of a second off the finishing time," said a flat voice behind us.

I turned to see the wizened visage of Clocker Callaway.

"How's the investigation coming?" he inquired without much interest, or at least without much inflection. "Do you think one of the handicappers killed Sam?"

I certainly didn't think Clocker was involved. "I doubt there would have been enough time for anyone to push through the crowd and get to the parking lot," I said.

"What if they took the shortcut?" he asked.

"What shortcut?"

"If you want, I'll show you."

"I definitely want," I said.

Clocker led us through a door near the pickers' section marked NO ADMITTANCE and down a long narrow corridor that ran parallel to the track. It was done in handsome gray cinder block, with doors on either side. At the end of the hall, just past the announcer's booth, we hit a stairway. We walked down and came to a pair of metal doors. I pushed open the one on the right and stepped out into the area where the police had found the rifle shell.

"Interesting, don't you think?" Clocker asked.

I nodded. It sure was.

Clocker looked at his watch. "One minute, twenty-nine seconds," he said. "With an average win time of two-ten and two-fifths, that would have left somebody forty-one and two-fifths seconds to get here."

"Give or take a fifth," Nate said.

"I wonder how many other people know about the shortcut," Herbie said. I wondered how Clocker knew about it.

There was trouble with a Jersey accent waiting for us when we got to the top of the stairs. "Can't you assholes read the sign?" Matt Caldwell snarled. "It says AUTHORIZED PERSONNEL ONLY."

Herbie and Clocker shrank back, but Nate took a step forward. "Actually, it says NO ADMITTANCE, but you are technically correct. Don't feel bad. With a little work, you could probably pass the civil-service exam."

"I'll do a little work on your face, asshole."

Nate smiled. "And you'd die trying."

Caldwell looked like he just might try until Dave Gwynn stepped out into the hall. "What's going on out here?" he asked.

"I caught these assholes sneaking around, Mr. G." Caldwell spoke through gritted teeth.

"Calm down, Matt," Gwynn said. He turned to me. "He's right. You're not supposed to be back here."

"I'm sorry," I lied. "I was just coming to ask you a few questions."

Gwynn looked at his watch. "I'm a little pressed for time right now."

"It'll only take a minute."

"Okay, come on in. But not all four of you." He turned to Caldwell. "Matt, why don't you show the others out."

"That's all right," Nate said. "I think we can handle it."

"Make it fast, buddy," Caldwell barked.

We watched as Nate set a leisurely pace down the hall, glancing over his shoulder occasionally and grinning.

"Do you want me to stay with you and make sure this guy doesn't try any funny stuff, Mr. Gwynn?"

"No, Matt, I don't think that'll be necessary."

Gwynn stepped over to a microphone and announced that there were fifteen minutes to post time. Then he sat down in a swivel chair and asked what I wanted.

"I'm curious about Tony Lunaviva's horses," I said. "Sam Natoli found out he was holding them back to keep up the odds."

"Hold on a second." Gwynn raised a hand. "Sam *thought* Lunaviva was holding them back. That doesn't prove that he was."

"Listen, Dave," I said. "I've noticed it after being here three days, and Sheriff Maszursky told me he noticed it. You're the racing secretary. Surely you must have noticed it, too."

Gwynn adjusted his baseball cap. "Off the record?"

I nodded.

"Well, you're right. I can see what's going on better than anybody. And I've taken it into consideration while doing the morning line. I don't know if you've noticed or not, but I've been setting pretty low odds for Lunaviva's horses, considering their past performance. But I can't do much more than that. I'm between a rock and a hard place here. I can't very well list them as favorites, because sometimes his horses really don't have a chance of winning. That would be misleading, too."

Gwynn was right. I had noticed that he was setting lower odds for Lunaviva's horses than you would have expected. But I also recalled Sam's telling me that the racing secretary wasn't above making some adjustments for his own purposes.

"But Sam did talk to you about it," I said.

"Oh yeah. We talked for a long while." The faintest trace of a smile appeared on Gwynn's face. "And Sam figured out his own way to take care of things."

"You mean by putting Lunaviva's horses on his sheet."

"That's right."

"What did you do after Sam spoke to you?"

"Are we still off the record?"

"Of course."

"I talked to Mr. Bonnardo about it."

"And what did he say?"

"He told me he'd look into it."

"And did he?"

Gwynn sighed. It was the sigh of a beaten man. "You can't tell anybody I said this, Renzler, but Biff Bonnardo and Tony Lunaviva are practically best friends."

"So you mean Bonnardo won't do anything about it."

"I mean you should draw your own conclusions."

"My conclusion is that Bonnardo runs a crooked little racetrack here."

Just then, the bugle for the post parade sounded. Gwynn swiveled to the microphone, flipped a switch on a control panel with his foot and introduced the horses. When he was finished, he turned back to me.

"I've been in this business a long time, Renzler. I worked at Jackson Park for a couple of years before I came here. Let me tell you something: At a small track, there's bound to be some funny stuff going on. It's the nature of the beast."

I was tempted to ask how he felt working for a beast like Biff Bonnardo, but that would have been a cheap shot. I figured Gwynn got an okay salary, and even if Sam hadn't told me, I would have been sure he supplemented it by cashing bets for himself. But with an invalid wife, he probably needed every penny of it.

A woman came into the booth and handed Gwynn a sheet of paper. He swiveled to the mike and announced two scratches and a couple of driver changes for the sixth and seventh races.

"I'm really getting busy here," he said. "Do you have any more questions?"

"A few."

"Are you going to be at Lunaviva's party tonight?"

"I wouldn't miss it."

"Well, if they can wait until then, I'll answer all the questions you want." He held up a can of Coke. "I'll be much better talking over a Scotch anyway."

"That sounds fine to me."

As I got up to leave, Gwynn said, "Renzler, if you talk to Mr. Bonnardo about any of this, I'd appreciate it if you'd leave my name out."

"You have my word," I said, not bothering to add how little some people think that's worth.

When I got back to the pickers' section, Nate asked about the agenda for the afternoon. I told him I had to make some calls.

"Great," he said. "That means we don't have to hang around this dump all day."

"Why don't you just call from here," Herbie said hopefully.

"There aren't any phones at the track," I said. "They're afraid people will call their bookies."

"Is that the reason?" Nate said. "I thought they were afraid people would order out for food."

We set up shop in Nate's room at Howard Johnson's. He kept a Nixon news vigil while I worked the phone. On our way over, I filled him in on my conversations with Dave Gwynn and Al Phillips.

I knew I wouldn't have a chance to ask Gwynn about getting a tape of the race until Lunaviva's party, so I called my friend Carol Robertson at WNBC and asked her to send me a copy. I didn't know if it was important, but I had to cover every angle.

"You sure have great timing, Renzler," Carol said. "We're all going crazy here on Nixon. He's going to resign any day. But I guess you probably wouldn't know anything about that."

"Sure I do. Nine o'clock tomorrow night."

"What? Have you heard something?" Carol's worst fear in life is being scooped on a story.

"No. But that's the time I've got in the pool I'm in."

She let out a sigh. "You'd bet on anything, wouldn't you?"

"Almost. And knowing how efficient you are, I'd bet you'll have that tape to me tomorrow."

"I don't know. I'm really busy."

"There's a dinner in it for you."

"Yeah. At some sleazy steak house."

"No. We'll go to a nice steak house."

"I can't. I'm going steady with somebody."

"Bring him along. I'll make him uncomfortable."

"I'm sure you would. Do you need the film of this race, too?"

"No, just the audio."

"Okay, I'll see what I can do."

The next call wasn't as pleasant, and it lasted a while longer. It takes some fancy footwork to dance through the red tape of the phone company, but I know all the steps. I've found that impersonating an FBI agent usually gets good results.

I got the info I needed, but it didn't tell me anything. The number Tommy Stevens had given me was his home listing, but he hadn't placed any calls to Sam Natoli. That didn't mean he hadn't made the threats; only that he hadn't made them from his house or mobile home or whatever he lived in. It also meant we were still at square one—too many suspects, too few clues.

After my talk with Al, I didn't think the next call was really necessary, but I made it just in case. Rolf Laxman was an old friend of mine who used to work at the *Daily News* before moving to Chicago and taking a job at the *American*. When it folded, he went over to the *Sun-Times*. By way of me, he and Al were friends.

Rolf's a guy who can talk your ears off, and I had to switch the phone from my right to left before getting down to the subject I was calling about. It turned out Rolf and Al hadn't seen much of each other lately.

"I guess you probably heard he left the *Trib*," Rolf said.

"No, I didn't."

"Yeah, one guy told me he quit, another guy said he was fired. I guess it all depends on who you talk to."

"When's the last time you talked to Al?" I asked.

"Jesus, not for a while. The last time, though, it was real funny. I ran into him and he was with this gorgeous chick. They were going shooting at the gun club in Lincoln Park and they invited me along. Al couldn't shoot worth a damn, but I'll tell you, this girl was something else."

I could feel my heartbeat quickening. "What was her name?"

"Hell, I don't remember. She was a knockout, though. I do remember that."

"Was her name Michelle?"

"Yeah, I think that's it. Michelle. That sounds rights. She was from out of town."

"Did you get the impression she and Al were dating?"

"Well, I sure hope so, for Al's sake."

"How long ago was that, Rolf?"

"Oh, I don't know. Three or four months ago, I guess."

"Thanks, Rolf," I said. "You've been a lot of help."

"Hey, hold on, Renzler. When are you coming out to visit?"

"When the Cubs win the pennant."

"Oh, great. When hell freezes over."

As I put down the phone, I had a sinking feeling that moment was coming sooner than anybody expected. At least for Al Phillips and Michelle Natoli.

"You're looking a little sickly o'er the pale cast of thought," Nate said as he watched me light a cigarette.

I glanced at myself in the mirror, then at the tube, where a grim-faced Alexander Haig was ducking questions from a fleet of TV reporters demanding to know just how rotten things were in the Oval Office. Nate was right, but I didn't look half as bad as Nixon's chief of staff. That wasn't much of a consolation.

26

We stopped for a pop in the HoJo's lounge before heading back to the track to pick up Herbie. We got there just as the contest standings were being posted. The Penzler-Moore-Phillips team had come through with another good day, due in no small part, I figured, to Al's use of Longshot Sam's info.

Timmy the Greek still held the lead with a bankroll of $1600, but Al had closed the gap between them to ten dollars. Clocker Callaway was third, but he was $400 behind Al. Amazingly, Serendipity's astrological system was working well enough to keep her in fourth place, just $50 behind Clocker. Toteboard Tommy was more than a hundred behind her in fifth.

The other pickers had less than they started with. Dr. Dave, in sixth place, was $300 down, followed by Lucky Lou, who had $500 left. His buddy Sol's nickname fit his disposition, as he watched his name being crossed off the list. Solly had gone bust. With two days to go, there were seven pro pickers left.

On the amateur side of things, out of the fifty-five contestants who had started, there were only thirty-seven left. Dark Penzler had surged into first, ahead of Sheriff Maszursky, but Herbie had smartly mixed up some of our picks so that Nate Moore was in third place. The kid was turning out to have a sneaky streak in him after all. All it took was for somebody like his uncle to bring it out.

As we started to leave, Al told me he was going to dinner with Michelle, her sister, and the dreaded Cove, then picking up the Greek before heading on to the party. "So I guess I'll see you there," he said.

"Fine with me, Al."

He grabbed my arm and studied my face for a moment. "Hey, is something wrong?"

I put on my poker face and shook my head. This wasn't the time or place to discuss the things we needed to talk about. "No, Al," I lied, "everything's just fine."

"We knocked 'em dead today, Renzler," he said, putting on his best sneer. "I wish you'd been here to see it."

"I wish I had been too, Al."

We went right to the Hofbrau, where Herbie savored his first beer in the bar while watching the TV news. Barry Goldwater was fending off the press with assurances that Nixon hadn't decided whether to resign yet and no head counts had been taken in the Senate to see how an impeachment vote would go. Inside the White House they were holding a wake, with Tricia and Julie home for a family dinner with Mom, Dad, and the duds—their husbands, Ed Cox and David Eisenhower.

"I bet that's a lively gathering," Nate said. "If only Checkers were still alive."

I was about to say it didn't sound any worse than Thanksgiving at my sister's, but I caught my tongue at the last moment. I didn't think Herbie would appreciate the comment.

The Nixon countdown was the spectacle I had been waiting for all summer, but now that it was here I wasn't enjoying it as much as I had hoped. Thank Al Phillips for that. Even Nate seemed subdued.

Herbie downed his second beer as the news ended, and we wandered into the dining room to stuff our faces with Wiener schnitzel. Herbie's friend Lucille had the day off, but a zither player was on hand to keep things lively, or at least curious. It was eight-thirty by the time we cruised up Route 46 past the Hi-Way Motel and came within sight of the world's largest donut. The sky wasn't completely dark yet, but the neon lights were already giving off a tasty glow.

The circular drive leading down to Tony Lunaviva's house sparkled with lights, and the bottom half was lined with cars. In addition to the handicappers, Lunaviva must have invited five hundred of his closest friends. A cloud of steam was rising from the coffee cup on the donut tower, and a string of lights along the patio made the round swimming pool look like—you guessed it—a donut. A rock band was set up on the far side of the pool; Nate said it sounded Like Tommy James and the Shondells. Neither Herbie nor I challenged him on the point.

"Boy-oh-boy, is this ever neat!" Herbie said as we parked at the top of the drive. He stumbled while getting out of the car, and I had a feeling my nephew was feeling his two beers.

"I'll bet the guy has the world's largest electric bill," Nate said as we walked down the steep hill toward the front of the house, where three Holey Toledos were sitting at a table and taking names.

It turned out only two of them were checking names. Matt Caldwell's brother was there to check their work. I thought they were doing a fine job, but he had a different opinion. He was quick to notice that there were two invitations and three of us.

"Hey, wait a minute," he said, standing up. "You didn't get an invitation from that guy." He pointed at Nate. "You can't just let anybody in."

"He's okay, he's a friend of Mr. Lunaviva's," one of the kids said. I didn't recognize him as Jimmy, the doorman, until I heard the lisp in his voice. Jimmy knew damn well that we weren't friends, but I guess the five-dollar bill I'd slipped him with our invitations was enough to buy friendship status. Apparently, the bribe had eluded his supervisor's eye.

"You know the rules," the Caldwell kid said. "Nobody's allowed in without their invitation."

"I left mine back at the motel," Nate said, throwing himself on the mercy of the court. "But I'm sure my name's on the list. Yeah, there it is—Track Jack Jones."

"See—I told you," Jimmy said. I suspected a little power struggle was going on between him and the Caldwell kid.

For a moment I thought young Caldwell was going to demand to see Nate's ID. But he just stood there glowering at Herbie.

"What are you looking at?" my nephew demanded. Like his mother, the kid seemed to get ornery on a couple of beers.

"Not much," Caldwell answered smugly.

"Stop making trouble with the guests, Mike, or I'm going to tell Mr. Lunaviva," Jimmy said.

"Go ahead and tell him. See what I care." Mike stalked off, no doubt in search of his brother.

"Don't let him bother you," Jimmy said. "He's a sorehead. He's always trying to pick fights."

We thanked him and started to head down the walk.

"Wait a minute," Jimmy's partner called after us, holding out three round stickers. "You forgot your name tags. You punch out the middle part and it looks just like a donut."

"Holy Toledo!" Nate said. "Do we return the centers to you so you can make them into munchkins?"

Jimmy shook his head. "You're thinking of Dunkin' Donuts."

"And you each get a Toledo pin," the other kid said, holding out three pins like the one we had found in Dino LaRussa's motel room.

"It's just like the Mormons," Nate said as he fastened the pin to his lapel. "They can make you a member whether you want to join or not."

Serendipity McCall was waiting for us at the edge of the patio, half in the bag and half out of a red dress. "Finally, the private eyes are here," she said, extending her hand with palm down. "Now maybe the party can really get started."

Nate kissed her hand playfully. I followed suit to avoid rubbing her the wrong way. When Herbie's turn came, he eyed it suspiciously, as if he thought she had stolen it from Saint Catherine of Siena.

"Go ahead, it's not going to bite you," Serendipity teased. "Now," she said, after the deed was done, "which one of you wants to dance with me first?"

I knew who wanted to dance with her last, so I excused myself to go chat with Dave Gwynn, whom I spotted talking to a leggy blonde under a tree over near the house. As I looked back over my shoulder, I saw that my nephew had gotten the nod. Or maybe it had been a prod. Whichever it was, I saw Serendipity McCall leading him onto the dance floor just as the band began singing, "My Baby Does the Hanky-Panky."

The blonde with Gwynn turned out to be Daphne Lunaviva. That meant that the woman I had seen Tony Lunaviva doing the frug with on my way over was somebody other than his wife.

Gwynn acknowledged my approach with a wave of his glass,

and Daphne turned and greeted me with a seductive smile. That's not to say she was trying to seduce me. It was just her natural expression. I figured she looked that way when she went to church.

"This is Mark Renzler," Gwynn said. "He's—"

"I know, I know," Daphne interrupted. "Mr. Renzler and I are old friends—aren't we?" She giggled. "He and his partner were here giving Tony the business yesterday. You know, Mr. Renzler, my husband would be very, very angry if he knew you were here."

"He's the one who invited me," I said.

"If I were you, I'd be careful he doesn't uninvite you."

"I promise to be on my best behavior."

She let out a laugh. "That and a dollar will get you half a dozen donuts."

"So how's your investigation coming?" Dave Gwynn asked. "I'm sorry I had to cut our meeting short today."

"That's okay, I understand. You were busy."

"Well, he's not busy now." Daphne laughed. "Unless you count working on getting loaded being busy."

"That can sometimes be serious business." I turned to Gwynn. "I'm wondering if you heard anybody coming down the hall past your office before Sam Natoli was shot. Either before or during the ninth race."

Gwynn shook his head. "I usually keep the door closed. Even if it was open, I doubt if I would have noticed. It takes a lot of concentration to call a race."

That I believed. But there was something else I was curious about.

"On Monday, you said you were sure the shot came from the parking lot. But the police think it was fired from the doorway beneath your office. I'm wondering—"

Gwynn put up his hand to stop me. "I wondered about that myself. It confused me at first, but then I figured out what happened. The shot sounded close, but not that close. Then I realized I had the windows shut. I usually keep at least one window open to let in some air. But it'd been raining, so I had it closed." Gwynn finished off his Scotch. "But it still sounded loud, I can tell you that. It really startled me."

"I know this is important and all," Daphne said. "But we're

supposed to be having a party here. Don't you think this could wait until another time?"

I gave her a look that wiped the smile right off her pretty face. Dave Gwynn did me one better.

"No, it can't wait, Daphne. If you're bored, why don't you go off and find somebody else to play with."

Daphne glared at Gwynn. If he was trying to hurt her feelings, she looked like he had succeeded. "All right, if that's the way you feel about it. I *will*."

We watched as she pranced away. "She's unbelievable," Gwynn said, shaking his head.

"You won't get any argument from me on that." As we walked to the bar to refill our drinks, I asked him whether the races were recorded.

"Oh, sure. We're required to by law. We record everything—all the announcements, scratches, driver changes, et cetera. Now with the video, we just tape the races." Gwynn took our drinks off the bar and left a dollar in their place. "Why do you ask?"

"Well, I heard it real quick on the TV news, but I don't think there was any gunshot on the tape."

"Oh no, there had to be. I think you must be mistaken. The TV people get the tapes from us."

"That's what I figured. So the sound of the gunshot should have been recorded."

"I should think so. Unless . . ."

"Unless what?"

"I don't know. I'm not an expert on these technical things. Maybe a gunshot is hard to identify or something."

"I'm not an expert either," I said. "But I've heard recordings of shots before and they definitely sound like shots."

"I see." Gwynn looked a little baffled.

"Is there a technician I could talk to who does the taping?"

I knew the answer before it came out of his mouth. "You're looking at him," he said. "Well, me and Mr. Bonnardo. Sometimes if he's in the booth with me, he does it."

"Do you remember which one of you recorded Monday's races?"

"Well, I recorded it. But Mr. Bonnardo's the one who gave it to the TV people."

"Do you mind if I come by tomorrow and listen to the tape?"

"No, not at all. Why don't you stop by before the first race. That way we can sit down and listen to it together. I'd be curious to hear it myself." Gwynn downed his drink and glanced at his watch. "Well, I better go find my wife."

And I thought I should go find my nephew.

"I ran into my partner first. "Having a good time?" I asked.

"Just super." Nate grinned and did a few dance steps that wouldn't make anybody forget Fred Astaire. "I was right about the band, by the way," he said. "It *is* Tommy James and the Shondells."

That was big news to me. "You haven't seen Herbie, by any chance, have you?"

Nate turned and pointed. "The last I saw him, he was sitting over there on the far side of the pool."

"He was probably hiding from Serendipity."

"*Au contraire*, Uncle Bad Vibes. The kid can cut a rug. You'd be amazed at the skills they develop in the CYO these days."

"All I ever learned to do was smoke cigarettes and get drunk behind the school."

"Two of your finer talents," Nate said. "Herbie was even dancing with Sam's ex-wife Candy. I think maybe she's into young bruisers."

"Or maybe she's into bruises."

"Speaking of which, I'm about to run off and take my lumps with Serendipity. She even volunteered to go up and get her car. I'm supposed to meet her out front."

"You're kidding." At least I hoped he was kidding.

Nate shook his head. "What can I say? She invited me to count her freckles. How can you refuse an offer like that?"

I thought it would be easier then getting drunk at a hockey game. "You're going to miss the band's big finale."

He shrugged. "They already played 'Crimson and Clover' before we got here."

"Jeez, that's too bad. I'm sorry I missed it."

Nate grinned. "Well, wish me luck."

"You're going to need it. Are you just going for the clap or do you want a standing ovation?"

"You are truly disgusting, Renzler," he said.

I figured he might have a different opinion in the morning.

27

I wanted to find my nephew before Matt Caldwell's younger brother did, but Al Phillips found me first.

"Have you seen the Greek?" he asked.

I shook my head.

"We just got here a few minutes ago. I went to the bar to get us a drink, and he slipped away. I told him to wait for me but he didn't."

"What's so important about finding the Greek?"

"Somebody stole all his handicapping stuff. Or at least he thinks they did. He may have just lost it. But he's convinced that Tommy Stevens took it. I tried to calm him down, but he said he was going to kill him."

I couldn't imagine that either of them would be able to inflict any damage, so I continued my search for Herbie. I found him sitting under a tree and gazing at the stars.

"How are you doing, Herb?" I asked.

"Great, Uncle Mark. I feel really great." He hopped to his feet quickly but almost fell over as he tried to get his balance.

I steadied him with my arm. "Did you have another beer?"

"Nope. One of the Holey Toledos gave me some of this green stuff. It tasted just like candy."

Uh-oh. That sounded like Chartreuse to me. "And did it give you a funny feeling in the back of your throat?"

Herbie nodded.

"How much of the green stuff did he give you?"

Herbie shrugged and held his thumb and index finger about three inches apart. "Just a little glass."

At 110 proof, a little glass could go a long way. I put my arm on his shoulder. "I think it's time for us to head home, Herb."

"Okay, Uncle Mark," he said. "But I feel pretty good."

That would change pretty fast.

"Do you think I might be a little drunk?"

I told him I thought that was a distinct possibility. And he wasn't alone. As we wound our way through the carpet of big drunks on Tony Lunaviva's patio, we passed Mr. Donut himself. He was shooting the breeze with his buddy Biff Bonnardo. They were so full of booze that they almost knocked us over with the hot gust of their conversation.

In view of Herbie's delicate condition, I decided to ignore our host for the evening. But he made that difficult to do.

"What the hell are *you* doing here?" Lunaviva demanded, staggering in front of me. "I thought I told you to stay off my property."

"I'm one of your guests." I smiled my charming smile and tried to sidestep him, but he moved over and blocked my path.

"Well, I sure as hell didn't invite you."

"He's in the contest, Tony," Bonnardo said. "He's the private detective that's—"

"I know who he is. He was out here harassing my wife and myself yesterday afternoon. I had to throw his butt off my property."

"Is that so?" Bonnardo's tone changed from reasoning to unreasonable as he glowered at me.

"I wasn't harassing him. I just thought it was curious that Sam Natoli was murdered with the help of a guy who worked for him. And he was killed after he figured out Lunaviva was holding back his horses to drive up the odds at *your* racetrack."

"That's ridiculous!" Bonnardo growled.

"It's bullshit, is what it is," Lunaviva added.

"No it's not. And you"—I pointed at Bonnardo—"must have known about it."

"Watch what the hell you're saying. I run an honest track."

"Your track's a shithole." I guess I was feeling the booze a little myself.

"Get the hell off my property!" Lunaviva shouted. Then he began calling for Matt Caldwell.

"We're on our way," I said. "Let's go, Herbie."

I turned to leave, and this time Bonnardo blocked the way, rocking on the heels of his black-and-white fence climbers. Knocking him over would have been easier than pounding the cream out of the co-star of Lunaviva's TV ad. That's if I didn't pass out from the double-threat fumes of gin and Hai Karate. But with Herbie on hand, I elected to take the high road, spinning around and heading off in the opposite direction while Bonnardo and Lunaviva shouted drunken insults from the low road.

The path of least resistance led to the center of another confrontation, this one involving Timmy Malkos and Tommy Stevens. When we happened upon it, the altercation was already subsiding. Lou Larson and Dr. Dave were holding Toteboard Tommy back, and Al Phillips had his arms around the belly of the Greek. Blood was trickling from Tommy's nose, and I figured the Greek must have landed one before they were pulled apart.

"I see you found him," I said to Al.

"I've got my hands full," he said, shaking his head.

"I'll say you do."

"Don't be a smart-ass. Reach into my pocket and grab the car keys. I've got to get him out of here."

Herbie helped Al restrain the Greek while I pulled out the keys. "Are you planning on dragging him?" I asked. "Or should I try to find a forklift?"

"You go get the car, and I'll get him out to the bottom of the circle," Al said.

"What does it look like?"

"It's Michelle's car. At the top of the hill. The black Fiat with LONGSHOT license plates. You can't miss it."

No, I guess I couldn't.

"Should I go with you, Uncle Mark?" Herbie's speech was slurred.

"No. You stay and give Al a hand with the Greek." I wasn't sure he'd be much help. I had to get the kid home pretty soon.

Al had parked the car right at the top of the circle, in a premium space for an easy exit. If I didn't have to pick them up, I could have turned right and gone out through the gate. There was plenty of room to pull out of the parking space, so I gave it a little burst of gas as I started down the hill. That turned out to be a very bad idea. I had never driven such a fancy car before, but I decided I'd prefer the Pinto any day.

At first I thought the brakes were just a little sluggish, then I realized they were very sluggish. By the time I realized they weren't working at all, I was cruising down the upper half of the donut at twenty-five miles an hour and gaining speed. I was out for a ride with nowhere to go.

I know some people are suspicious of foreign cars, but I didn't think the problem was attributable to poor workmanship. Somebody at the party had cut the linings on Al's brakes.

I pulled up the emergency brake. That did no good at all. I downshifted into first. That helped a bit.

The engine belched as the transmission ground in protest, just like the Pinto does when asked to climb a hill. The car jerked, slowing momentarily as it stalled out, but gravity was doing its part to make sure the laws of nature were upheld.

The lights of the donut flickered ahead of me like the runway at an airport. Unlike at an airport, the lights weren't in a straight line. I had about ten seconds before I reached the bottom curve of the driveway, and I didn't waste them on a Hail Mary. I honked the horn furiously and flashed the high beams on and off to warn the partygoers who were gathered in front of the house and preparing to go their separate ways.

There were cars parked on both sides, but I could see an opening along the lower part of the loop on the far side, beyond the house and in front of the donut tower. I could ram the cars, but that wouldn't stop my momentum, and I'd probably lose control and end up mowing down the throng.

I figured my best bet was to keep the car on the inner part of the curve and hop the curb at the opening. If I could avoid hitting the legs of the tower, I could drive for miles on the open pasture. Or at least a thousand yards out to the colossal barn where Tony Lunaviva kept his collection of prize Mustangs or broken-down geldings.

That, of course, was a longshot.

As I turned the bottom rim, the car shook and veered to the right. I thought it might flip over. Give me the small turning radius of a Corvair any day. But I kept the steering wheel turned tight, and the little wop box stayed upright.

My horn-and-lights action seemed to have worked. The

crowd was backed away from the curb when I hit the bottom of the donut. I glimpsed the terrified faces of my nephew and Al Phillips flying past me. As I rounded the far turn, the beams of the donut tower came into my field of vision like the goalposts on a football field. I thought I was home free.

Then I saw Timmy Malkos.

The Greek loomed up larger than life in the center of the windshield, frozen in his tracks. I swerved to avoid him at the last instant, but he was too big and too slow a target. He lost his balance and fell forward as the car hopped the curb, landing on the hood with a sickening thud. For a split second, his huge head was framed in the windshield, but the force of the car lifted him upward and sent him floating through the air like a medicine ball. There was a smear of blood where his face had struck the windshield.

My head lurched to the side and hit the window, and I heard a snap of metal breaking as the car rammed into the left post of Tony Lunaviva's monument to the almighty donut. The Fiat hurtled on ahead as the tower careened down in front of me, meeting the Greek about ten feet off the ground. I saw him land in the world's largest coffee cup just to my left as I continued on, speeding right through the center of the world's largest donut the instant before it hit the ground.

The car rolled to a stop about a hundred yards out in the pasture. I could have turned it around and driven slowly back, but I decided to hoof it. My heart was pounding and I felt a little woozy as I got out and planted my feet on good old terra firma. My head throbbed and I could tell from the lump near my eye that I was going to have a shiner to challenge Herbie's in a short while. Luckily, it was my left eye. That's the one that's only for decoration.

By the time I got back to the driveway, a crowd of people was gathered around the giant coffee cup and peering over the rim at Timmy the Greek. There was a huge vertical crack running down the side of the cup that would take the world's largest tube of Elmer's Glue to repair. But the damage to Timmy Malkos was irreparable. I could tell from the unnatural angle at which his head was turned that the Greek had suffered a broken neck.

The first person I focused on was Sheriff Maszursky. That

could have been because he was the biggest guy there, or it might have had something to do with his bellowing "What the hell happened?"

"Somebody cut the goddamn brake linings," I shouted back. "That's what happened."

"Are you okay?" he asked.

"Under the circumstances—yeah."

"It's a miracle you weren't killed," Al Phillips said.

Thank God for big favors.

Herbie came over and gave me a bear hug. "I said a prayer for you, Uncle Mark." Maybe that explained it.

"I think you ought to call McReynolds," I told Maszursky. "I don't think this was any accident."

He nodded. "That's already been taken care of."

"Jesus Christ!" Al said. "Somebody was trying to kill me *and* the Greek." He turned and scanned the crowd. "Where the hell's Toteboard Tommy?"

"Which one is that?" Maszursky asked.

"The ugly guy with the big schnozz," Al said. "He had a fight with the Greek a little while ago."

Sheriff Maszursky shouted orders at one of his deputies. It was the first time I had seen Matt Caldwell all evening. "Find this Toteboard Tommy. And I want the names of everybody at the party. And spread the word: Nobody leaves until after the police get here."

Maszursky wheeled and shouted at the crowd to stand back. I moved off to the side with Herbie and Al.

"Uncle Mark, all of a sudden I don't feel so good."

Herbie's hands were folded over his stomach, and his face was turning the color of Chartreuse. The booze alone was probably enough to do him in, but seeing another dead body couldn't have helped.

I turned to Al. "Will you be able to get back okay? I'm going to take Herbie home."

"Yeah, don't worry about that. But don't you think the police will want to talk to you?"

"I think the morning will be soon enough."

28

I let Herbie sleep in while I went to meet Nate for breakfast at HoJo's. I had filled him in on all the fun he missed at the party when I gave him his wake-up call.

"Well, don't you look pretty," he said, admiring my black eye.

"Not any worse than you do," I replied.

"Well, I had a long night too."

"Spare me the details."

"You know me. I wouldn't want to cheapen the experience by talking about it." Nate stretched his arms and yawned. "But let me tell you, that Serendipity is quite the independent woman. Did you know she *lives* in that van of hers?"

I didn't, but it didn't surprise me. "Don't tell me you spent the night in that thing?"

He shook his head. "I came inside like a good boy. She stayed out in the lot. She had to get up early and change the oil. She does all her own repairs. If you're nice to her, I bet she'd tune up that junker of yours."

"No, thanks. She probably sets the timing according to the phases of the moon."

He grinned. "Well, I can assure you, she gives a very good grease job."

"I thought you didn't want to cheapen the experience."

"Sorry. I just couldn't resist."

In more ways than one.

"Are you certain somebody tampered with the car?" Nate asked.

I nodded. "I'd bet my life on it."

"You almost did," he said, wiping his mouth on the sleeve of his shirt. "So I guess one of the handicappers is behind the killing of Sam, after all. The leaders are going down one by one."

"Not necessarily. But I'm sure one of them is responsible for the death of the Greek. And they were trying to kill Al at the same time. Somebody must have seen them arrive."

"How could the killer be sure the Greek would go home with Al?" Nate asked.

"He couldn't be. But it was a good bet. And even if the Greek did go home in a different car, Al would have still been nailed. The Greek was just a bonus."

"It was a pretty risky way to do it," Nate said. "That car could have run over a lot of other people at the bottom of the driveway."

"Some people are willing to take risks when they're playing for fifty grand. Besides, the car was parked at the top of the circle. It wasn't necessary to drive down to the house to exit. All they had to do was turn right through the gate and they would have been out on the road. That's where the killer expected them to crash—out on one of those winding hills. If Al was hitting the booze like he's been known to do, nobody would have wondered about the brakes. They would have figured he lost control of the car." I lit a cigarette. "I wonder where Toteboard Tommy was when Al and the Greek got there."

"I think you might be missing something, Renzler. Aren't you forgetting your buddy Al?"

"What do you mean? It was Al's car that was tampered with."

"Right. And who did Al ask to drive it? You. The private detective. Probably the only guy here who could figure this whole thing out. And he knew you were getting close yesterday when you talked to him about Michelle."

Nate had a point there. If I was willing to consider the notion that Al had killed his best friend, there was no reason to think he wouldn't try to kill me. But I still had my doubts.

"I don't know, Nate. If Al was planning on killing Sam, it doesn't make sense that he'd invite me out here to begin with."

Nate took a bite out of a piece of black toast. He likes his breakfast charred. "Don't assume people who commit murder make sense," he said. "That's a quote from a friend of mine."

I nodded. Renzler's first law. At least that's what Nate likes to call it.

"Look at it this way," he said. "Who had the best chance to tamper with the brakes? Al. He told you the Greek slipped away while he was getting a drink. I don't think he was at the bar. I think he was out messing with the brakes."

"But it was only by chance that Al asked me to get the car."

Nate shook his head as he pushed away his plate. "I think he would have been able to come up with something."

I took a mouthful of coffee, followed by a deep breath and the last drag off my cigarette. "Let's get out of here. I want to call McReynolds."

"Are you going to tell him what I just laid out for you?"

"Not yet. But if you're right, I'm going to strangle Al Phillips with my bare hands."

"Better use gloves," he advised. "That way you won't leave any prints."

Nate rousted the hung-over Herbie while I called the police station. Tom McReynolds didn't bother with any of the social amenities when he got on the line.

"Where the hell did you go last night?" he demanded.

"My nephew was sick. I had to take him home. I wasn't feeling so good myself after my little Evel Knievel stunt."

"I thought Maszursky ordered you to stay there."

What could I say to that? "I'm sorry, it was an emergency."

"You know, Renzler, I don't think you have much respect for the law."

That wasn't the first time I had been told that by a cop. "Did you talk to Tommy Stevens?" I asked, trying to change the subject.

"Of course I talked to him! I talked to all of them. I was up half the night, for Chrissakes. The only one I didn't get a chance to question was Serendipity McCall. She left before it even happened."

"Do you have any prime suspects?"

"Are you kidding? Everybody in the contest is a suspect, except for Al Phillips. And I think this disproves your theory that Mr. Lunaviva was involved. I hear you were giving him trouble last night."

"I beg your pardon. *He* was giving *me* trouble."

"That's not the way I heard it. Now I want you to get your butt down here and give us a statement in half an hour. You got that? No excuses."

"Okay, I'll be right down."

"And by the way, Renzler. I finally got the report from the state of Nebraska on that white Mustang."

"Missouri," I said.

"Same difference. It was registered to a lady by the name of Michelle Wyatt. Does that ring any bells for you?"

It sure did. She was the sister of a lovely young woman named Melanie Wyatt, whom I had met at Longshot Sam's funeral ceremony the day before. But I wasn't about to tell that to McReynolds.

"No, not a one," I said. If I hadn't gotten so much practice lying to nuns at an early age, I probably wouldn't have been able to pull that one off.

"It could be a married name or a maiden name. We're running a check with the state of New Jersey. We should have something by this afternoon. You wouldn't happen to know Michelle Natoli's maiden name, would you?"

"I think it's Johnson," I lied.

Herbie came through the kitchen as I put down the phone. "Hi, Uncle Mark. I see you got a shiner just like me."

"And I've got a hangover just like you, too," I said as I dialed the number to Michelle Natoli's house.

I let the phone ring ten times before hanging up. Then I told Herbie to hurry up and get dressed. My visit to the police station would have to wait awhile.

Al Phillips was coming out of the Winners Circle when we got to the clubhouse. "What a mess," he said, shaking his head. "We just had an emergency meeting. There was talk that Bonnardo was thinking about suspending the contest, but it turns out he's gung ho to go on with the thing. Then we had another vote on whether to cancel for today in honor of the Geek. It was Serendipity's idea."

"She's a thoughtful girl," Nate said.

Al rolled his eyes. "The vote was six to nothing."

"I thought Serendipity was for it," Nate said.

"No. It turns out she just thought it would be a nice idea to take a vote on it."

Just then the new love of Nate's life came out the door. I thought he recoiled slightly when she waved. I'm sure she looked less attractive in the cold light of day and without a gallon of booze coursing through his veins. But he did the gallant thing, marching right over to meet her.

I suggested to Herbie that he go for a hot dog.

"I don't think I'm ready to eat anything yet, Uncle Mark."

"Well, why don't you take a stroll anyway. I need to talk to Al alone for a minute."

"So, what's up?" Al said as we watched Herbie shuffle away.

"Where's Michelle?" I asked.

"She drove her sister and the nerd to the airport. Why do you ask?"

"Because I want to talk to her."

"She should be back home in an hour or so. You look like something's bothering you."

"Yeah, something is bothering me, Al." I didn't try to hide my irritation.

"Oh, Jesus." Al sighed. "Well, do you want to talk about it?"

I did, but Dave Gwynn was approaching us. "Yeah, Al," I said. "I want to talk to both of you—right after the races are over today."

"Sure, Renzler, whatever you say." Al turned on his heels and walked away.

Gwynn extended his hand as he reached me. "I heard you had quite a ride last night. You're lucky you weren't killed."

I nodded. I wasn't feeling too lucky.

"Just between you and me, I think we should suspend this whole contest until we figure out what the hell's going on. But I'm afraid Mr. Bonnardo doesn't see it that way."

I told Gwynn I agreed with him.

"Well," he said, "would you like to go listen to that tape?"

"That sounds like a fine idea."

I followed the racing secretary through the NO ADMITTANCE door. Instead of going to the announcer's booth, we entered a room next to it and to the right that overlooked the track.

"This is Mr. Bonnardo's office," Gwynn explained. "We keep all the tapes over here."

I watched as Gwynn tilted his head to read the dates on a long row of cassette tapes stacked on end in a cabinet along the wall. His fingers stopped, then continued, then stopped again. "That's funny," he said at last. "It's not here."

"Are you sure?"

Gwynn nodded. "I remember putting it right there."

"What are you looking for?" asked a voice behind us.

I turned to see Biff Bonnardo. He didn't look too pleased to see me. The feeling was mutual.

"I was trying to find the tape of Monday's races for Mr. Renzler," Gwynn said. "He thinks it might be important for his investigation. But it's not here."

"Well, I sure the hell don't have it," Bonnardo said.

I refrained from pointing out that nobody had said he did. That took considerable restraint on my part.

"Besides," Bonnardo said to Gwynn, "what's he doing in here in the first place?"

Gwynn looked a little baffled. "I thought you said we should help him."

"Well, I changed my mind—now that I found out he's been harassing Tony Lunaviva."

I didn't see any gain in going back over the same ground we had covered the night before—especially with Gwynn there.

The track announcer looked at me with eyebrows raised. I spoke to him, but looked at Bonnardo. "That's okay, Dave," I said, "I'm getting another copy from a TV station. I'll be able to listen to the tape—with or without his help."

Bonnardo glared at me. "Fine. Now why don't you get out of my office and quit bothering my staff."

On my way out the door, I turned and glared. "Thanks so very much for your cooperation, *Biff*," I said.

29

Nate and I were waiting outside Michelle Natoli's house when she pulled into her driveway in a black Mercedes. Apparently, Sam Natoli had assembled quite a car collection of his own.

It was ten minutes past noon and five minutes after White House press secretary Ron Ziegler's announcement that Nixon would address the nation live on TV at nine o'clock that evening. If Sulky Sol was still in town, I'd be collecting on the pool. That wasn't much consolation for the mood I was in.

"It's expected that the President could be announcing his resignation," the newscaster said.

"That's it, go way out on a limb, buddy," Nate told him. "Regardless of what all we have to do tonight, I intend to be parked in front of the tube when it happens," he said to me.

"That makes two of us."

Michelle Natoli looked pleasantly surprised to see us. "What are you guys doing here?" she asked, smiling.

"We wanted to talk to you," I said.

"Sure, why don't you come inside. Do you want some lunch?"

I was about to say that wouldn't be necessary, but Nate told her he wouldn't mind. As Michelle unlocked the door, she said, "I can't believe what happened last night. It sounded terrible. Al told me all about it this morning. He didn't get home until two A.M."

"I'm sorry about your car," I said.

"Who cares about the car? I'm just glad you and Al are all

right. I can't believe somebody tried to kill him. I don't understand what's going on. Everything's so crazy."

Nate and I exchanged looks. This wasn't going to be easy.

"I thought maybe you could help us with that," I said.

Michelle looked puzzled. She looked beautiful when she was puzzled. "What do you mean?"

"I mean we have a few questions to ask you."

"Okay," she said, smiling anxiously. "Go ahead."

"I don't know exactly where to start."

She let out a nervous chuckle. "Is something wrong?"

"Why don't you start with the car," Nate suggested.

That seemed like a good idea. Jump right in.

"What car?" Michelle asked.

"Your car," I said.

"My car? You mean the Fiat?"

"No. I mean the white Mustang that Danny Moreno drove away from the track in on Monday afternoon. The one Danny's killer drove to the Hi-Way Motel Tuesday night. The one that was found torched behind a Holey Toledo on Route 46 a little while after Danny was killed."

Michelle looked at me incredulously. "I don't know what you're talking about, Mark."

"Don't you own a white Mustang?"

"I did. But it can't possibly be the same car."

"I'm afraid it is, Michelle."

"But it can't be!"

"Why not? Do you know where it is?"

She nodded. "Bernie's got it."

"You mean Bernie Rich?"

"That's right. Sam gave it to him a couple of months ago. We never drove it. We had the Fiat and the Mercedes, so Sam asked if it was all right if he gave it to Bernie. His car broke down, and I guess he was a little short of money. I said sure."

"And you never switched the registration from Missouri to New Jersey?"

Michelle shook her head. "We were going to, when the insurance was up and all, but then Sam gave the car to Bernie."

"I think maybe we should talk to Bernie," Nate said.

That sounded like a smart idea. I got on the horn while Michelle began heating up leftover lasagna.

"Hello, Renzler, what can I do for you?" Bernie asked cheerfully when he got on the line.

There was no cheer in my voice. "What happened to the car, Bernie?"

"What car?"

"The white Mustang with Missouri plates that Sam gave you."

"Oh, that car." Suddenly Bernie didn't sound so cheery. "Jeez, I was afraid that might come up. I guess I should have said something about it earlier."

"You haven't said anything about it yet, Bernie. What happened to the car?"

"Well, it's a long story."

"Give me the short version, Bernie."

"I sold it."

"To who?"

"Whom," Nate corrected as he handed me a beer.

"To Tony Lunaviva. He collects Mustangs."

"When?"

"About a month ago, I guess. Actually, I sold it to his wife, Daphne. She was planning on giving it to him as a gift."

"You sold a car that you didn't own?"

"Well, I knew Sam wouldn't mind. I was planning on telling him, but . . . well, you know."

No, I sure as hell didn't. "What about the title?"

"Sam was supposed to look for it. He couldn't find it when he gave me the car. It's no big deal. You can always write away for another one."

"That's just swell, Bernie. You sold her the car without changing the title."

"Well, it's not like she was going to drive it. She was planning on getting it fixed up before she gave it to him. I was going to talk to Sam about it, but then—"

I hung up before Bernie could finish his sentence. "He sold it to Lunaviva," I said.

"Why, that little rat," Michelle said. "I could kill him."

"That explains a lot of things," Nate said.

I nodded, but I thought Michelle still had some explaining to do. Now was as good a time as any.

"I don't know how to put this, Michelle, but you and Al were the only people besides us who knew where Danny Moreno was the other night."

A wave of disbelief spread over Michelle's face. She looked unbelievably beautiful. "You don't think *we* killed him, do you? You must be joking!"

I shook my head. "I don't know what to think. I just know that you were late getting to the airport to pick up your sister. And I know—"

"I don't believe it! Did she tell you *why* we were late?"

I shook my head.

"We were there on time. But Cove, Mr. Efficiency himself, gave us the wrong airline. We were in the wrong damn terminal!"

If Michelle was putting on an act, she was a very good actress. I could tell that even my skeptical partner was impressed with her performance.

"Do you have any *more* questions?" she asked.

Nate did the dirty work for me. And he looked sheepish doing it. "Uh, we heard you visited Al in Chicago a few months ago. You went to a rifle range and—"

"And Sam was out there with me! He had to take care of some business, so I went to lunch with Al." The tears began to roll down Michelle's cheeks. Given the chill in her expression, I expected them to freeze like icicles. "You think *I* shot Sam!"

"No we don't, Michelle." I reached out to take her hand, but she wouldn't let me have it. I can't say that I blamed her.

"You guys are amazing. I loved Sam! Al was his best friend. How could you possibly think that . . ."

"We didn't think it," I lied. "We just needed to hear it from you. You have to understand: Somebody did a very good job of making it look like you did it."

"Somebody like Tony Lunaviva, maybe," Nate added.

Maybe, but I had a feeling somebody might be trying to frame the donut king, too. If Lunaviva killed Sam, I didn't think he'd be dumb enough to use one of his own cars for the getaway. And he wouldn't have torched it at his own donut stand.

"I don't care," Michelle said. "Just the idea that you would even suspect it!"

We watched in silence for a few moments while Michelle

busied herself setting the table. That seemed to indicate she was calming down.

"Somebody used *your* car, Michelle," I said. "The lady who drove away from both murder scenes fits your description."

"But I didn't do it!"

"No, but the police are going to think you did once they track down the license. I think it's a good idea to get you out of here for a day or so."

Michelle shook her head. "I'm not going anywhere. I'm staying right here in my own house." She sounded like she meant it.

"Then you're going to jail," I said. "And I don't think Bernie Rich will be able to get you out."

That seemed like a strong challenge to her stubbornness. She appeared to be thinking it over as she took the lasagna out of the oven.

"Well, what about you?" she asked. "I thought you were supposed to be helping."

"And we will. But we can only help if you do what we say."

"Okay," she said at last. "What do you want me to do ?"

"You can stay at my apartment," I said. "It'll only be for a day or two."

"But it will seem like an eternity," Nate added. I shot him a glance worthy of Charles Manson. "Unless of course you like cats."

"I hate them," she said. But she was smiling again.

I was feeling better myself. "In that case, it will seem like two eternities."

Michelle wanted to stop by the track and let Al know what was going on, but I thought that might be pressing her luck. I promised to talk to him as soon as we got back from New York.

I didn't know how soon McReynolds would learn the identity of the car owner, but once he figured it out, I was sure he'd put a watch on Michelle's house. We took two cars, leaving the Pinto in a lot outside a run-down building two blocks away that Michelle said was the community center.

While we were making the switch, I noticed a black van that had pulled out behind us when we left Michelle's house stopped across the street. I didn't get a good look at the driver, and I wasn't even sure he was following us. But I didn't take any chances. I gunned the engine on the Mercedes as soon as we hit a straight stretch of road near a golf course, then Michelle guided us to the highway through a development called Tall Oaks that seemed noteworthy for its lack of trees.

The traffic gods were on our side, and it only took an hour to get back to West Seventy-second Street. It seemed like years since I had been home, but we didn't linger for long. Just long enough for Michelle to get acquainted with the cat and for me to get reacquainted with my gun. I had a feeling I was going to need it.

I apologized for the deplorable living conditions, and Michelle answered with an apology of her own. "I'm sorry I got so upset with you guys before," she said.

"We're the ones that should be sorry," Nate replied.

We picked up a six-pack for the journey back to Jersey and finished it off by the time we picked up the Pinto and got back to Garden State Downs. On our way in, I noticed a black van parked in a space reserved for racetrack employees. It was locked, and I wasn't about to break it just to check the registration. I had a pretty good idea whose it was, anyway.

We peered in the window and saw a *Playboy* rabbit logo hanging from the rearview mirror and two eight-track tapes on the dashboard next to a CB radio.

"Black Sabbath and Alice Cooper," Nate said. "Judging by the bad taste, my guess is it belongs to Matt Caldwell."

"Yeah, mine too." I didn't know the bands, but the leopard-skin seat covers were enough evidence for me.

"I wonder who told him to tail us," Nate said.

I had an idea about that as well. "I'd be willing to bet even money it was Biff Bonnardo."

We didn't see the track owner or security director inside, and we didn't make a point of looking for them. We got to the clubhouse with three minutes to post in the ninth race. I filled Al in on what had happened, and we got out of there before the race was over. As soon as McReynolds matched Michelle with the car, I figured he'd go looking for Al, too.

"I owe you an apology," I told him as he got into the Mercedes and prepared to head into the city to see Michelle.

"Don't worry about it," he said, sneering. "It's just horseshit on the backstretch now."

"What's that supposed to mean?" Nate asked as we watched Al drive away.

"I think it's track lingo for 'water under the bridge.'"

"Renzler, if you know that, I think you've been hanging around the racetrack too long."

I had a feeling he was right.

30

"Uncle Mark, remember I've got choir practice from seven to eight-thirty."

"I remember, Herb." Actually, I had managed to forget it. "How about we head over to the Hofbrau for an early dinner?"

That was fine with him, but Nate wanted to head home to HoJo's to watch Nixon resignation updates. We made plans to meet in the lounge shortly before the golden moment of nine o'clock.

After Herbie's encounter with Chartreuse the night before, there was no call for surreptitious beer procurement in the bar. He had sworn off the sauce—at least on nights when he had choir practice.

It turned out Herbie shared his father's compulsiveness about being on time and I wanted to hit the house to see if Carol Robertson had sent the tape, so we downed our dinner in half an hour. When Lucille delivered our check, she said, "I thought you'd be interested to know that your friend Matt Caldwell is out in the lot. I was looking out the window and I noticed him waiting in that black van of his."

I pulled back the curtain and peered out the window to see Mr. Garden State Downs rocking back and forth behind the steering wheel. I figured he was listening to one of his tapes. "Thanks a lot, Lucille," I said. I let her know just how interested I was by leaving an extra five on the table.

I thought about confronting Caldwell right away, but I decided to spare my nephew any unpleasantness that might result. I'd have my chance to chat with the security guard after choir practice was underway.

Caldwell stayed a few blocks behind us all the way to Herbie's house. Carol Robertson, bless her sweet heart, had come through with the tape, but it wasn't any help without something to play it on. My sister and brother-in-law had every modern convenience you could imagine, right down to an electric toothbrush. But when it came to stereo gear, they were still stranded in the hi-fi age.

I waited to make sure Caldwell continued tailing us before straying too far from the house. If he had any notions about ransacking the place, I'd have to change my timetable for confronting him.

"I don't understand why he's following us around in the first place," Herbie said. He sounded a little nervous.

"Somebody told him to."

"But who?"

"My guess is Biff Bonnardo, the owner of the racetrack."

"Is he the one that killed Longshot Sam?"

"I'm not sure. He could be. One thing I am sure of—there were several people involved."

"So it was a conspiracy."

"Exactly."

"Have you figured out who all was in on it?"

"Not yet. But I should have a pretty good idea once I listen to the tape." I didn't bother to add that I might get some even better ideas out of Matt Caldwell.

"I don't understand what's so important about the tape."

I wasn't sure myself. At first Nate's comment about the gunshot had merely aroused my curiosity. Now that the track copy was missing, there was more than curiosity at stake. Judging from Bonnardo's reaction, I seemed to have stumbled onto something important.

"I think somebody may have erased part of it," I said.

"You mean like President Nixon did with the Watergate tapes."

"Yeah, Herb, something like that." I chuckled. That hadn't occurred to me until he mentioned it.

When we reached the entrance to the Neumann Prep minor seminary on Black Oak Ridge Road, I noted appreciatively that the good fathers who built the school had been thoughtful enough to locate it across the street from a tavern. It could have been a strategy to keep the kids ever mindful of the near occasions of sin, but I suspected it had more to do with the price of land in the area.

The driveway leading to the school also led to a new housing development up the hill beyond it. Caldwell must have thought we were going back there, because he turned in a few hundred yards behind us. I surprised him by taking a sharp right into the parking lot at the last moment. He ducked down low as he continued past the school and up the hill. Only a guy as dumb as Caldwell could have thought somebody else would be too dumb to notice him.

"Okay, Herb, I'll meet you right back here at eight-thirty."

"Are you going to go buy a tape recorder? You could get one at that shopping center we passed over by the traffic circle."

That wasn't a bad idea, but I had a better one. "No, I'll be down across the street at the Wayside Inn. And I think I'll have a little chat with our friend Matt."

Herbie nodded. "Be careful, Uncle Mark."

"Don't worry, Herb. I think I can handle him."

He grinned. "I didn't mean that. I mean not to drink any Chartreuse."

"I learned that lesson a long time ago, Herb."

As I pulled into the small gravel parking area outside the tavern, I decided Herbie's notion made more sense. There wouldn't be time to buy a tape recorder after I picked him up, and the stores might be closed when Nixon's speech was over. Besides, I enjoyed teaching Matt Caldwell how to tail someone.

I noticed an improvement in his skills as he followed me to the shopping center. Inside the store, a helpful kid wearing a Holey Toledo button insisted on demonstrating several models. My plan was to play the tape right there, but it occurred to me that Herbie might be able to use a tape recorder for his music. Call me Mr. Thoughtful. But I still managed to disappoint the sales kid by opting for the bottom-of-the-line model.

I spotted Caldwell's van parked two rows away when I got into my car. I made a point of driving right by it to make sure he didn't miss me. He didn't.

I stayed in the car a few minutes and played the tape before going into the tavern. That probably confused Caldwell, but it clarified some things for me.

Nate had been right. There wasn't any gunshot on the recording. I couldn't hear any glitch to indicate it had been erased. That either meant somebody had done a good job of splicing, or the gunshot hadn't been recorded in the first place. It also meant someone was lying. As I entered the saloon, I was pretty sure I knew who.

I ordered a beer and mulled some things over. It was the first chance I'd had to relax by myself for a few days, and it helped clear out my head. Something Nate had said that morning suddenly struck me as curious. As I sat there drinking, I guess you could say I had an epiphany of sorts. After a talk with Matt Caldwell, I thought I might have everything figured out.

I wandered over to the window and looked outside. Caldwell, the crafty devil, was parked in the lower level of the school parking lot. His tailing skills were improving, but he still had some lessons to learn.

I smoked a cigarette and drank another beer before exiting the bar by the rear door. There was an embankment in back that led down to one of the last farms in North Jersey. I marveled at the sight while strolling parallel to the road a few yards down the hill. I walked about a quarter of a mile before crossing the road and cutting back up through a wooded area to the school. As I came down the far side of the building, I could hear the choir singing Handel's *Messiah*. Evidently, they were getting an early start on Christmas.

Matt Caldwell was in the driver's seat when I approached the van, rocking from side to side as he played drums on the steering wheel and sang along with a rock song that sounded like a tribute to Sodom and Gomorrah.

"Hello, Brother Matthew," I said, walking right up to the door. "Thinking about studying for the priesthood?"

If Caldwell was amused by the remark, he didn't show it. I figured he just hadn't heard it. I didn't bother repeating.

"What the fuck?" Caldwell opened the door quickly, but not quickly enough to hit me. I took a step back, waited for him to start getting out, then crushed the door on his leg. He grunted in pain, and I released the pressure just long enough for him to push it open again. Then I closed it.

"I could have a lot of fun doing this," I said. "But I'm a little pressed for time, so why don't you get out slowly and put your hands up."

Caldwell grimaced as he wobbled out of the van. I backed up along the side of it to give him some room. I didn't think I needed the gun, but I held it on him just in case. They say you can never be too careful.

And they're right.

I turned the instant I heard the footsteps behind me, but it was still an instant too late. Matt Caldwell's brother had a smile on his face and a crowbar in his hand. I didn't know why he had stayed in the back of the van, and at that point the question was purely academic.

He used the crowbar on my hand first, knocking the gun to the ground and causing you wouldn't believe how much pain. The next shot was to my head, a glancing blow, and I managed to wheel and raise my left arm in defense. But there was no defense against the kick to my kidney that came courtesy of big brother. I slumped over from that, so the younger one's next effort with the tire iron landed across my back. Matt Caldwell spun me around for good measure and gave me two solid shots to the ribs, one for each of his hands.

"Get the handcuffs, Mike," he ordered.

That sounded like a good idea under the circumstances. Any alternative to the tire iron was fine with me. Not that they asked for my opinion.

Any thought I had of slipping away slipped right away as soon as I felt Matt Caldwell's hands pull mine back behind me. The guy was one strong son of a bitch.

"I nailed the jerk-off," Mike said jubilantly as he opened the rear door of the van.

"You sure did, buddy," his role model replied as he pushed me face down onto the sporty gold shag carpeting inside. They paused long enough to slap hands and grunt at each other before closing the door behind me.

One glance was all it took to explain why Mike Caldwell had stayed in the back of the van. His brother had put a lot of imagination and effort into decorating it. And it was clear that he wasn't one of those pussies who read *Playboy* and *Penthouse*. The walls of *his* van were lined with *Gallery*'s "girl next door."

If you've never seen any of these, take my word for it—if one of those girls moved in next door to you, you'd move out the next day. I figured young Caldwell spent a lot of his time slamming the ham. The only thing I couldn't figure out was how he could concentrate with the music blaring. It poured out of four speakers, a sure sign that Matt Caldwell had quad.

"Man, that was fantastic, man," Mike said as his brother lowered the volume. "Is that what it was like over in Nam?"

"Uh-uh. Nam was much better. Over there you got to kill gooks."

"Are we gonna kill *him?*"

"We don't have no choice."

I didn't think it was worth wasting my energy to present other choices at that point. My only hope was that Caldwell took his marching orders from a more reasonable authority. That seemed like a pretty safe bet.

Matt grabbed the microphone to his CB radio as he pulled onto the road. "Breaker-one-niner, this is Big Dick," he said. "We kicked us some butt up on Black Oak Ridge Road and we're haulin' it back home. Do you read me, Peckerhead?"

I didn't think there was any response from Peckerhead, but it was hard to tell amidst the garbled chorus of Jersey accents talking in phony Southern drawls about double-nickels and Smokey the Bear.

"Do you think he heard you?" Mike asked hopefully.

"Nah. Probably not. He never uses his radio. I'm the one that had to think up a handle for him in the first place." And what a handle it was.

Caldwell cranked the music back up and we drove for ten minutes down the highway before pulling off onto a side road. A minute or so later he stopped the van.

"Okay, out, asshole," he said as he opened the back door.

I slid along the floor and lowered myself to the ground. As soon as my feet touched, Matt Caldwell planted one of his on the back of my knee. I crumpled and fell forward, but I managed to keep my chin up when I hit the ledge, earning myself big savings in dental fees. Caldwell grabbed my arms and pulled me back up, then gave me a shove toward the ugly green shack he called home.

I didn't know where we were, but it wasn't a neighborhood

I'd want to visit. There were eight small houses on a dead-end gravel street, each one more ramshackle than the next. According to a signpost, it was called Manhattan Avenue. *Brooklyn* would have been stretching the imagination far enough.

Caldwell kicked open a broken screen door with peeling paint and pushed me into what passed for the living room. It was clear that he reserved the lion's share of his decorating budget for the van. The furnishings consisted of a card table, two folding chairs, a color TV, and an aluminum bookshelf that served a more practical purpose than storing the great works of Western civilization. On it were about six quarts of motor oil, some coffee cans containing nuts and bolts, two bottles of rotgut booze, and a collection of eight-track tapes. But the thing that interested me was an almost empty bottle of Chanel Number 5. I thought it was curious that Caldwell used the same scent as Longshot Sam's wives.

"Nice place you've got here," I said.

Bad idea. For that I got another kick in the pants and a smack across the chops. But some good did come out of it. When I fell down, I ended up with the best seat in the house—a red beanbag chair badly in need of reupholstering.

Matt Caldwell went into the next room, which I assumed was the kitchen. I never got the full tour of the house. I heard him talking on the phone, and I could tell from his defensive tone that somebody was giving him a hard time. But I couldn't hear what he was saying; his brother had the TV set on at high volume and was madly flipping the channels in search of an alternative to news previews of Nixon's impending resignation.

"What's all this crap?" he muttered.

I considered the possibility of trying to enlighten him, but decided there wasn't enough time. Matt Caldwell returned with a can of Rheingold in his hand.

"What'd he say?" his brother asked.

"He'll be here in a little while. We're supposed to give this jerk a drink," he said, nodding at me. "He's gonna have himself a little car accident."

"That's cool. Can I have a beer?"

"Sure. They're in the fridge."

Caldwell took a bottle off the bookshelf. It was a label I didn't recognize—Wayne Cork & Bottle, State Highway 23. I think the year on it was 1974, but part of the label was torn off, so I couldn't be sure.

"I hope you like whiskey, asshole," he said.

I nodded. "I see you serve only the best."

I think that one went over his head. He leaned mine back. "Open up, faggot. Here she comes, down the hatch."

All things considered, I think I would have preferred a few more belts with the crowbar. I got down about four shots' worth before I started to gag.

"What's the matter, you a wussy?"

I guess maybe I was. "I could use a beer chaser," I said.

Caldwell laughed. "You're a real smart aleck, aren't you?" He cocked his hand and delivered a stinging blow to the left side of my head. It dazed me, and I thought I might pass out.

No such luck. He grabbed my hair and pulled my head back, pouring down some more booze until the bottle was empty. "Now I'll show you how we finish off the bottle," he said, stepping behind me.

A moment later, I felt a shot on the back of my head. Behind me, I heard Matt Caldwell's sinister laugh. Before me, I saw Dick Nixon's somber face. The moment I'd been waiting for all summer had finally arrived, but I was about to make an early departure.

"My fellow Americans . . ." Nixon said.

That was the last thing I heard before I passed out.

31

I guess I should start by introducing myself. My name is Herbert Richard Derkovich, Jr. I live on Brookside Avenue in Pompton Plains, New Jersey. I am sixteen years old, and next year I will be a junior at Neumann Prep.

Uncle Mark asked me to write this part of the story because he was unconscious when a lot of important stuff was happening. Uncle Mark is the neatest guy I know, but he has some pretty strange ideas. Like asking me to write this. I don't know why he writes everything down. My dad says his books don't sell very well. I don't know if they are good or not, because my dad won't let me read them until I graduate from high school. But Mom said I could read one next time he goes on a business trip as long as I don't tell him about it.

I like to write things, and I hope I don't sound conceited if I say that I am very good at it. I got A's in English all during freshman and sophomore years. I think the talent comes from my mom, who is the only person I know except for Father Conroy who can explain the difference between a participle and a gerund.

Another thing strange about Uncle Mark is what a slob he is. I have never been to his apartment in New York City, but you wouldn't believe what a mess his car is. The floor and the backseat are covered with beer cans, coffee containers, and Holey Toledo bags. I even saw some ants crawling around in one of them because he didn't finish the doughnuts. By the way, that's the correct way to spell it, but most people do it wrong.

If you think Uncle Mark is strange, you wouldn't believe how weird his friend Nate is. I used to call him Uncle Nate, but now I know better. He always asks me about sex and why I want to be a priest and stuff like that. I think his problem is that he isn't married. I don't think he even has a girlfriend. Uncle Mark has been married a lot. It seems like every time I see him, he has a new wife.

I hope it doesn't sound like I dislike Nate, because he is a nice man who means well and can be very funny sometimes. He is also very smart and is probably the strongest guy I ever saw except for Father Conroy. Uncle Mark is smart too, but he doesn't sound like it because he always says "um" and "you know" when he talks.

Anyway, I guess I should tell you what happened. I was in choir practice, in my usual spot in the back row, because that's where the baritones are supposed to stand. Father O'Brien was busy giving instructions to the tenors because they always need extra help, so I was looking out the window when I saw Uncle Mark walking up to the black van in the parking lot.

It was really exciting when Uncle Mark started bashing Matt Caldwell with the car door, but then I saw his ugly brother who I can't stand, Mike Caldwell, sneak up behind Uncle Mark and hit him with a crowbar. I hate to miss choir practice, especially now because we are getting ready for Midnight Mass on Christmas, but I yelled out, "They're beating up Uncle Mark!" and I ran out of the room right away to go help him. I heard Father O'Brien yelling at me, but I didn't have time to explain.

By the time I got outside, they were putting Uncle Mark into the van. I ran down the parking lot after them and said a Hail Mary while doing so, but by the time I got to where they were, they were already pulling out onto Black Oak Ridge Road. I was afraid Uncle Mark might be dead and I got really upset and was almost starting to cry, but I said another Hail Mary and an Our Father and said some ejaculations while running to Uncle Mark's car. I think I might have been bawling by then, but probably not, because I was mostly mad at Matt Caldwell and his ugly brother and I was so mad I wanted to kill the both of them.

Uncle Mark's keys were right on the floor where he always leaves them. I don't understand why he does that, but I was sure glad they were there. I don't know how to drive yet and I won't even get my learner's permit for another year, but I always watch my dad when he drives and sometimes my mom lets me park the car in the garage for her and I back it up and down the driveway when my dad's away on business trips. There are so many idiots on the road these days anyway that you know it can't be too hard.

I almost backed into another car when I started to back up onto Black Oak Ridge Road, but once I got going it wasn't too hard. But I had to go real fast to catch up with Matt Caldwell's black van. I was lucky that the lady who almost hit me turned off at the corner of Jacksonville Road or I never would have been able to catch up with them, because she was going really slow. I had to exceed the speed limit to do so.

The only scary part about it was when I came to the traffic circle at Route 23 and Ratzer Road, which is very dangerous. You have to merge and the cars really come whipping along there. My mom hates it so much that she always takes the long way on Newark-Pompton Turnpike instead of going around the circle. But it wasn't really that bad when I did it. The only problem was that Uncle Mark's turn signals don't work and I was afraid the police might stop me because there was a cop waiting there. But he was probably on his way to Holey Toledo. My dad says that's all cops ever do, drink coffee and eat doughnuts.

The van kept going down Route 23 until they turned off at the bottom of the hill after you pass the Getty station. I was following right behind them, but when they turned left on Ryerson Avenue and went over the railroad tracks, I slowed down because I thought they might be stopping at one of the houses back there. It is a real bad section where poor people live back near the Pompton River, and it always gets flooded in the springtime. Sometimes it floods so bad that the houses get covered with water and they have to rescue the people in boats.

I stopped the car when I saw them getting out of the van, and parked it on the next street over so they wouldn't see me. After they went inside I went over and stood on the side of the house and peered into a tiny window. It was a tiny house, just like all the other houses around there, and it couldn't get much sunlight because there was only that one little window.

I could see Uncle Mark inside on a beanbag chair. He had handcuffs on and Matt Caldwell was forcing him to drink a big bottle of liquor. It wasn't Chartreuse, but I bet it was just as bad. From the way he was gagging, it probably didn't even taste good. I thought about going to find Nate or call the police, but I was afraid they would take him somewhere else while I was gone. I wanted to go right inside and beat up the both of them, but they were both pretty big and Uncle Mark would not be able to help me, being he was drunk and had handcuffs on.

Matt Caldwell was being real rough, but Uncle Mark kept making wisecracks like he always does. Some of them were pretty funny. But then Caldwell slugged him on the back of the head with the liquor bottle after Uncle Mark drank it all. I just stood there praying, because there was nothing else I could do.

In a little while a car pulled up in front of the house, and a man and lady got out of it. I didn't get a good look at them because I was afraid they'd see me, so I went and hid in the backyard. I waited until I heard them go inside and then I went back to the window.

The man and lady were standing in the corner, so I couldn't see them. The lady didn't say anything, but the man did. He was really bawling out Matt Caldwell. He yelled almost as loud as Father Rafferty, the headmaster at my school. And believe me, he can really yell.

"You idiot!" he screamed. "I told you to *follow* him, not kidnap him. Don't you understand anything?"

Matt Caldwell turned all red in the face, just like my friend Mike Murphy does when Father Rafferty yells at him. "But we didn't have any choice, Mr. B.," he said. At least I think he called him Mr. B. It was pretty hard to hear. He might have called him Mr. D.

"Okay, here's what I want you to do," the man said. When he lowered his voice, I realized he sounded just like one of the men who work at the racetrack. "This guy drives a Pinto, right? When those get hit in back, the gas tank explodes. So what you do is you put him in the car and drive him up near the Boonton Reservoir. You find an isolated spot, give him a little love tap so it looks like somebody hit him, then you torch the thing."

"You mean hit him with my van? What if it blows up?"

"Then that means you didn't do a very good job," the man said.

"But I don't want to hurt my van!" If I wasn't so worried about Uncle Mark, I would have thought it was pretty funny that Matt Caldwell was only worried about his dumb van. If the van blew up, then he would be dead too. I got the impression that the man wouldn't mind if that happened.

"Why can't we just torch his car and leave it at that?" Matt Caldwell asked.

"Because I said so! I want this to look like an accident. Now where's his car? I'll help you load him in it."

"It's parked outside a tavern up on Black Oak Ridge Road."

"What the hell is it doing there? You mean you didn't bring it?" Father Rafferty never yelled that loud.

"Don't worry. We'll go back and get it."

"What about his nephew?"

"He went inside the school across the street. He was wearing some stupid robe." When I heard that, I really wanted to sock Matt Caldwell.

"You idiot! What the hell is he going to think when he gets outside and finds the car with nobody around? Get the hell back there right now and get that car!"

As soon as I heard that, I turned and ran as fast as I could back to Uncle Mark's car. At first I got lost in all the dead-end streets back there near the river, but after a minute or so I found Ryerson Avenue again. I had to hurry to Howard Johnson's and find Nate, but it looked like we would be able to save Uncle Mark after all. I guess my prayers had been answered.

32

I thought about driving straight back to school and going to find Father Conroy up in the rectory, because he's really strong. But there was a chance he wouldn't be there. Howard Johnson's was right on the way, and I knew Nate would be waiting for Uncle Mark, so I stopped there first.

It was real dark in the bar, but I didn't have any trouble finding Nate. He had that lady Serendipity with him, the one they call the Daily Double on account of her big bosom. She was sitting right on his lap and he had his arm around her. In the other hand he was holding a drink. They were laughing real loud. The bar was crowded and noisy, but they were the loudest ones there.

When I first went into the bar, I also saw Mrs. Marshall, this lady who lives across the street from us. My mom says she is not a decent woman. I never knew what Mom meant before then and she would never tell me, but I understood as soon as I saw Mrs. Marshall. She was sitting next to a man I didn't know, but he sure wasn't Mr. Marshall. Not only that, but he had his hand right on Mrs. Marshall's leg.

I looked away as soon as I saw her. She looked at me, but luckily she didn't seem to recognize me. I think she was drunk.

Nate saw me and recognized me right away. "Well, well, if it isn't Father Herb," he said. He calls me that sometimes to tease me about becoming a priest. I don't like it when he does so, but Father Conroy says if people make fun of your vocation, you should ignore them. It just makes your faith stronger, which is exactly how I feel when Nate teases me.

"Hi, Herb," Serendipity said. "Do you want to dance?"

"No, thanks." I like to dance, but I didn't like dancing with her. She wears this perfume that makes you feel like you have to throw up. And I sure didn't feel like dancing right then.

"Where's your uncle?" Nate asked.

"He got kidnapped by Matt Caldwell and his ugly brother and we have to save him right away."

"What?" Nate started to get up, but when he did so, Serendipity lost her balance and fell off the barstool and landed on the floor. If things weren't so serious, it would have been pretty funny, because luckily she wasn't hurt.

I helped her to her feet while Nate got off the barstool. He looked real wobbly when he stood up, too. He even fell backward against the bar.

"You're drunk," I said. I knew I should have gone right to the school and gotten Father Conroy instead.

Nate put his arm around my shoulder. He does that a lot. I don't really like it, but I never say anything because I don't want to hurt his feelings. "How very perceptive of you, Herbie," he said. "In fact, I'm downright shitfaced." (I didn't think I was allowed to put that word on paper, but Uncle Mark said I should because that's what Nate said and you're supposed to write exactly what happened.)

I practically felt like crying. "Uncle Mark is in trouble, and you're just sitting around getting drunk. And my name is Herb, for your information." I guess I was yelling at him.

"Calm down, kid, I'll sober up," he said. "You can count on old Uncle Nate in the clutch. Just tell me what happened."

I told him the whole story while we went to the car. I started to run, but he told me to slow down. When we got to the car, I thought he was going to drive, but he said he couldn't.

"But I'm not old enough to drive," I said.

"How did you get here?"

"I didn't have any choice. There wasn't any adult around to do it."

"Just pretend there still isn't an adult around," he said. That didn't make me feel too good. I wished Father Conroy was with us. I knew that he wouldn't be drunk.

Nate kept shaking his head and slapping himself in the face while I drove along Black Oak Ridge Road.

"Why are you doing that?" I asked.

"To sober up. What I really need is some coffee."

"Uncle Mark has a thermos full of it in the backseat."

"Great. Now wish me luck trying to find it." He turned around and started picking through all the bags and wrappers and junk. Uncle Mark's car is really a mess. Nate grinned when he found the thermos, but when he unscrewed the cap he groaned and said, "Yuk!" For a moment I thought he was going to throw up.

"What's wrong? Is it cold?"

"Not just cold. *Old.* You'd have to use carbon dating to estimate the age of this stuff."

I didn't know what he was talking about. That happens a lot with Nate. "If you really have to have some, we could stop and get some to go," I said. "But I think we should hurry up before they get there."

"No need to stop now, Herb," he said. "One whiff of that stuff did the trick." He grinned at me. He was trying to make me feel better, but I could tell he was still drunk.

Nate reached into his shirt pocket and took out a pill and put it in his mouth. I asked him what it was.

"Aspirin," he said.

"I never saw an aspirin that looked like that before."

"It's a special kind of aspirin called Dexedrine. It works just like aspirin, only better. Do you want one?"

"No, thanks. I don't have a headache."

My hands were shaking when I turned into the parking lot outside the Wayside. I was feeling real scared and Nate must have noticed.

"Don't worry, Herb," he said. "I've gotten your uncle out of tighter jams than this before. This one's a piece of cake. But I'm going to need your help. Do you think you can handle Caldwell's little brother?"

"Sure, no problem." At least I hoped I could. Mike Caldwell looked like he was pretty strong. But the thing that worried me about him was that he was mean, too.

"Then we've got nothing to worry about." Nate opened the trunk of the car and took out a tire iron and a flashlight. "You take this," he said, handing me the tire iron.

"Am I supposed to hit him with it?"

"He hit your uncle with one, didn't he?"

"Yeah, but—"

"Have you ever been in a fight before, Herb?"

"Not really. I sort of got into one with a kid from the DePaul football team at a CYO dance. He was picking on a friend of mine."

"What happened?"

"He swung at me, and I got him in a headlock, but then Father Conroy broke it up."

"No, no, no." Nate shook his head. His breath was really smelly from all the liquor. "No headlocks, Herb. This isn't the CYO dance and Father Conroy isn't here. This is the real thing. You use your feet and you use your elbows. You go for the throat and you go for the nuts. Do you understand?"

I did, and all of a sudden I got a real sick feeling in my stomach.

Nate put his arm around me and walked me to the side of the building. "We'll stay right here until they get out of the van," he said. "Then when I give the word, we sneak up on them. I want you to take the punk, but the first one you see, you clobber them with this." He smiled. "These cretins won't know what hit them, will they?"

I shook my head. I didn't know what cretins were. "What if they have a gun?" I asked.

Nate licked his lips. I don't think he even thought of that. "Well, we've got something better," he said. "We've got the element of surprise."

He didn't sound too sure. "Do you want me to run up to the school and get Father Conroy to help us?" I asked. "He's really strong."

"Herb, the only thing we're going to need Father Conroy for is to deliver the last rites to the Caldwells."

Nate leaned his head back against the wall and closed his eyes. "You're not going to go to sleep, are you?" I asked.

"No, I'm just catching a little rest."

I closed my eyes and started to say the Rosary. I didn't even get halfway through the Apostle's Creed when Matt Caldwell pulled up in that stupid black van of his. My mom says people that drive vans are all idiots. I think she's right.

My hands were all sweaty. I was never so scared in my whole

life, except for when I was outside the house watching Caldwell beat up Uncle Mark.

He parked the van right next to the corner where we were crouching. When Mike Caldwell got out on the side near us, he was only about ten feet away. I could see his ugly face real clearly. I gripped the tire iron and thought about how ugly his face was and how he had hit Uncle Mark. I wanted to get myself mad, because that was the only way I would be able to hit him with it.

They walked to the back of the van to open the door, and Nate scooted over to the driver's side. I crouched on the other.

"Okay, Herb, let's go," he whispered.

My heart was pounding real fast and my mouth felt dry as I ran along the side of the van. On the other side, Nate yelled, "Merry Christmas, motherfucker!"

I got to the back of the van just in time to see Nate go charging at Matt Caldwell. He swung at him real hard, but he missed by a mile and went flying right past him. As he did so, Matt Caldwell gave him a kick and knocked him off balance. Nate fell to his knees and Matt Caldwell was about to go over and kick him again, but Nate laughed and threw a handful of dirt in his face, then charged at him and tackled him.

Mike Caldwell started to run over to help his brother, but I came up on him from behind. "Over here, you imbecile," I said.

He turned and that was my chance to clobber him across the face with the tire iron. But I just couldn't do it. Instead I hit him with it on his arm. He groaned and I could tell he was hurt, but I hit him again just in case. When he grabbed his arm in pain, I dropped the tire iron and slugged him right across his ugly face. That was the first time I ever hit anybody in the face. He fell down and I was about to jump on top of him, but I looked over and saw Matt Caldwell on top of Nate.

I started to run over and help him, but Mike Caldwell stuck out his foot and tripped me. As I fell down, he grabbed me with his hand right where it hurts and wouldn't let go. He was really a dirty fighter. I swung with my elbow as hard as I could. It hit him right in the jaw and sent him flying backward.

As I got up and went to help Nate, somebody behind me yelled, "Watch out, Herb!" At first I thought it was Uncle

Mark but when I turned and looked, who did I see coming out of the bar but Father Conroy!

It was a lucky thing he yelled, because Mike Caldwell had the tire iron in his hand and he was about to swing it right at my head. I ducked down and rolled into him and he went flying over the top of me.

"You little bastard!" Father Conroy yelled as he ran over to Mike Caldwell and grabbed the tire iron out of his hand and threw it on the ground. I never heard him talk like that before.

Then he pulled Mike Caldwell up off the ground and threw him against the side of the van like he was a basketball. You wouldn't believe how strong Father Conroy is. Mike Caldwell hit his head against the van and fell down, but Father Conroy pulled him to his feet and punched him right in the stomach. He knocked the wind out of him just like he was letting the air out of a tire.

"What the hell's going on here, Herb?"

"These two guys kidnapped my Uncle Mark and they're going to kill him, Father!"

Father Conroy looked into the back of the van, where Uncle Mark was trying to slide out on his stomach. You wouldn't believe all the dirty pictures they had up on the walls in there. Then Father Conroy ran over to the spot where Nate was standing over Matt Caldwell, who was turned on his side. Before I could say anything, Father Conroy slugged Nate right on the chin, knocking him backward.

"No, Father, you hit the wrong guy!"

Father Conroy turned and looked at me, and when he did so, Matt Caldwell grabbed his ankles and tripped him. Father Conroy hit the ground real hard, and Matt Caldwell crawled on top of him. He grabbed his head and was about to start hitting it against the ground. I couldn't believe anybody would do that to a priest!

"The tire iron, Herb," Father Conroy called out.

I grabbed it with two hands and swung it over my head like a sledgehammer. I slammed it down as hard as I could and hit Matt Caldwell right in the middle of the back. He screamed in pain and rolled over.

Father Conroy's face was bleeding when he got up, then you

wouldn't believe what happened next. He kicked Matt Caldwell right where it hurts!

Uncle Mark looked real wobbly when he got out of the van. Nate looked wobbly when he got up, too.

"This is my Uncle Mark, Father. He's the private detective from New York City. And this is his partner, Nate."

"I'm John Conroy, Herb's Latin and Greek teacher," he said. He smiled and put out his hand.

Uncle Mark couldn't shake Father Conroy's hand because he had handcuffs on, but Nate did. "Are you sure you aren't his boxing instructor?" he asked. He grinned and rubbed his chin. "That's some right hook you have, Father."

Father Conroy laughed. "I think it was a left."

Nate reached down and pulled the ring of keys off Matt Caldwell's belt. "I'll have you out of those cuffs in a jiffy, Renz," he said.

"How was Nixon's speech?" Uncle Mark asked Nate. "I missed the whole damn thing." He seemed more upset about missing the speech than he did about getting beat up.

"You missed a classic performance," Nate said. "One that I'll always treasure."

"Are you okay, Uncle Mark?" I asked. "He made you drink a whole bottle of liquor and then he hit you with the bottle."

"Remember how you felt last night, Herb? I feel exactly like that, only a hundred times worse."

"Wow, that's pretty bad."

"We should get you to a hospital," Father Conroy said. "It looks like they worked you over pretty good."

"No, that's okay. Nothing that a dozen Alka-Seltzers, a bottle of Pepto-Bismol, and a gallon of coffee won't fix."

"What about you, Father?" Nate said. "Are you all right?"

"Just a scrape," he said. "The bastard tried to grind my face into the ground. I got the wind knocked out of me when he tripped me." Father Conroy looked at me just like he does when he wants you to conjugate a verb. "Don't tell anyone you heard me talk like that, Herb."

"No, Father, I won't."

"Well, I guess I should go inside and call the police," Father Conroy said. "I can't believe they're not here yet."

Uncle Mark shook his head. "If it's all the same to you,

Father, I'd just as soon leave the cops out of it for now. We've got some questions to ask these two first. They're involved in a murder case."

"Well, to be honest about it, I'd prefer not to get involved myself. I can see the newspaper headline already: LOCAL PRIEST IN TAVERN BRAWL. I don't think Father Rafferty would be too pleased about that, do you, Herb?"

"No, Father, I don't." I didn't think he would be too happy if he found out that Father Conroy was in the Wayside Tavern in the first place. But I wasn't about to say anything.

"And, Herb, I wouldn't be too pleased if word of this got out around school. Let's just keep it between you and me, okay?"

"Yes, Father."

"And don't forget the Man upstairs," Nate said.

Until then, I wasn't sure if he believed in God. I was sure glad to find out that he did.

33

I'd like to thank my nephew for taking over the narration while I was out of circulation. He writes pretty well for a kid who's only sixteen. Much better than I did when I was his age, as a matter of fact.

With too many cars and too few sober drivers on hand to operate them, Father Conroy volunteered to take the Pinto across the street to the school. Nate and Herbie tied up the Caldwell brothers and gagged them with Matt's custom wallpaper before dumping them in the back of the van. Herbie was nervous about driving the big rig, so Nate did the honors. He said he wanted to drive, but I had a feeling he liked stripping the gears on Matt Caldwell's pride and joy. Given my delicate condition, I can't say I enjoyed it any more than Caldwell did.

It was eleven o'clock when we got back to my sister's house. I opted for the cathartic properties of Alka-Seltzer over the protective coating action of Pepto-Bismol. Despite the intense short-term unpleasantness, by the time I stepped out of a hot shower I felt almost like a human being again, albeit a weak one.

I had a pair of lumps that made my head look like it was growing hockey pucks and a few new bruises on my face to go with my shiner. My ribs were sore, and my hand still throbbed from crossing paths with Caldwell's crowbar. I thought a bone might be fractured, but I was able to hold a coffee mug, so it couldn't have been an important one. A little medical attention was probably in order, but in the meantime I had the best medicine in the world working for me—the emotional lift that

211

comes with feeling lucky just to be alive. It seemed like I'd been getting far too much of that treatment lately.

Good sense dictated that we get a good night's rest, but I was getting a surge of energy from the caffeine and the knowledge that we were getting closer to figuring out who killed Longshot Sam. Not to mention that Nate had slipped me a hit of speed when my nephew wasn't looking.

"Are you sure Caldwell called the guy Mr. *B?*" I asked Herbie after he finished reporting on the meeting he had overheard.

"I think so, Uncle Mark. But I'm not positive. It was hard to hear all of what they were saying. He might have said Mr. D. or Mr. T."

"Well, it looks to me like Biff Bonnardo is our guy," Nate said. "And if he is, that would mean sweet little Candy is our mystery girl in the white Mustang."

"That would fit," I said. "But how did she get hold of the car? Maybe Mr. *T* is in on it with him."

"Not necessarily," Nate said. "Maybe Dino stole it. After all, he worked there."

"And maybe it was never there to steal. Maybe Daphne never gave it to Tony." I shrugged. "I think Mr. Caldwell can probably explain some things for us."

Nate shook his head. "I tried a little friendly persuasion while you were in the shower. G. Gordon Liddy would be an easier nut to crack." Nate did an imitation of Matt Caldwell's Jersey accent. "When I was in Nam, I didn't talk to the Viet Cong, man. And if the Cong couldn't get me to talk, I sure ain't gonna say nothin' to a pussy like you."

Nate rolled his eyes. "We might be able to get to him by pressing his brother, but I'd feel awful sleazy working over a kid—even if the kid is a monster."

"I'll do it," Herbie said. I had a feeling that seeing his Latin teacher kick Matt Caldwell in the balls outside a tavern had given my nephew Herbie a new perspective on the practical uses of violence. Or maybe he had learned it from the nuns in grade school.

"That won't be necessary, Herb. But how would you like to go for a little ride?"

"It's pretty late, isn't it, Uncle Mark?"

"One o'clock," Nate said. "The night's still young, Herb, just like you."

"Where are we going?" Herbie asked.

"A couple of stops. The first one is Garden State Downs."

"Uh, maybe it is getting a little late," Nate said.

"I'll buy you breakfast." I've never known Nate to turn down an offer of food or drink.

"Breakfast! At this hour?"

"There's a whole other world out there after midnight, you hep-cat," Nate said.

As I expected, nighttime security at GSD was even less extensive than the stellar system employed during the day. There weren't any guards on duty. Even if there had been, we had the director of security with us.

Under the threat of corporal abuse to his younger brother, Matt Caldwell relented and told me how to get inside without setting off the alarm. He probably realized I would have been able to figure it out myself. All it required was entering through the side door by using one of his many keys.

Caldwell's van was equipped with a flashlight the size of a space capsule that had an illumination power to rival the glow of the sun. Nate stayed in the van with the brothers grim while Herbie and I used the sunbeam to light our way up the stairs to the inner sanctum of Biff Bonnardo's racing palace.

It took us half an hour to locate the tape of Monday's races, but that was because we started out looking in the wrong place. When I found it, I knew who killed Longshot Sam. And it suddenly dawned on me just who had helped him do it.

"Is it time for breakfast now?" Herbie asked when we got outside to the van.

"Not yet. It's time to find out for sure who killed Dino LaRussa."

"And just how are you planning to do that?" Nate asked.

"By paying a call on the old geezer who works at the Hi-Way Motel." I told him and Herbie about the bottle of perfume I had seen in Matt Caldwell's house.

"That's odd," Nate said. "I had him figured for a Brut kind of guy. But that might explain the Holey Toledo pin we found in Dino's motel room."

I nodded. "I wonder if it was his or his little brother's."

"I don't understand what you're talking about, Uncle Mark."

"You will when we get there."

"Knowledge comes to him who waits, grasshopper." Nate winked at Herbie. "That's a quote from a philosopher named David Carradine."

"No, it's not. It's from a TV show called 'Kung-Fu.' I saw it once. Mom thinks I'm too young to watch it because it's so violent."

I did the driving and this time we avoided the back roads. It took a little longer, but the delay had nothing to do with traffic from the mall. Even in Jersey the shopping centers have to close sometime. It was just hard to get the van up to fifty-five while driving in second gear. In addition to his other problems, Matt Caldwell was going to need some transmission work.

When we peered into the office window, I could see that the clerk was sleeping through the "Joe Franklin" show. At least I thought it was "Joe Franklin." There was a chance Tony Lunaviva's commercials also ran on another channel. We managed to rouse the old guy just as Tony popped his head through the cream donut. As we watched him walk unsteadily to the door, Nate said, "One of the benefits of working a job like this is that it doesn't stretch your wardrobe budget. That's the same outfit he was wearing on Tuesday."

"Same checkered shorts," I said. "It could be a new undershirt."

"Let's be sure to ask him."

The old guy switched on an outside light so he could get a good look at us. "We were here Tuesday night," I shouted to refresh his memory.

"Sure, I remember," he said as he unlatched the door. "What can I do you fellas for now?"

Nate pushed the door open and stepped inside. "You could start by telling us the truth," he said.

The old guy took three steps back. Judging from the look on his face, I had a feeling this was the last night of wear he'd be able to get out of the shorts. Nate can be pretty intimidating. With our matching black eyes, Herbie and I probably looked a little threatening, too.

"What do you mean?" the old guy stammered. "I told you everything I know."

I shook my head. "I don't think you did, Mister . . ."

"Evans," he said. "Charles Evans. You can call me Charlie if you want. Most folks do."

"You told the police that a woman was here right before that guy was killed the other night, Charlie."

"Yessir, I did. That's because—"

"That's because somebody paid you to tell them that," Nate said. "Isn't that right, Charlie?"

"Well, not exactly. I mean . . ." Charlie scratched his head as he looked from Nate to me and back to Nate. "How'd you fellas know that?" he said at last.

"We watch a lot of cop shows on TV," Nate said.

"Who paid you, Charlie?" I asked.

"I don't know his name, mister, I swear I don't. He was a big fella, though. Mean and scary. He come around here Monday evening and gave me twenty dollars and said if I saw that fella that got killed come in here, I was to call him right away. I didn't know he was going to *kill* him, I swear I didn't. He had another guy with him, a younger fella. I just thought they was taking that other fella for a ride in that van of theirs. I knew he was a troublemaker and I figured he must've got in some kind of trouble, but I didn't know how much. I didn't even know they killed him until you fellas come and told me about it." Charlie raised his hand as if he were taking an oath. "I swear, that's the God's honest truth."

"And why didn't you tell that to the police?"

"I was gonna, but after I went and told you the story, I didn't think it would look too good, changing it and all. And besides, that fella told me if I said anything to anyone about it, he'd come back here and kill me. And after I seen what he done to that other fella, I believed he would've, too."

Charlie pleaded a little more when he saw I didn't look convinced. "I got a cousin down in Paterson, mister, that was a witness to a murder one time. And the police told him they'd make sure he got protection if he testified. Well, that murderer got out on bond and the next thing you know, I don't got a cousin anymore. So who's gonna protect me, that's what I want to know."

I nodded, and some of the fear drained out of Charlie's face.

I turned to my nephew. "Would you mind helping Nate get our baggage out of the van?"

Herbie looked puzzled.

"He wants us to bring our guests," Nate explained.

"Was there a woman here with them the other night, Charlie?" I asked.

He shook his head. "No, sir, I made that up, just like he told me to."

"You said Dino LaRussa—that's the guy who got killed—used to come in here with a blonde. Is that true?"

"Yessir, it is. They come in here a couple times. I come up with the idea of adding that part myself, on account of the big fella told me to say it was a redhead. I thought that might throw you off a little." Charlie cracked a crafty smile. I suspected he had seen more TV cop shows than Nate. "And let me tell you, she was one of our best customers."

"You mean she used to come in here with someone else?"

Charlie nodded. "That's right. A middle-aged fella with glasses. At least I think it was the same lady."

"Did the guy wear a baseball cap?"

"Yessir, he did. Boston Red Sox, I think it was."

Charlie was wrong about that part, but I didn't bother to correct him. Just then Nate tapped on the door, using Matt Caldwell's forehead as a knocker. Herbie giggled as he followed Nate's lead with Caldwell's brother. The kid was in bad need of a new role model.

"That's the fella, all right!" Charlie said. "And that's the kid that was with him!"

Matt Caldwell snarled something thoughtful, but the gag muffled his speech.

"Sounds like he's feeling talkative all of a sudden," Nate said. "Shall I remove the restraining order?"

I shook my head. "Let him choke on his words for a while."

As we turned to leave, Charlie looked at me hopefully. "Listen, mister," he said, "do you think there might be a little something in this for me? I mean, being I told the truth and all?"

"You already got your payoff, Charlie," I said. "And it was a big one. You're lucky this guy"—I nodded toward Caldwell—"was dumb enough to let you keep living."

Charlie nodded sadly. "Do you think I'm gonna get in trouble with the cops?"

"Yeah, Charlie, I'm afraid you are. They don't like people lying to them about murders."

"Don't worry, Charlie," Nate said. "You won't be in half as much trouble as your cousin."

34

We found an all-night diner called the Pompton Queen on Route 23, just past the shopping center where I had bought my tape recorder. Herbie was delighted, though a bit confused, at the prospect of being able to order anything he wanted in the middle of the night. After lengthy deliberation, he settled on bacon and eggs, pancakes, fries, and a cheeseburger.

"Excellent restraint, young man," Nate said. He nodded toward a refrigerator case full of pies topped with meringue stacked higher than the bills back home on my desk. "I admire a guy who makes sure to leave room for dessert."

The speed had pretty much killed my appetite, so I limited my order to an English muffin. Nothing can curb Nate's hunger, so while he and Herbie were chowing down, I went to the phone booth and made a long-distance call.

It seemed like weeks since I had spoken to Track Jack Jones, though it was only a couple of days. They must have been eventful ones for him, too, because he didn't remember me at first.

"Oh sure, Renzler," he said after I refreshed his memory. "Sorry about that, bro. I got some trouble with names and faces. Especially white ones. Sometimes I just can't tell you people apart."

Track Jack let out a laugh and I chuckled along with him. "I'm sorry to be calling so late," I said, "but it's important."

"Late? For you, maybe. But I'm kind of a night owl."

"That's what I was hoping."

"So what's happening out there? Did things calm down after I left?"

"No. In fact, it got even crazier. Somebody killed Timmy the Greek."

"Somebody killed the Greek! You're shitting me, man."

"I'm afraid I'm not. And whoever did it tried to kill Al Phillips, too."

"*Un*believable. Do the cops have any idea who did it?"

"I don't know about the cops. But I've got a pretty good idea myself." That reminded me of the point I had to check with Nate. In the excitement of the evening, I had managed to forget about it. "But the reason I'm calling you is that I know who killed Longshot Sam. It was Biff Bonnardo."

"You mean the dude that owns the racetrack?"

"That's the one. And the woman who drove away in the car on Monday afternoon was his girlfriend—Sam's ex-wife, Candy. The problem is, I need your help to prove it."

"Me? Why me?"

"Because you're the only one who can identify her."

"You mean you want me to come out there?"

"That's right."

"No way." I was afraid he'd say that. I can't say that I blamed him. "No way I'm going back out there and mess with that honkey security guard."

"You don't have to worry about him. He won't be there. He's taken a little vacation." I didn't see any need to explain what really happened to Matt Caldwell.

"Sorry, bro, I don't think so. Besides, I didn't get a good look at that lady anyhow. I was high as a kite on account of smoking that trash that Serendipity gave me."

"It was her dope?"

"Why, sure. That girl's practically a walking drugstore. You surprised?"

"Not about that. I'm just surprised she didn't go out to her van with you."

"That's because I wouldn't let her. She was making a play for me, you see, so she was being real nice. But that's one girl I wouldn't mess with. Especially not after she went and slept with the Greek last year. Who knows what you'd catch? Besides, I'm not into white meat."

"And I take it you're not into coming out to New Jersey for a few hours."

"No, sir, I am not."

"There'd be some dough in it for you."

"How much dough, bro?"

"A grand. And I'd cover your travel expenses, too."

"Is that so?"

I lit a cigarette while I listened to Track Jack think over my offer. I could almost hear the dollar signs clicking in his head. Guys who make their living picking horses have a hard time turning down clams over easy.

"What if I can't identify her?" he asked. "Do I still get the scratch?"

"Of course. I'm not paying you to lie. I'm just trying to get you out here to have a look."

"Make it two grand," he said.

"Fifteen hundred."

There was a long pause while he thought about asking for seventeen-fifty. "All right, bro," he said at last. "Being I liked Sam and all. Besides, I got to collect on that Nixon pool from Sulky Sol."

"Wait a sec. I won the Nixon pool. I had nine o'clock tonight."

Jack laughed. "Tough luck, bro. He don't officially resign till noon tomorrow."

I wasn't about to argue over the phone, but you could be sure I'd put up a stink when payoff time came around. I told him I'd meet him outside the Winners Circle at 11 A.M.

"You mean tomorrow morning?" he asked.

"Don't look now, Jack, but it's actually today."

When I got back to our booth, my nephew was finishing off his second slab of pie. Judging from his expression, I had a feeling that the law of diminishing returns had taken effect about halfway through the first piece.

"You look kind of glum, Herb," I said. "Ready to go home and get some sleep?"

Nate shot me a warning glance. "Herb's feeling a little depressed."

"What's the matter? You didn't like the chow?"

Herbie shook his head. "The food was fine, Uncle Mark. I'm

just sad that Mom and Dad are coming home day after tomorrow. I won't be allowed to do any of this neat stuff anymore."

"Well, there's still plenty of excitement ahead of you," I said. I couldn't think of any examples for him, but I was certain something would come up. The way his uncle was feeling, a day of watching the grass grow would be far too eventful.

"That's right," Nate added. "Just think of how exciting things are going to be with Gerald R. Ford as President of the United States." He looked at me. "There is a downside to this Nixon resignation, you know."

I nodded. "But the biggest downside to me is that I missed the speech."

"Don't worry. I'm sure they'll rebroadcast the whole thing on PBS."

"What's PBS?"

"The Public Broadcasting System."

"Oh, that's right. I still think of it as educational TV."

There was a light on in the rectory when we stopped by Herbie's school to pick up my car. I had a feeling Father Conroy was up watching a little late-night TV. Nate followed in the Pinto while Herbie and I drove Matt Caldwell's van.

"Are you sure there isn't something else bothering you, Herb?" I asked. The kid seemed pretty glum.

"Not really. I was just thinking about Father Conroy."

Although my brain was dark, a little light went on in the back of my head. Herbie was grappling with the discovery that his hero was human. "It upset you to see him outside the tavern, didn't it?" I said.

Herbie nodded. "I'm glad he showed up and all. If it wasn't for him, I don't know what would have happened. But I didn't think priests were supposed to do that kind of stuff."

"You mean drink at bars?"

"Yeah. And talk the way he did. It was like he wasn't a priest. He was totally different from the way he usually is."

"That's because he has a life outside of school, just like you do," I said. "I should think seeing him like that might make you feel better about becoming a priest yourself."

"Why's that?"

"Because you have to make so many sacrifices going in—like

not being allowed to get married and have a family. I think it would be comforting to know that you don't have to give up all life's pleasures. Besides, the more familiar you are with the outside world, the better you'll be at understanding the problems of your parishioners."

Herbie nodded. "That makes a lot of sense, Uncle Mark. Did you ever think about becoming a priest?"

"No, I didn't, Herb."

"Not even for a minute?"

"Well, maybe for a minute."

"You didn't become a priest because you wanted to become a baseball player, right?"

"Yeah, that's right, Herb." I couldn't see any gain in telling him that I just wanted to get laid.

We drove Matt Caldwell's van to the safest place I could think of. We didn't want anybody to break in and steal his CB radio. We parked it in the lot outside the Pequannock police station.

By the time we got back to the Derkovich shack on Brookside Avenue, my nephew was snoring like a drunken cardinal after a papal coronation party. "The kid's had a long day," Nate said as he pulled him out of the backseat. Nate would be a great father if he could start out with a kid who was already thirteen.

"He's had a long *week*," I replied. "And so has his uncle, for that matter."

I passed out before my head hit the rack and slept the sleep of the dead. Four hours later, I realized that the dead have it better than we do in some ways. They don't have to bother with unpleasantries like waking up.

"Uncle Mark, do you want me to light a cigarette for you, too?" Herbie asked.

I opened my eyes to see the human alarm clock holding a cup of steaming coffee. "No, that's okay, Herb. I think I'll wait until I've had my aspirin."

"Do you want regular aspirin or the kind Uncle Nate takes?"

I didn't know what he meant, but I was touched to find out that Nate had found his way back to avuncular status. "I think regular aspirin will be just fine for now, Herb," I said.

My aching bones could have used a day in a sauna, but they had to settle for twenty minutes in a warm shower. I figured being in hot water with Tom McReynolds would provide added therapeutic benefits, and when I rang him on the horn, the police chief blew off a lot of steam while letting me know just how little esteem he had for me.

"Where the hell have you been?" he demanded. "I've been looking all over for you! You were supposed to be down here yesterday!" I was holding the phone about a foot from my ear in anticipation of his assault, but that was still a yard short of the distance required to prevent temporary hearing loss.

"Sorry," I said. "I got real busy."

"Yeah, I'll bet you were busy. I don't know how you do things in New York City, Renzler, but out here in New Jersey, we do things by the book."

I didn't see any gain in asking if that was the same book he was planning to throw at me.

"Let me guess what you were so busy on," he said. "You were aiding and abetting a fugitive in a murder investigation."

"I was? Who?" I've been told plenty of times that I'm not nearly as smart as I think I am, but I like to think that playing dumb is one of the things I do best.

"Don't play dumb with me, asshole." I guess I was wrong about that, too. "Tell me you didn't know that Michelle Wyatt and Michelle Natoli are one and the same person."

"I didn't know," I lied.

"You're lying, you two-bit shamus!" Evidently, McReynolds had watched too many old movies on TV.

I didn't challenge him on either score. With all the lumps I had on my head already, taking a few more wouldn't hurt.

"Michelle Natoli—*your* client—killed her husband. She's also wanted for the murder of Danny Moreno. And that guy Al Phillips was in on it, too. They were shacking up together down at her house in Packanack Lake. Only he took off with her. I suppose you're going to tell me you don't have any idea where they are."

"No, I'm not. I have a very good idea where they are."

That one stopped him in his tracks. "You do? Where?"

"They're at my apartment in Manhattan."

"What the hell are they doing there?"

"I don't know. I think they wanted to take in dinner and a show, but they might have gone to a Yankees game."

"*Bull*shit. Listen, Renzler, you can't possibly be as dumb as you sound."

"Thanks for the compliment. At least I'm smart enough to know that Al Phillips and Michelle Natoli didn't kill Longshot Sam."

"And I suppose you know who did."

"As a matter of fact, I do." I gave McReynolds a quick wrap-up and asked him to set up a meeting in the Winners Circle at eleven o'clock.

"That sounds a little unorthodox," he grumbled. Maybe the book they did things by in Jersey was the Koran.

"Would you expect anything else from me?"

"No, I sure the hell wouldn't. I'm just glad I only see you once every twenty-five years. Who all do you want me to invite?"

"Just round up the usual suspects," I said.

"Huh?" I guess *Casablanca* wasn't one of movies McReynolds had seen.

I gave him a list of names, and he recited each one after me as he wrote them down. I resisted the temptation of spelling them out. I knew he wouldn't like that. When he finished, I said, "By the way, we caught the guy who killed Danny Moreno."

"What do you mean you 'caught the guy'? I thought a woman did it."

"Nope. The killer intimidated Charlie Evans, the desk clerk at the motel, to lie about it."

"And just how the hell do you know that?"

"I talked to Charlie. He didn't know Danny was dead when we first questioned him. When he found out he was, he was scared he'd get in trouble for changing stories. By the way, Charlie should be at the meeting, too."

"Sure, sure. Now who the hell is it and where the hell is he?"

"It's Matt Caldwell and—"

"What? You mean the security guard?"

"That's right. And his brother helped him."

"Why the hell didn't you turn him over to us?"

"I did. They're in that black van that's parked right outside your office window."

"I don't believe it."

I didn't stay on the line to find out which part he didn't believe. I hung up and called my apartment.

Michelle Natoli's dulcet voice was a refreshing change from the jackhammer tones of Tom McReynolds. I told her it was safe to come back to New Jersey and gave her a thumbnail on the meeting.

"You're so wonderful," she gushed. She wouldn't get any argument from me on that.

"By the way," I said, "do you think you'd have time to buy a red wig?"

"A wig? What for?"

"It's too complicated to explain now, but I'd like you to get a wig that resembles your hair. I thought you'd have a better chance finding one in Manhattan than I would out here. Not to mention how foolish I'd feel."

She laughed. "No problem. But not in New York. I'll just pick one up at the Willowbrook Mall. Anything else?"

"Yeah," I said. "While you're at it, why don't you buy a blond one, too."

35

Despite my problems with punctuality, this was one meeting I managed to get to on time. In fact, I had a few minutes to spare. I used them to head off Track Jack Jones and Charlie Evans and tell them to wait down the hall from the Winners Circle. And I had enough time left over to sneak a glance at the contest standings.

Clocker Callaway had taken over the lead from Al on the pro side, while Penzler and Moore had slipped to third and fourth in the amateur. Apparently, Thursday hadn't been a very good day. But I was feeling optimistic that we could turn things around. I figured Gerald Ford would be feeling the same way when he was sworn in as President at noon.

While I waited by the entrance to the Winners Circle, Tom McReynolds gave a warmup pitch, explaining why the meeting had been called and urging everyone to be patient and cooperative with me. Just in case they weren't, there were a couple of cops on hand to keep order. And if additional backup was needed, we had the towering presence of Sheriff Maszursky.

There was a lot of whining at the conclusion of McReynolds' remarks, and I waited for the grumbling to die down before I stepped into the room. A couple of people were surprised to see me, and not pleasantly. Most of them didn't like me to start with, and I tried to head off some of the ill will by arming myself with two dozen belly bombs from Holey Toledo. That wasn't enough of a gesture to make me any new friends, but I could tell from the smile on Tony Lunaviva's face that at least one person might be having second thoughts about me.

As I put the donuts on a table in the center of the room, I glanced around and took silent attendance. Lunaviva and his wife sat in a booth along the middle of the wall. Biff Bonnardo and Candy Miller were in the booth next to them. Dave Gwynn chose to stand at the far end of the bar, while Serendipity McCall, Toteboard Tommy Stevens, Dr. Dave Higgins, and Lucky Lou Larson were crowded together two booths away from the track owner and his party. Clocker Callaway sat alone near the front, and Al and Michelle were in Sam's spot at the back.

"Are they all here?" McReynolds asked me as the guests began to go for the donuts.

I nodded. All except Sulky Sol Epstein, and his presence wasn't necessary.

Any diplomatic gains achieved by my donut initiative were lost as soon as Dr. Dave Higgins sampled the fare. "Yecch! What are these things made of—sawdust?"

Those in the know looked to Lunaviva for a reaction, but Nate had the first response. "If that's all it is, you're lucky," he said. "A friend of mine found a rat tail in his."

"Hey, you watch your damn mouth," Lunaviva said, holding a powdered-sugar donut in one hand and pointing with the other.

"Okay, so maybe I exaggerated a little," Nate said. "It was only a mouse."

Biff Bonnardo came to his friend's defense. "I own this place," he said to Nate. He hooked his thumb toward his chest, apparently unaware that jelly filling was leaking out onto his white silk tie. "I could have you thrown out of here if I wanted."

"And I'm the police chief," McReynolds said. "If you'd like, we can all go down to the station."

That idea didn't meet with much approval, except from Dr. Dave, who muttered, "Maybe we'd get Dunkin' Donuts down there."

"Now I don't want any lip out of anybody," McReynolds warned. "So why don't you all be quiet and let Renzler get this over with."

I lit a cigarette, picked up my coffee cup and stood by the door. Public speaking has never been of my talents, and I tried to keep my thoughts in order by focusing on the prettiest face in the room—Michelle Natoli's. Unfortunately, the ugliest face in the room interrupted before I could get started.

"Hey, what happened to you, Renzler?" Toteboard Tommy called out. "You look like you got run over by a dump truck."

"He got attacked by Matt Caldwell and his brother—that's what happened," Herbie said.

"What? Where is Matt?" Bonnardo asked.

"He's in jail, Mr. Bonnardo," McReynolds said. "Which is where you're going to end up if you don't be quiet and listen."

Bonnardo wasn't used to having people talk that way to him, but I'd been giving him some practice. He looked stunned by the police chief's retort, but he didn't say anything. I was a bit surprised myself.

McReynolds nodded at me and I took a deep breath. Everyone looked at me expectantly. I had their attention and respect. Sometimes I just love being a detective.

"We all know Longshot Sam was killed by a rifle fired from near the parking lot Monday afternoon," I said. "A guy named Danny Moreno, who worked for Tony Lunaviva, lured Sam down to the rail, then got away in a white Mustang driven by someone who resembled Sam's wife, Michelle. It turns out the car was owned by Michelle, but Sam gave it to someone who sold it to Mrs. Lunaviva for her husband's collection. But—"

"Hey, wait a second, what are you talking about?" Lunaviva was up out of the booth and gesturing at me with both hands. "I don't know anything about that car."

"Just sit down and be quiet," McReynolds ordered. The police chief's respect for the donut king seemed to have waned a bit. I had a feeling old Sheriff Maszursky had given him an earful about the erratic performances of Lunaviva's horses.

"But he's lying."

"Sit down and shut up," McReynolds repeated.

I wasn't about to acknowledge it, but I was thankful for Lunaviva's interruption. It clarified a point in my mind.

"I talked to Danny Moreno when he called Michelle and tried to shake her down for money to split town," I said. "Moreno knew I had identified him, and the person he was working for knew he was a liability. So he hired Matt Caldwell to kill him before he could tell his story."

"What? Matt Caldwell killed Moreno?" Biff Bonnardo shook his head. "I don't believe it." If you could believe his reaction, neither did Tony Lunaviva.

"But I did manage to get some info out of Moreno first," I said. "He told me that one of Sam's wives was involved and that the shot wasn't fired from the parking lot. He was also afraid Tony Lunaviva was going to kill him."

"*Bull*shit!" That was Lunaviva.

"*Shut* up." That was McReynolds.

I smiled at the cop. "Thank you," I said.

"Don't mention it."

"Longshot Sam had figured out that you were holding back your horses," I said, speaking directly to Lunaviva now. "And Danny Moreno was tipping him off."

That got Lunaviva's dander up again. "That's a damn lie!"

"No, it's not!" This time it was Sheriff Maszursky who came to my aid. "You've been pulling funny business with your stable ever since this place opened. I know it, you know it, and *he* knows it." Maszursky pointed at Bonnardo, then turned back to me. "Sorry if I'm stealing your thunder," he said.

"That's okay, Sheriff. I like your style."

All of a sudden, everybody in the room was chattering away. While McReynolds restored order, Maszursky said to me, "If I wasn't picking so many winners here, I would've called the State Racing Board a long while ago."

"I think it finally might be time to do that," I said.

"I intend to." He grinned. "*After* the contest is over."

"Continue, Renzler," McReynolds said.

"Longshot Sam knew what you were up to and so did the person who set out to kill him," I said to Lunaviva. "It was planned carefully so that you'd look like a suspect. It was planned so carefully, in fact, that even Moreno thought you were the one behind it."

Now that Lunaviva was off the hook, a smile spread over his face. It disappeared faster than you could say "Bavarian cream."

"The reason Moreno thought he was working for you was because he was driven away from the track by your wife," I said.

"Me!" It was the first time I had heard Daphne Lunaviva speak in a tone other than boredom. "You're crazy! I didn't do anything!" She looked to her husband for help. "Tell him to stop this, darling."

"Sorry, Daphne," I said. "I was on to you the first day you spoke to us. You made a point of saying how much you disliked Moreno. You also made a point of telling us how mad Tony got when you told him you saw Moreno talking to Sam. If Tony was in on it with you, you wouldn't have said that."

Lunaviva rose to his wife's defense, but this time he remained seated. He was clearly having some doubts himself. "Wait just one minute," he said. "The lady that drove away had red hair. How can you—"

"I'll explain that in a few moments," I said.

To my left I saw that Herbie already had the red wig out of the box. "Is it time for this, Uncle Mark?"

"No, not yet, Herb. But it is time for this," I said, turning to the tape recorder and pulling the two cassette tapes out of my pocket.

"Moreno was the one who tipped me off that the shot wasn't fired from the parking lot," I said. "At first I thought he was mistaken, because the shell was found near the door to the track personnel area. Then I figured that must have been the spot he meant. If the shot came from there, it seemed likely that somebody who worked at the track killed Sam.

"One possibility was Matt Caldwell. He was a Green Beret and knew how to shoot. He was also quick to jump Track Jack Jones and accuse him of killing Sam. But Caldwell couldn't have done it because he's too dumb to pull off something that was this well planned.

"Since Mr. Bonnardo and Mr. Lunaviva are friends, and since Sam was on to Lunaviva's scam, I thought they might be in on it together. Or I thought you"—I pointed to Bonnardo— "fired the shot from your office, and then had Caldwell hide the gun."

"I did nothing of the sort, and I resent this kind of talk."

I looked at McReynolds, who looked at Bonnardo. "Please keep quiet, sir," he said.

"But Mr. Gwynn was sure the shot came from his left," I said. "So Bonnardo couldn't have shot Sam from his office, because it's located to the right of the announcer's booth. It was only by chance that I realized the tape of the race was the key piece of evidence."

I pressed the button on the tape recorder and played the last fifteen seconds of the race. I shut it off right after Dave Gwynn flubbed the name of Lunaviva's horse, then corrected it and said, "Glazed Donut—in front."

"Sam was shot just before the horses reached the wire," I said. "But there was no gunshot on the tape." I looked to the bar, where the track announcer was lighting a cigarette. "There's a good reason for that, isn't there, Dave?"

Gwynn eyed me with his usual cool expression and spoke in a calm voice. "I don't have any idea what you're talking about, Renzler, but I don't like the implication."

Of course he did and of course he didn't. He knew there were problems when Matt Caldwell didn't show up for the meeting and I did. He knew I was closing in on him, but he had stood there stone-faced, watching as the circle around him got smaller and smaller. I suspected that Dave Gwynn had once been a military man himself.

"Sure you know what I mean, Dave. Because you're the one who shot Longshot Sam."

36

It was one on one between Dave Gwynn and me.

"You planned the whole thing, and I have to admit, it was a brilliant plan," I said. "It took incredible cunning to murder a guy at a racetrack with so many people around. Most people would think you'd never to able to get away with it in front of so many possible witnesses. They'd even think you were stupid for trying. But you knew better.

"You knew because you've sat up in that announcer's booth countless times, watching the people down below you. You knew you wouldn't be shooting Sam in front of anyone—you'd be shooting in *back* of them. Because you knew that when the horses are pounding down the stretch for the wire, everyone is watching the race, and nobody is looking back at the grandstand. And you knew that better than anyone."

I glanced around the room at all the baffled faces. Only one person remained expressionless—Dave Gwynn.

"With the parking lot so close to the grandstand, nobody would have suspected that the shot was fired from inside the building," I said to the room. "And even if someone did, the last person they'd suspect would the race announcer."

I turned back to Gwynn. "It was a foolproof plan, Dave. Only one thing went wrong, and that was something you couldn't have planned on. You had no way of knowing that one fool would get in your way—me. The only reason we're all here today is that I saw Danny Moreno talking to Sam. If I hadn't been watching when he took Sam down to the rail and said something that made him turn around, nobody would have noticed Moreno slipping away. Nobody would have any idea who shot Longshot Sam."

The faintest trace of smile appeared on Dave Gwynn's face. "I can see how you came up with this theory, Renzler. It would be almost flattering in a way—if it wasn't so preposterous."

Ah, that's what they always say. "It's not preposterous, Dave. Now the one thing that did present a problem for you was the sound of the shot. Even at a low-rent track like this with bad attendance, there's enough crowd noise that the sound of a single shot wouldn't attract attention. Everybody's concentrating on the race, and they wouldn't think about it. Or if they did, they'd just figure it was a firecracker or a cherry bomb.

"But if the shot were amplified over the PA system, then you'd have a problem. So you had to switch off the microphone or cover it up for an instant. I know you wear a lot of hats at this place, but shooting Sam, calling the race, and covering the mike took some fancy footwork. It occurred to me that Matt Caldwell might have helped you with this, but—"

"He couldn't have," Dr. Dave said. "Me and Tommy saw him downstairs in the grandstand making time with that little beauty queen. Didn't we, Tommy?"

I used the interruption to light a cigarette and catch my breath.

"Yeah, that's right," the toteboard man mumbled through a wad of powdered sugar and flour. I wasn't counting, but it had to be at least his fourth Holey Toledo.

"I know how he did it," Bonnardo said. "The microphone and tape recorder are hooked together. You can turn it on with a foot control."

"Just like Rose Mary Woods," Nate muttered, referring to the woman who had achieved her fifteen minutes of fame by erasing eighteen and a half minutes of tape.

"Exactly," I said, looking at Gwynn. "I noticed that setup when I talked to you in the booth. Aside from the parimutuel board, it's the only modern technology at this whole track."

Gwynn gave me a cold stare, then shook his head and pointed to the track owner. "*He's* the one who did it. I'd lay odds on it." He spoke directly to Bonnardo. "You're the one who said we should kill Sam Natoli, but I wouldn't go along with it. You did it and now you're trying to frame me. You sneaked down the stairs and shot him from the doorway."

I wanted desperately to believe Dave Gwynn. Of all the possible suspects, excluding Al and Michelle, Gwynn was the one guy I had hoped wouldn't turn out to be the killer.

"You're a damn liar," Bonnardo said, gesturing at the track announcer and inadvertently spreading the jelly filling from his tie onto his sleeve.

I shook my head. "It took me a long time to figure things out, Dave, but when I did, I realized there were little tip-offs all along the way. Sam got death threats before the contest. He thought they were from Tommy Stevens, but you were the one who made the calls. In case something went wrong, you wanted to plant the idea that one of the pickers was plotting to kill Sam, which is why you warned him not to compete in the contest. When Tommy spoke up at the orientation session, you mimicked his voice perfectly. It's not that you were trying to frame him, but I realized your voice could have been mistaken for his.

"And then there was the car. I think it was by luck that you found out you could get hold of Michelle's car. So you told Daphne to buy it. In the unlikely event that someone saw Moreno getting away, that would cast suspicion on Michelle."

Gwynn shook his head again. "You seem to be forgetting something, Renzler. You're forgetting that *I've* been cooperating with you." He nodded toward Bonnardo. "Unlike *him*."

"That's true. You have been cooperative, Dave. But that's because you knew I'd suspect Lunaviva or Bonnardo before you. When I came forward and screwed things up, you had to go to plan B. You told me what a great guy Sam was and how Bonnardo was preventing you from stopping Lunaviva's little scam. You were pretty smooth about implicating both of them. And you were very clever at using every piece of information you could.

"When you ordered Caldwell to kill Moreno, you thought to have him torch the car behind a Holey Toledo to make the cops think about Lunaviva. You also had him scare the motel clerk into saying a red-haired woman in a Mustang had been there to see Moreno. That one you botched, by the way. You got too hung up trying to plant clues. You should have just told

Caldwell to bump off the clerk, too. Caldwell, you could trust. He's not very bright, but he did survive a POW camp. And what would one more dead body cost you? Nothing. That part was very sloppy, Dave."

I took out the tape I had found the night before and put it into the tape recorder. "I got the first tape I played from one of the TV stations," I said. "This is the tape that was on file here at the track."

"Wait a second," Bonnardo said. "Where did you find that?"

"In your office, with the rest of the tapes."

"But I thought it was missing." Bonnardo's expression turned from bafflement to annoyance in nothing flat. "And just how did you get into my office?"

I winked at Herbie, then told a half-truth. "I had the director of security with me."

"Is that tape recorder going or what?" McReynolds asked.

"That's the point, Chief," I said. "He erased the tape."

"It's been going for forty-seven seconds already," Clocker Callaway said.

"Don't worry," Nate assured him. "Rose Mary Woods's record is still intact. This is only blank for that race."

"That would be two minutes, eight and two-fifths seconds, if I recall the win time correctly," Clocker replied.

I waited to make sure no one challenged that important point before continuing. "Even after Matt Caldwell screwed up last night and kidnapped me, you had it figured out," I said to Gwynn. "You knew that the tape was the only piece of evidence left against you. When I first asked you about it, you stole it. But after you told Caldwell to kill me, you went right to the track, erased the tape, and put it back in Bonnardo's office where it belonged. Then, after I was dead, if the cops asked any questions, you'd be able to tell them about Bonnardo going crazy when you and I were looking for the tape in his office.

"It was right after that incident that you told Caldwell to follow me. And your timing was perfect, because Bonnardo was the one who had just blown his stack. I didn't realize it was you who sent Caldwell after me until I found the tape. If Bonnardo had killed Sam, he wouldn't have put it back there. He would have hid it in your office to implicate you."

I turned to Herbie. "Caldwell didn't say Mr. B. last night. He said Mr. *G.*"

"What?" McReynolds looked puzzled. "I don't understand this Mr. B and G stuff, Renzler."

"I do," Clocker Callaway said. "That's what Caldwell called Gwynn the day he stopped us in the stairwell."

Michelle Natoli had been sitting and watching quietly, but now she stood up. For a moment, I thought she was going to walk over to Gwynn and confront him close up, but Al put out his arm to hold her back. "I thought you liked my husband, Mr. Gwynn," she said. "Why did you kill him?"

Gwynn looked away and didn't answer. I did.

"For money, Michelle," I said. "He has an invalid wife and a girlfriend with expensive tastes to support. At a track like this, the racing secretary can clean up, because he's the one who sets the odds. And Dave was doing very well for himself, thanks to Lunaviva, who was tipping him off about when his horses were going. That's how Tony was able to get away with his scam. He had the cooperation of the racing secretary and the track owner."

I looked at Lunaviva and Bonnardo. "Isn't that right, fellas?" They sat there speechless, but if looks could kill I was dead a thousand times over.

"But Sam was in the way," I said. "It wasn't just Lunaviva's horses. There were other entries whose odds Dave had adjusted. But Sam had it figured out." I looked at Gwynn. "I think Dave did like Sam. But he liked money even more."

"Mr. Gwynn, is there anything you'd like to say?" McReynolds asked.

Gwynn looked past the head cop and right through me. His blue eyes narrowed, and with the chill in them, they looked a little like sapphires. There was an emotionless quality to him that was almost scary. I wondered if he always had been like that or if losing his son in the war and having a wreck for a wife had made him that way.

"It's totally ridiculous," he said at last. "Even if I did shoot Sam, which I didn't, how would I have been able to get rid of the rifle?"

"Good question," I said. "You had some help. It was a tall order, so you needed a tall guy."

"Is it time for the wig now, Uncle Mark?"

"Yes, it is, Herb." I turned to Nate. "Would you bring in our surprise guests?"

"It would be my pleasure."

37

"Track Jack!" Serendipity gasped as the big guy entered the room. The other pickers seconded the emotion. Old Charlie Evans didn't rate any reaction at all.

I kept my eyes on Dave Gwynn. Not only did he look startled to see Track Jack, but he winced as he realized it was all over.

"What's he doing here?" Biff Bonnardo asked.

"I'm here to help nail your white ass, sucker," Track Jack said. "And after the reception I got here last time, I'm going to enjoy doing it."

"Who the hell do you think you are?"

"Sit down and relax, please, Mr. Bonnardo," McReynolds said. "We're almost done here." The police chief shot a glance at me. "We are, aren't we?"

I nodded. Right at the top of the stretch and heading for home.

"Jack was out in the parking lot when Sam was killed," I said after the crowd quieted down. "He had the best look at the woman who drove Danny Moreno away." I took the red wig from Herbie. "Would you mind putting this on, Daphne?" I asked.

Daphne Lunaviva was on the verge of tears. "Yes, I would mind," she blurted. She turned to her husband for support. "Tell them I won't do it, honey. This is an insult. That wig is so ugly!"

That didn't have anything to do with her reservations, but

the donut king was still feeling loyal. It was a halfhearted effort, but he did speak up on his wife's behalf.

"Yeah, I don't think this is necessary," he said.

"Just put on the wig, please, Mrs. Lunaviva," McReynolds said. "I'll decide if it's ridiculous or necessary."

Track Jack spent a few moments staring at Daphne before shaking his head. "I told you it wouldn't work, bro," he said. "I really didn't get a very good look at her."

I nodded. "Even if you had, Jack, I doubt you would have identified her. Because you were in on it with them."

"Say what?"

"You and Gwynn were in on it together."

"Gwynn! What's this shit you're handing me, bro? I thought you told me Bonnardo was the one that killed Sam."

I smiled. "If I had told you Gwynn did it, would you have come out here?"

Jack didn't respond to the question directly, although his comment pretty much answered it. "Why, you lying mother-fucker! You stung me!"

"Shut up," Gwynn snarled through gritted teeth.

"Damn! I *knew* I never should've come back out here," Jack muttered.

"Then why did you?" Lucky Lou asked.

The big guy was silent, so I took the liberty of answering for him. "He was greedy," I said. "He couldn't resist the idea of making some fast money." It was the common denominator that united all of the pickers.

"You can take the wig off now, Daphne," I said. Then I turned to face the racing secretary. "Jack's the one who helped you get rid of the rifle. He stood in the doorway and you handed it down to him through the side window as soon as the race was over. Then he took a few steps out into the lot and stashed it under Serendipity's van."

I spoke to Jack. "Were you trying to implicate her or did you just put it there out of convenience?"

Jack didn't answer, so I turned back to Gwynn. "You made one other mistake when you talked to me, Dave. You told me you used to work at Jackson Park. I realized you and Jack must have known each other in Detroit, but you acted like you had never met. It's ironic that the person who saw him was your wife. It's also ironic that your assistant, Matt Caldwell, almost killed him. I thought Caldwell might have been in on it with you, but he couldn't have staged a beating like the one he gave Jack. You must have been going crazy when you got down to the rail Monday afternoon."

Gwynn let out a sigh, but he didn't say how he felt. I turned to Track Jack. "How much did Gwynn pay you?" I asked as I lit another smoke. "However much it was, it couldn't have been enough to cover what you went through." Although Jack didn't reply, he looked like he was inclined to agree.

I spoke to Charlie Evans. "Do you recognize the man who used to come into the motel with that blonde?" I asked.

"Yessir, I do. He's the fella you were just talking to." Charlie pointed at Gwynn just in case there was any doubt.

"And what about the blond woman he used to come there with?"

Charlie looked at Daphne Lunaviva for a moment, then focused his attention on Candy Miller. "That's the lady, right there," he said.

"Which one?" I asked.

"The red-haired lady sitting across from the fella with all the slop on his tie."

"What? That's a lie!" I wasn't sure which part of the allegation Biff Bonnardo was taking issue with, because he glanced down at his tie before rising to his feet. But I knew which part surprised me.

"Are you sure?" I asked, looking from him to the frightened face of Candy.

"Sure I'm sure."

"But you told us she had blond hair," Nate said.

Charlie Evans held out his hands, with palms turned up. "She did then, but she don't now. What can I say?"

"See—I told you!" Daphne Lunaviva was up out her chair with her fist raised at me. Her husband stood up with her.

I ignored them and spoke to Sam's third wife. "Do you have something to tell us, Candy?"

"I don't understand any of this," she said. It was the first time I had heard her speak, and her voice was cracking. "I didn't do anything, I swear I didn't." Candy looked frantically at Dave

Gwynn, but he glanced away. "Dave, tell them!" she pleaded. "Tell them!"

"Do you need the blond wig now, Uncle Mark?"

"Good thinking, Herb, but I don't think it's necessary." I looked at Candy, who was struggling to choke back tears. "Dave can't speak for you, Candy, because he doesn't want to implicate himself. So you better say something on your own behalf."

She nodded as she gazed helplessly at the racing secretary. Before she could speak, Charlie Evans came unintentionally to her rescue.

"I don't know if it's important or not," he said, "but that lady there used to come into the motel, too." This time he pointed at Daphne, whose expression changed instantly from triumph to defeat. "Only she used to come in with a short, fat guy," Charlie said. "Name of Bernie, I think she called him."

"Not Bernie the attorney," Nate said.

"Oh my God," Michelle gasped.

"Yeah, I think he did say he was a lawyer once, now that you mention it." Charlie chuckled. "And let me tell you, they sure made a lot of noise together."

I shot a knowing glance at Nate, who returned it in the form of a grin. If Charlie Evans had heard them, they must have been *very* noisy.

"You're lying!" Daphne shouted, then turned to her husband and tried to sell him with her big blue eyes. "This old guy's wacko, darling," she pleaded. "Don't believe him."

This time even Tony wasn't buying.

"Bernie the attorney is the guy who sold Daphne the car," I told him.

The donut king nodded sadly as he sat back down and gripped his head with his hands. He looked like a guy with the world's biggest headache. The cause of it stood over him, biting her lip as tears streamed down her face.

"Then which one used to come in with Dino LaRussa?" Nate asked Charlie Evans.

"Who's that?"

"The guy who was killed in room six," Nate said.

"Oh, that was the lady that was just screeching at your friend," Charlie said.

"I had it wrong," I said, turning to face Dave Gwynn. "I thought you were having an affair with Daphne. But it was Candy you were involved with, wasn't it?" By that time I guess I should have known it was pointless to ask Gwynn any questions.

I looked back at Candy, who was still weeping. "Did you know Dave killed Sam?" I asked.

Candy shook her head. "We were planning on going away together. That's all I knew. Dave said he was expecting to come into some money soon." As she looked from the cold tile floor to the cool-eyed Gwynn, a wave of recognition began to wash over her face. As Al Phillips had said, Candy was cute as a button, but she had a brain about the same size.

"My inheritance!" she said. "That's the money you were waiting to get. *After* you killed Sam! That's why you made me wear that blond wig when we were out together and told me to go out with *this* jerk." She hooked her thumb toward the startled Bonnardo, who now had a little egg on his face to go with the jelly on his tie. "You said your wife was getting suspicious, but it was really because you didn't want anybody to know about us in case of this."

Gwynn closed his eyes and shook his head. He was a beaten man, but he wasn't giving in to any displays of emotion.

I shook my head in amazement. "I was wrong," I said to Gwynn. "You didn't get rid of Sam because he was cramping your betting style. You were hoping to make the big score all at once."

I turned to Candy. "He was trying to protect you," I said. It wasn't my place to defend Dave Gwynn, but even though he had killed Michelle Natoli's husband and tried to kill me, there was some small part of me that managed to feel sorry for him. I guess it was my timeworn habit of rooting for the underdog. Or my sense of what a living hell his life had been since his son got killed and his wife went nuts on him.

Candy started to speak, but Sheriff Maszursky interrupted her. "You might want to stop right there, miss, and hope he finds a good lawyer."

"And I can recommend one," Michelle said, getting up from her dead husband's booth and walking to the center of the room. She was weeping as she confronted Daphne Lunaviva.

"I hope they lock you up and throw away the key, Daphne," she said. "But more than that, I hope you see Sam in your dreams every night."

As I looked into Michelle's eyes, it occurred to me that it took Sam Natoli five picks to find himself a true winner. Too bad he hadn't lived long enough to enjoy it. But as she turned and embraced Al Phillips, I took some consolation in the thought that although Michelle had lost one winner, she had found another guy who was at least in the money.

38

"**I** think the gruesome twosome are going to have trouble finding dates for a while," Nate said to me as we watched Biff Bonnardo and Tony Lunaviva leave the room with their former squeezes. They were followed by Track Jack Jones, Dave Gwynn, and half a dozen cops.

As Toteboard Tommy and Dr. Dave got up to leave, Tom McReynolds signaled for them to remain seated. "We're not quite finished yet," the police chief said.

"What now?" Dr. Dave asked.

"They didn't tell us which one of them killed Timmy the Greek," Serendipity McCall said.

"Yeah, that's right," Lou Larson added. "Who killed the Greek?"

"Who cares who killed the Greek?" Toteboard Tommy grumbled.

It was obviously a rhetorical question, but that didn't stop my nephew from saying, "I do." If his career plans didn't change, it would probably be the first and last time he got to say it.

I turned to face Serendipity. "It's curious that you're the one who brought it up," I said.

"What do you mean?"

"Because you were the one who wanted to take the vote on canceling the contest after the Greek was killed."

"What's wrong with that? I did it out of respect."

"That's a good one, Red," Dr. Dave snorted.

"What's so funny about that?"

"You voted against your own motion," Lou Larson reminded her.

"So what? I just did it as a gesture."

I spoke to Al Phillips. "Do you remember who saw you and the Greek drive up to Lunaviva's party together?"

Al bit his bottom lip for a moment until his top one curled into his customary sneer. "Yeah, now that you mention it," he said. "She was getting into her van when we pulled up. We parked right in front of her, as a matter of fact."

"Don't look at me like that." Serendipity got up from her booth and turned in a circle. "Why are you all looking at me? It's probably that Gwynn guy who did it."

I looked at Nate and checked on the point I'd been meaning to ask him since the night before. By now it didn't really matter. I already knew what the answer would be.

"You told me Serendipity liked to work on her car," I said. "How did that come up?"

Nate shrugged. "She told me. And"—the color drained out of his face as Serendipity looked at him hopefully—"her hands!" Nate shook his head. "How could I have missed it?"

"They had grease on them, didn't they?" I said.

Nate nodded.

"I don't know what you're talking about," Serendipity lied.

"Sure you do," I said. "You're the one who tampered with the brakes on Al's car. That's why your hands were dirty."

"That doesn't prove anything! I was working on my van that day. I had an oil leak. It's hard to wash that stuff off."

"But you managed all right before the party," I said. "I know, because I kissed your hand."

"I had to fix something when I went to get Zodiac." There was a mix of fear and loathing in the Daily Double's eyes as she searched the room for a supporter. She didn't find one.

"You had something to fix, all right," I said. "You were trying to fix it so that you won the contest. You were in fourth place and you realized that with the Greek and Al out of the way, you'd be in the money. You'd even have a chance to win."

"No, no, that's not true! I didn't have anything to do with it."

"You're lying," Al said. "You killed the Greek, and you tried to kill me, too."

"No, I didn't!"

"It wasn't something you planned," I said. "You just saw them there, and it was too good a chance to pass up. You couldn't be sure the Greek would go home with Al, but even if he didn't, you'd at least be able to knock one of them out of the way. You didn't like Al to start with. You tried to cozy up to him but he kept rejecting you. And everybody knows you hated the Greek. I don't know why exactly, but—"

"I can tell you why," Clocker Callaway said in his customary monotone. "Because the Greek gave her herpes."

"That's a lie!" Serendipity shrieked. "It's a damn lie! You don't know what you're talking about." For my partner's sake, I hoped she was right.

Just then I heard a noise near the doorway that sounded like a coin being dropped into a fountain from five thousand feet. When I turned, I realized it was the sound of Nate's heart sliding into his throat.

"What's herpes, Uncle Mark?" Herbie asked as Nate slipped quietly out the door.

I could have told him to ask Uncle Nate, but I draw the line on sarcasm once in a while. I ignored the question and turned my attention toward Serendipity, who was gyrating and gesturing in the center of the room. If an O'Jays song had been playing, you might have thought she was dancing.

"I hate all of you!" she squealed. "All of you! And *you!*" She pointed at me. "I hate you most of all! Never trust a Virgo. *Never!*"

"My God, this gal is really loony tunes, isn't she?" Sheriff Maszursky said beside me.

I nodded. I thought she just might be crazy enough not to know what she had done. "What do you expect from somebody who handicaps horse races through astrology?" I said.

"*Really?*" That detail seemed to startle the sheriff more than anything else he had heard.

"Is that enough for you?" I asked McReynolds.

He nodded. "Yeah, I think I've got plenty."

"Good. If you don't mind, I think I'll take a stroll."

Lou Larson followed me and Herbie out the door. "Good work, Mr. Private Eye," he said.

"And quick, too," Clocker Callaway added. He checked his watch. "Forty-eight minutes and fifteen seconds."

"Thanks," I said. I looked at Lucky Lou. "Now there's a little matter of a pool I wanted to discuss with you."

"No, no, don't look at me. That was Sol's idea. He's got all the money. If you want, I can give you his address."

"Let me guess," I said. "It's a post-office box."

"Yeah, that's right. How'd you know that?"

"Uncle Mark knows everything," Herbie said, smiling proudly.

I put my arm around his shoulders. Five days before, I barely knew the kid. Getting to know him was the best thing that had happened to me in a long time. He was smart, thoughtful, and good-natured. I didn't know if he'd go through with his career plans. To be honest, I hoped he wouldn't. But if he did, I felt sure he'd make one hell of a goddamn good priest.

"You were wonderful," Michelle Natoli said as she rushed over and put her arms around me. I wouldn't have minded staying in that position for a week or two, but the embrace only lasted a minute. As she pulled away she said, "How can I ever thank you?"

"You could probably start by buying him a beer," Al said with a sneer.

He held out his hand, and I shook it. We looked at each other, that man-to-man look that tells you who your real friends are, and I wondered how I could have suspected that Al had killed his best one. In some ways, I had almost come to dislike Al. And even though I still regarded him as a friend, I realized we wouldn't be seeing or talking to each other much anymore.

Beside me, Herbie was getting the full body treatment from Michelle. That would be something to tell the other altar boys about when school got back into session.

"Well, if you'll excuse me, I've got to go find Nate," I said.

"I'll come with you, Uncle Mark," Herbie said, extricating himself from Michelle's embrace. Despite all I had done to enlighten him that week, the kid was still in the dark about the best things in life.

We found Nate exactly where I expected him to be. He was leaning against the bar, a bourbon in one hand and a butt in the other. Nate always drinks bourbon when he's in a contemplative mood.

"Don't look at me like that, Renzler," he said, waving at me with his cigarette.

I told him I didn't know what he meant, then I ordered a beer and started to look at him like that again.

"All I did was count her freckles. I swear, that's all I did."

I took a swallow of my beer. Damn, it tasted good. Even if it was flat racetrack swill.

"That's between you and her," I said.

"And don't forget the Man upstairs," Herbie added.

"Let's hope he's still on our side when the races start today," I said.

"Oh, that's right." Nate stretched his arms and yawned. "We've still got another whole day of that nonsense to go through."

"Cheer up," I said. "We could win a lot of dough."

Nate shrugged. "I think I'll just ask the bartender here to turn on the TV so we can count how many platitudes our new President uses in his first address to the nation."

"What's a platitude?" Herbie asked.

"It's a jellyfish withering on the shores of the sea of thought," Nate replied.

"You're certainly waxing profound," I said.

"It's a quote from Ambrose Bierce." Nate looked at Herbie. "There's a writer I bet they don't let you read over at the junior seminary."

Herbie shot me a mystified glance. Old Uncle Nate was acting weird again.

"Do you think Ford will pardon Nixon today?" I asked.

Nate shook his head. "No way. He'll wait awhile to assess the mood of the electorate. Only then, when he's absolutely sure everybody's against it, will he go ahead and give him a pardon."

"Would you be interested in making a little wager on when it happens?" I asked.

"Why, of course. You know me. I never turn down a bet."

"Do you mind if I get in on this action?" Herbie asked.

I looked at Nate. "Do you think he's old enough?"